Divided Loyalties

In the dining room, A.P. and Jeremy were engaged in a heated exchange.

"How dare you behave the way you are doing with Mary Lou?" A.P. demanded.

"Why not ask her why she was so snotty with me?"

"I won't have you using words like that with relation to her."

"What are you? Her protector? She strikes me as well able to stand up for herself," said Jeremy.

"That doesn't mean I have to let you insult her."

Jeremy scanned A.P.'s expression. "You're in love with her, aren't you?"

A.P. gazed at the flickering candles in the silver candelabra and made no reply.

"Does she know?"

He shook his head.

"Mary Lou Dryden isn't the girl for you, A.P."

Also by Maisie Mosco

Out of the Ashes
Almonds and Raisins
Scattered Seed
Children's Children
For Love and Duty

Published by
HarperPaperbacks

MAISIE MOSCO

NEW BEGINNINGS

HarperPaperbacks

A Division of HarperCollinsPublishers

HarperPaperbacks   *A Division of* HarperCollins*Publishers*
10 East 53rd Street, New York, N.Y. 10022

A hardcover edition of this book was published in Great Britain in 1991 by HarperCollins*Publishers*, U.K.

Cover illustration by Donna Diamond

First HarperPaperbacks printing: January 1993

Printed in the United States of America

HarperPaperbacks and colophon are trademarks of HarperCollins*Publishers*

10 9 8 7 6 5 4 3 2 1

Acknowledgments

My editor, Kate Parkin.

Stephen Mosco and Jane Mosco,
for assistance with research.

In memory of Lillian and Nat Malimson

THE FAMILY

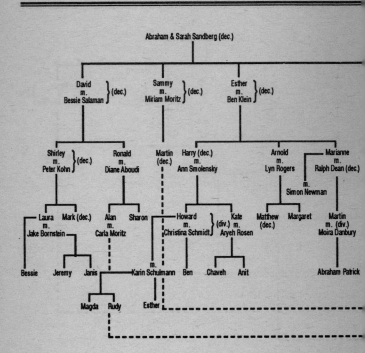

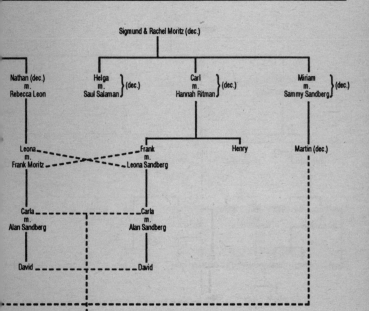

Sigmund & Rachel Moritz (dec.)

Nathan (dec.)
m.
Rebecca Leon

Helga
m.
Saul Salaman } (dec.)

Carl
m.
Hannah Ritman } (dec.)

Miriam
m.
Sammy Sandberg } (dec.)

Leona
m.
Frank Moritz

Frank
m.
Leona Sandberg

Henry

Martin (dec.)

Carla
m.
Alan Sandberg

Carla
m.
Alan Sandberg

David

David

The greatest thing in the world
is to know how to be one's own

—Montaigne

PART ONE

INHERITANCE

Chapter
1

*O*n a bleak, October day in 1988, the gallery at the House of Lords was dominated by a family group, assembled to hear the maiden speech of one of their own.

To the elders of the family, the new peer of the realm looked alarmingly young for his responsibilities. To his contemporaries, the grandeur pervading the atmosphere was out of key with the life he had so far lived, nor could they easily envisage him robed for State occasions, a jeweled coronet atop his fiery hair.

For the lad himself, a sense of unreality prevailed, though some time had passed since the death of his maternal grandfather had metamorphosed Abraham Patrick Dean, better known as "A.P.," into Lord Kyverdale.

While the debate after which he would be called to speak proceeded, A.P.'s gaze roved to the gallery, where his grandmothers were seated side by side. Irene, Lady Kyverdale and the author Marianne Dean had never liked each other, he reflected, but today they were briefly united.

He was an only grandchild to both – and the older generation had expectations for their descendants. That had certainly included Grandfather Kyverdale, to whom A.P. had never felt close. Inheriting the title had seemed a bit of a lark.

But a lark it wasn't, as A.P.'s Jewish father would put it. The Kyverdales were steeped in history, one of the oldest Catholic families in the land. And his lordship had been a prominent Member of the House, taking his duties seriously. Not one of the dodderers who treat this place as somewhere to drop in for a snooze, A.P. thought, glancing around the opulent Chamber.

Well, he said to himself, the Kyverdale heritage is now vested in *you*, to make of it what you will.

That evening, A.P. returned to Oxford for a celebration with his friends. His cousin, Jeremy Bornstein, a fellow undergraduate at New College, traveled with him from London and the two went directly to the Trout Inn, where the party had begun without the guest of honor.

"We should've waited for his lordship to arrive and order champagne," said Gary Potter, a miner's son from Newcastle whose brilliance had won him a scholarship.

A.P. submitted to the mock deference that followed, which he had known would be in store for him. Nor was it in every case good-natured. Inherited peerages were anathema to some of those present. To Gary in particular, and how wouldn't they be? thought A.P., though Gary wouldn't be a pal of mine if he held it against me personally.

While the party grew more boisterous, A.P. did his best to join in. Suddenly there was a hollow ring to his inheritance. Perhaps because everything about it was rooted in the past.

Kyverdale Hall was a bastion of the aristocracy set in acres of parkland and A.P. was now its guardian for his lifetime, following in the footsteps of his ancestors. So much for his telling himself to make of it what he would, he was thinking when Jeremy was called to the telephone.

Jeremy returned to the bar ashen-faced and momentarily unable to speak. "I shall have to leave," he eventually told A.P. "The call was from my dad's secretary. She's been trying for hours to reach me and the college porter advised her to try the Trout —"

"Never mind that," A.P. interrupted, "what's the matter?"

"I haven't taken it in yet," Jeremy muttered. "It's Laura and Dad — she flew to Venezuela to join him — yesterday. He had some business to attend to there and then they were going on a cruise. The first real holiday they'd managed to take together for years. That's why they weren't in the gallery to hear your speech —"

"Laura rang up to explain and to wish me luck," said A.P.

A pause followed before Jeremy went on. "There's been some sort of accident in Caracas. Laura and Dad — they're both dead. How am I going to tell my sisters?"

A.P. conveyed to their friends that Jeremy had received bad news, put a comforting arm around his shoulders and together they left the inn.

"What you need is a few minutes to pull yourself together," said A.P., "while I fetch the car. Then I'll drive you wherever you need to go."

"You're a real pal," Jeremy declared.

"You've been that to me since your father's marrying Laura brought you into my family," A.P. replied before striding away.

Jeremy remained by the rustic bridge, gazing down at the river, recalling the times he and A.P. had stood here together, tankards of ale in their hands, watching the trout glitter in the sunlight. His mind was still refusing to accept that his parents were dead.

Though Laura was his stepmother, a true mother was what she had been to Jeremy and his sister Janis. As Dad was a real father in all but the blood sense to Laura's daughter, Bessie.

Oh dear God – poor little Bessie, Jeremy thought. How would she, still a schoolgirl and obsessed by her own plainness, manage without the parents who had seen her through anorexia and were still bolstering her recovery?

Were. Laura and Dad were no more. And Janis was doing her own thing – whatever that was – in Australia. Until she got fed up with it and took off for somewhere else!

Resentment that his elder sister was not here when he needed her surged through Jeremy. He had never quite forgiven her for suddenly ending her engagement to Kurt Kohn. Not just suddenly, but inexplicably, and Kurt had afterwards returned to his native Vienna, a good deal more scarred by the experience than Janis had seemed.

Jeremy forced himself to switch his mind to what he must. And this wouldn't be like it usually was with deaths in the family, the older members arranging the funeral and the younger ones turning up at the cemetery, as they had when Laura's Great Uncle Nat died peacefully in his sleep, last year.

For this funeral, the bodies must first be flown to England. Bodies? Laura and Dad? That vibrant woman still in her prime, and the go-getter whose deals, worldwide, had made him a millionaire?

Jeremy wanted to put his head in his hands and weep, but there was no time for grieving. Too much to do and to sort out. Like who his sister Bessie would now live with; a girl of fourteen couldn't live alone. And the family home in Hampstead. Would it have to be sold?

But first things first, he thought, as A.P. brought the car to the roadside. Tomorrow, he would fly to Caracas to bring his parents home.

It had yet to occur to Jeremy that he, like A.P., was now the recipient of an inheritance, nor could he then have envisaged the far-reaching consequences of his father's entrepreneurial dealings.

But for Jeremy and A.P., though neither could have expressed it in words, it was as if they had grown up that day.

Chapter
2

fter Jeremy had called her, Janis went to make herself some tea. Why wasn't she sobbing her heart out? she asked herself. She'd had too much practice in keeping her feelings locked inside her. The last time she'd shed tears was the August afternoon when she went to confide to A.P.'s Grandma Marianne her true reason for breaking it off with Kurt – and Marianne would never tell.

Since then, Janis had roved from place to place, supporting herself with an assortment of fill-in jobs. As if she was killing time between the past she'd run away from and she knew not what.

While she waited for the kettle to boil, resting her back against the counter dividing the kitchen from the living area, her fragmented life since leaving home flickered before Janis's eyes. She had briefly been a nanny in California, a florist's assistant in Paris, receptionist at a hairdressing salon in Madrid, and chauffeuse to a crusty old lady in

Bombay. Among other things. But, put together, what did it amount to?

Aimlessness! Was she to have no sense of purpose for the rest of her life? And the more wasteful her meaningless existence seemed for her parents' deaths. More positive people than Laura and Jake would be hard to find – and the real reason Janis wasn't shedding tears for them had to be that shock had numbed her.

She carried the mug of tea to the tiny balcony and fixed her gaze upon the view of the ocean visible between the rooftops. This district of Sydney was largely a young people's bedsitterland and fine for me, she reflected, for the transient I've become. Though her place was a flat, sooner or later she'd be moving on. Jeremy said she had itchy feet. But it wasn't quite that. It was something inside her that kept her on the move.

She had arrived in Australia three months ago and had spent some time with Laura's old schoolfriend, Peggy Morris, who now lived in Melbourne. The home comforts, though, had palled when Peggy tried to mother Janis. If mothering could help what ailed Janis, Laura would happily have supplied it, as she had from the day she married Jake Bornstein.

When Peggy's mothering included introducing Janis to "suitable" young men, Janis made her escape to Sydney, where she was now working as a waitress in a coffee shop. Since she had a degree in psychology, she could, if she wished, seek employment in that field, but Janis could summon no more enthusiasm to anchor herself professionally now than she had been able to throughout her travels. Whenever she forced herself to give the matter serious consideration, a lethargy of spirit overwhelmed her and she always concluded by asking herself, "What's the point?"

But if ever I put down roots anywhere, Sydney would be

a good place, Janis reflected now. She hadn't gone short of companionship from the young people she had met at a Reform Synagogue service, some of whose parents hailed from South Africa, as Janis herself did. Her father's remarriage was the reason he had moved his family and his office to London.

He did it for Laura, Janis thought, though in other ways it was Laura who deferred to Dad. Or had she just known how to handle him? Better than Janis's mum, who died in her thirties, had . . .

Janis couldn't recall ever hearing her mum and dad rowing, but there'd been times when she'd sensed that all was not well between them. Laura and Jake, on the other hand, used to have tiffs that didn't leave the air heavy with animosity.

Janis was sure that they'd been happy together, that all their differences had been about their children, all three of whom had in their own way contributed to the aggro.

Well, it's too late for regrets now, Janis told herself as she went to pack a suitcase. Tonight she would be on her way back to London. Jeremy had said that Dad's secretary would arrange Janis's flight, so she could just pick up her ticket at the airport.

No doubt the ticket would be first class, as befitted a millionaire's daughter, though Janis had refused to accept money from her father while she roamed the world, and he must have spent sleepless nights worrying about how she was getting by. Laura, too.

Remember we're always here for you, they'd said each time she called them. Now, that sole security in her life was no longer there and Janis had never felt more alone.

Chapter 3

*B*essie's initial reaction to the news that would change
her life was absolute refusal to believe it.

"God wouldn't do that to me," she insisted to
Jeremy.

"I'm afraid that He has, love."

"You're making it up, Jeremy! And why are you suddenly
calling me 'love'?"

Jeremy glanced around the familiar living room – cozy,
despite its spaciousness – his gaze halting briefly on the sofa
where he and his sisters used to sit when watching TV
together. He could not bring himself to look at the twin
armchairs that his parents had usually occupied, and turned
to give Bessie a compassionate smile.

"I'm not used to you being so nice to me, Jeremy," Bessie
went on.

"And you're not always nice to me, are you?" he said,
trying to lighten the atmosphere. "But that's how brothers

and sisters are with each other sometimes – and right now, Bessie, I'm as sorry for you as I am for myself."

Laura's mother, Shirley, who had been staying at the house with Bessie while her parents were away, intervened. "Let me deal with her, Jeremy. The child will be my responsibility from now on."

"I'm not a child!" Bessie responded.

Shirley ignored the interruption. "I'll be taking her back to Manchester to live with me," she told Jeremy, while rising to put her arms around Bessie. "We'll be a comfort to each other – and when I look back on my life, one way and another it's been nothing but loss after loss."

Bessie broke away from her embrace, dark eyes flashing. "I don't want to live with you!"

"We'll be on our way north immediately after the funeral," Shirley informed her. "You're all I've got now, and I'm all you've got."

Bessie's defiant expression crumpled. "God *did* let them get killed, didn't He? I'm never going to forgive Him for it," she added, fleeing from the room.

A silence followed her departure, Shirley rolling her damp handkerchief into a ball, Jeremy surveying the photo portrait of his father taken by Laura before their marriage.

"If you'll excuse me," he said, turning to Shirley, "I have a plane to catch."

"What I can't excuse," she answered, "is your taking everything into your own hands. I'd have liked my darling daughter to be buried up North, where Bessie and I could visit her grave often."

Jeremy ran a hand wearily through his disheveled, dark hair, aware too of the stubble on his chin. He hadn't had time to shave that morning. "You and Bessie weren't up yet when I arrived, Shirley, and I didn't want to waken you –"

"To tell me I've lost my daughter he didn't want to waken me!"

"All right, so I was putting off telling you. And meanwhile I rang up our rabbi and made the necessary arrangements –"

"Without consulting your elders, you had no right to!"

"But it turned out to be what Laura and Dad wanted. I learned from the rabbi that they'd reserved graves in the Reform cemetery, side by side."

"Your father probably got his secretary to fix that up, he was that sort of man," Shirley said coldly, "and there's a lot of him in you – though I didn't use to think so."

"I'll take that as the compliment it wasn't intended to be," Jeremy told her. "Fortunately for her husband and children, there was nothing of you in Laura," he added before leaving Shirley alone with her anguish.

When shortly afterwards Marianne arrived, Shirley found herself weeping on her cousin's shoulder.

"We've never been friends, but you have to be sorry for me now," Shirley said through her tears. "First I lose my son, then my husband, and now this . . ."

"I wouldn't put it that way about your husband," said Marianne. "Divorce isn't death and you were as keen to be free of Peter as he was of you."

"It wasn't like that!" Shirley blew her nose and calmed down. "After we lost our son – and then Laura ran away to London and you took her in –"

"You're never going to forgive me for that, are you?" Marianne interrupted. "Though it was decades ago."

"What does it matter now if I do, or not?" Shirley said bleakly. "Laura's leaving home put the coffin lid on my marriage. All right, so divorce isn't death, but a marriage can die and mine did."

She added with bitterness, "My ex-husband will probably bring his new wife to his daughter's funeral."

"Peter's been married to Hildegard for years," Marianne reminded her.

"But Laura was his daughter and mine, and I can't bear to tell him she's gone, Marianne. Would you mind making the call?"

Briefly Marianne felt herself back in her former niche, the person upon whom everyone in the family relied. Before she made her escape to Bermuda and a blissfully peaceful life.

"But check with Jeremy, first," Shirley advised. "He may have taken it on himself to ring up Peter, like he did with the rabbi. His father isn't yet in his grave and already that boy is running the show!"

Marianne said after a pause, "If I were you, Shirley, I'd be grateful and let him get on with it."

"Well, you were always the younger generation's staunchest supporter, weren't you? Encouraging them to run wild, instead of warning them like their parents would."

"Encouraging them to be their own person, you mean," Marianne rejoined, "which is everyone's right."

"But you won't get your hands on Bessie," said Shirley. "I'll make sure of that. Don't you dare invite that child to stay with you in Bermuda. She might not want to come back."

Marianne thought of the life in store for Bessie under Shirley's roof, hemmed in by the parochial attitudes from which Laura, at the age of sixteen, had fled.

Shirley, elegant as always in her habitual black, was looking at Laura's framed photography on the walls, some of which had featured in major exhibitions.

"Bessie and those damned pictures are all there is to show for Laura's being on earth," she said, twiddling her pearls.

Marianne countered, "I wouldn't say that. She took on Janis and Jeremy —"

"And look how they've turned out!"

Marianne let that pass.

"I was proud of Laura, don't think I wasn't," Shirley said, glancing again at the photographs on the walls. "But I never approved of how she lived her life. How could I, when she broke all the rules? Deliberately getting herself pregnant when she was still single, just because she fancied having a child – Disgracing the family like she did."

"But it isn't a disgrace any more."

"It was then," Shirley said vehemently, "and *I* had to live through it. My daughter coming to visit me with a bulging belly and no wedding ring. And Bessie doesn't even know who her real father is."

Shirley gave Marianne a piercing glance. "Did Laura ever tell *you*?"

"Not exactly."

"What does that mean?"

"That she didn't tell me his name."

"But you know something about him, don't you?" Shirley said with asperity. "And that's how it's always been in our family. The kids telling their secrets to you, and you laughing behind their parents' backs."

"Only if it was a laughing matter," Marianne answered calmly, "and what we're discussing isn't."

She got up to gaze through the window at the view of Hampstead Heath, her heart aching with sadness for Laura, who had made this house a home for Jake Bornstein and his motherless children. For Bessie, too.

To do so, Laura had had to learn to bend her life and her career to accommodate others, succeeding though it had not been easy.

"You still look like a kid, yourself," Shirley remarked, surveying Marianne's petite figure clad in a gray trouser suit. "From the back," she added cattily. "And I forbid you to tell Bessie what you know about her real father."

"I wouldn't dream of it," said Marianne, "though in my opinion she's entitled to know the little I do."

"*Your* opinion!" Shirley flared. "You never side with the ones you should!"

"That could be because I haven't forgotten what it's like to be young."

Lying on her bed, a snapshot of Laura clutched in her hand, Bessie's sorrow was tinged with resentment. Why did all the bad things have to happen to her?

Though she was now fourteen and her appearance mature, emotionally she was still the insecure child she had always been and now recalling the series of au pairs who had looked after her when she was little.

While my mummy went all over the world taking pictures for magazines! she thought. Mummy couldn't have really cared about me.

The resentment had centered upon Laura, who had not in those days adapted her life to motherhood, flitting back and forth between foreign assignments and home like a bright butterfly whose presence, or absence, had lightened, or shadowed, Bessie's horizon.

"I didn't even have a daddy," Bessie told the rag doll she had never abandoned, "and when my mummy got me one, I had to share her with his children."

The treacherous thoughts that Bessie had stemmed for too long, never expressed, caused tears of self-pity to cascade down her cheeks. "I haven't even told my best friend, Val, what I just told you," she said to the doll, "and what I said doesn't mean I don't love Janis and Jeremy. I do, but it was nice when they'd both left home and I had Mummy all to myself."

Bessie got up to get a paper tissue from the dressing table, dried her eyes and gazed in the mirror. A girl no longer the fatty she once was, but who would never be pretty, gazed back at her. How was she ever to get a boyfriend? Val already had one and Bessie felt like a gooseberry when she sometimes went with them to the cinema and saw them holding hands.

If she had to go and live in Manchester with her granny, she wouldn't even have Val, the only one of her school-friends who hadn't minded being seen with her when she dieted till she looked like a scarecrow.

For two pins, I'll do it again! she thought mutinously. Now my mummy is gone, who'd care?

She communicated this to Jeremy when he came, showered and shaved, to see her before leaving for the airport, and received a dressing-down.

"Janis and I will have enough on our plates, with all there'll be to sort out," he capped it, "without us having to worry about you being anorexic again."

"*Would* you worry about me?"

"You're our sister, aren't you?"

"But not really."

Jeremy sat down on the bed beside her. He didn't have time to dally if he was to catch his plane, but this was important.

"There's a lot more to what being a sister, or a brother, means than just the blood tie bit, Bessie, and our parents would be very upset if they'd heard what you just said. They worked hard to make us the real family we became – though I didn't give that a thought till now."

"Shall we still be a family now they're gone?"

"I'd say that's up to us. Wouldn't you?"

Chapter
4

*A*fter driving Jeremy to London, A.P. could not bring himself to return immediately to Oxford, nor to contemplate two more years amid the dreaming spires. It was as though his disenchantment with his inheritance had permeated his carefree undergraduate life.

En route they had stopped at a transport cafe and if Jeremy had not had his own troubles, right now, A.P. would surely have unburdened himself to his friend. Instead, they had sat silently drinking cup after cup of coffee, each immersed in his own thoughts, and A.P. privately envying the uncomplicated lot of the truck drivers dropping in for a quick snack. Who the heck would want to be a lord?

Other than Jeremy, though, who could A.P. talk to about the way he suddenly felt? Well, certainly not his parents. If there was one thing that Martin and Moira Dean would agree about, it was their son's staying the course till he'd got his degree.

Am I thinking of dropping out? If so, to do what? Devote myself to being Lord Kyverdale? No way!

He had parked the car at South End Green and sat staring through the windscreen unseeingly, while the mid-morning traffic sped by. On an impulse, he started the engine and headed for Islington, where his dad's old friend, Bill Dryden, now lived. Bill directed documentary films and his home was his office. If he wasn't out on location, he wouldn't mind giving A.P. some time and his advice. A.P. had a crisis, and what else were godfathers for?

It was Bill's daughter, Mary Lou, who opened the door, her jeans and the tip of her snub nose smudged with red paint.

"Thank goodness it's only you!" she greeted A.P. "I must look a dreadful mess —"

"For the moment, I thought it was blood. That you'd been doing a Lizzie Borden."

"I have more subtle ways of dealing with my parents than taking an axe to them," she said with a grin as A.P. followed her into the house.

"I wouldn't have thought they'd require dealing with," A.P. replied.

"Exactly *my* impression of yours," said Mary Lou, "but that's always the way, isn't it? That generation seems capable of understanding everyone's children but their own. Don't trip over the can of paint!" she warned too late.

The can now lay on its side and A.P. was paddling in a gooey pool.

"Lucky for you we don't yet have carpets down in our new house!" Mary Lou exclaimed. "Or this is one time you might not find my parents so understanding."

"What are you painting red?" A.P. asked, glancing at the white walls.

"Not the town! I've used up all my allowance, so I offered to be their interior decorator in return for some hard cash. They want a scarlet ceiling – some sort of middle-aged last fling, no doubt – and I was stirring the paint when you rang the blasted doorbell, A.P.!"

Mary Lou glared down at the pool on the floor. "Just look at what you've been'n gone'n done!"

"I'd be happy to clean it up."

"And me to let you – only I daren't risk the splotches you might make on the walls while wielding a mop. You always were a clumsy clod, A.P. I remember you dropping a cream cake at one of my birthday parties, when we were little, and knocking my chocolate milkshake all over my frilly frock when you bent down to pick the cake up."

"And you still hold that against me?" said A.P. "How about the time our families shared a holiday flat, and you put a dead hedgehog in my bed?"

"That was a joke."

"Not to the one who got pricked by it! What kind of girl would do that, I thought."

"I was only eleven."

"But it changed my entire impression of you," A.P. revealed. "Till then, I'd thought you were a sweet little girl and how wrong I was! Returning to the present, would you mind if I dripped my way out of the paint I'm standing in – before I stick to the floor!"

"I have a better suggestion," said Mary Lou. "Lean on my shoulder and take off your shoes, one at a time, and step carefully onto dry land."

"Have you ever known anyone take off their shoes *two* at a time?"

"My dad sometimes does, when he gets home from working on location and just drops into a chair. If it's him you came to see, you'll have gathered that he isn't in," Mary Lou added while A.P. stood poised on his right leg, removing his left shoe.

"Well, I didn't come to see *you*," he said when with her assistance he was seated, shoeless, on the stairs.

"Though our parents would probably be thrilled if you had," she answered with a laugh. "You and I teaming up is probably one of their shared fantasies. Better the devil they know!"

"But not from our point of view!"

"Found yourself a girlfriend at Oxford?" Mary Lou inquired.

"I haven't looked for one."

"Waiting to meet the eyes of the right girl across a crowded room?" she teased.

"Well, I'm certainly not interested in the one-night stand scene."

"Me, neither."

"That doesn't surprise me. You're a well brought up Catholic girl."

Mary Lou changed the subject. "How are you bearing up to being Lord Kyverdale, A.P.?"

"As a matter of fact, not too well."

Why had he confided in her? A.P. asked himself. Perhaps because they'd known each other all their lives, and the family association went further back than that. Mary Lou's father had been a childhood friend of A.P.'s mother – and had introduced her to Martin Dean when he and Martin were fellow undergraduates at Oxford.

Later, the Deans and the Drydens had lived on a commune together. Before A.P. and Mary Lou were born. Though they had not seen much of each other in recent years, their friendship had remained solid.

"Being a lord isn't for me!" A.P. went on ruefully.

"That's some conclusion to come to the day after your maiden speech in the House," Mary Lou replied. "My dad said you were very impressive."

"I was scared stiff."

"You won't be once you've got going," Mary Lou encouraged him.

"But I can't see myself getting going."

"Are you saying you don't want to?"

A.P. made no reply.

"I wouldn't have expected you to get cold feet," said Mary Lou.

"Then I'd better put my shoes back on," he joked feebly.

"Ha-ha!" Mary Lou scanned his gloomy expression. "Want to tell me what's wrong? Come on, I'll make us some tea and a sandwich."

A.P. let himself forget that his best shoes were still amid the paint and followed her to the kitchen, registering that she was still the pocket Venus Jeremy would surely call her. Petite and shapely, like her American mother.

They had not seen each other since Mary Lou returned from a two year film course in California, where she had lived with her maternal grandparents.

"Glad to be back?" he asked.

"Well, I can't say I don't miss the surfing and the beach boys! But don't let's digress from what you need to get off your chest."

Mary Lou put the kettle on to boil, fetched a granary loaf to the scrub-top table and began slicing it. When A.P. sat down opposite her, she told him to get off his butt and open a can of tuna.

"You're as bossy as ever," he observed. "That time our families shared a holiday flat —"

"I didn't let you get away with sitting watching me wash and dry the dishes."

They shared a laugh, and suddenly A.P. found himself able to tell Mary Lou how he felt about his inheritance, and that doing so helped crystallize his muddled thoughts.

"It's because you're the sort who needs a challenge," she said after a silence.

By then they were munching the sandwiches and Mary Lou absently licked some mayonnaise from her fingers.

"Plodding along in your ancestors' footsteps isn't one," she went on, "though if you'd been raised at Kyverdale Hall, you'd have been conditioned to that being your duty."

"I doubt it."

"The person you are doubts it," Mary Lou answered, "but if your grandfather had raised you, in the way his father must have raised him, you'd have grown up believing that their way was the only way."

She got up to refill the teapot, her expression thoughtful. "How I see it, A.P., is that you have three options. Stick with tradition; do a Tony Benn – by which I mean chuck it all up and declare yourself a non-aristocrat; or stay Lord Kyverdale, but do it *your* way."

A.P.'s mind returned to his thoughts in the House, yesterday: that the heritage was his for his lifetime, to make of it what he would. Had he the courage to wreak change where tradition had for centuries held sway?

"If I went for the third option," he replied, "I would first have to find out what my way is."

Chapter 5

*W*hen Jeremy saw a posse of journalists and photographers at Caracas airport, he assumed they were awaiting the arrival of a celebrity. Then a smartly-dressed young woman appeared at his side and gripped his elbow.

"I am Maria Santander, press secretary to the company your father was here to meet with, Mr. Bornstein. And you and I are going to have to fight our way through that crush. There is nothing I can do about it."

"How did they know I was coming?"

"From your father's London office, which is how I myself knew. He was well-known in the world he moved in – and those reporters are like bloodhounds. They want to know exactly what he was here for."

"Why not tell them and get it over with," Jeremy managed to say before the reporters surged around them.

"I am afraid, Mr. Bornstein, that it isn't as simple as that.

Millions of dollars are at stake. It would be best for you to say nothing. Leave the talking to me."

Jeremy's jet lag was compounded by bewilderment and disbelief when the first question was flung at him – by an American journalist: "Any idea who bumped off your parents and the other guy?"

Bumped off?

Maria Santander kept a firm hold on his arm, expertly stonewalling the quizzing as she propelled him through the throng and into a chauffeur-driven limousine, whose dark-tinted windows made him feel like a character in *The Godfather.*

"I was told that my parents were killed in an accident," he said, as the vehicle glided away.

"An *incident*," Maria answered. "A car bomb, to be precise. If it is any consolation, their deaths were instantaneous."

"It isn't." Well, not right now. Jeremy was seething with rage that terrorists had taken them from him. Blown them to smithereens – but why?

"I am truly sorry," Maria said to him.

"Thanks."

"And please believe that my company will do everything possible to smooth your path while you are here. Arrangements have already been made to fly the coffins home."

"Since I'm here to escort them, it will have to be *re*arranged!" Jeremy said sharply.

"As you wish, Mr. Bornstein. Your parents' effects have been collected from their hotel suite and are now in my office," she added.

Dad's leather-backed hairbrush and Laura's silver one. Clothes for the holiday they'd looked forward to having together. Her travel slippers and his. All neatly packed. Like their wearers now were, in the two coffins. What was left of them.

Jeremy felt his stomach heave. "Would you please ask the driver to stop the car? I need some air."

A moment later, he was throwing up at the roadside, aware of the mountainous terrain through which they were traveling, that a cluster of shabbily dressed men and women, pails of water in their hands, had paused at the bottom of a steep track to eye him curiously, and that Maria Santander was beside him.

"Please excuse me," he muttered when she handed him a paper tissue to wipe his lips.

"I understand."

The hell she did!

"They are carrying water to their homes," she said conversationally when the watchers went on their way.

While trying to pull himself together, Jeremy noted the shanties crowded together on the mountainside and that those who had halted to stare at him were now passing others, also clutching pails, heading downward. Some of the women were carrying babies, strapped to their backs.

"Why isn't there running water in their homes?" he asked Maria. "How can they live like that? And in those broken down huts –"

"They themselves are to blame for their plight," she answered with a shrug. "Everyone in Venezuela thinks life will be better for them in Caracas and most of our country's population has settled here."

When they resumed their journey, she offered Jeremy some brandy. "It will make you feel better."

"No, thanks."

He eyed the cut glass decanters and glasses in the limousine's cocktail cabinet, the gold-plated taps on the miniature sink emphasizing the sharp contrasts between immense wealth and the dire poverty he had just seen.

What a sheltered life he'd lived. A millionaire's son who'd walked around blinkered, he was thinking, when Maria told him she had canceled the hotel reservation his father's secretary had made for him.

"Why?" And why did he feel antagonistic toward her when she was being so helpful?

"The journalists will be waiting there for you."

"Will it be any different wherever you're taking me to?" Who was she protecting? Jeremy, or the company she worked for? From the first, she'd been anxious that he might say the wrong things. But what about?

"In the home of our late chairman, the press cannot get to you," she said. "Senor Mendez, too, was killed in the incident."

The "other guy" that the American reporter had mentioned.

"His family have invited you to be their guest."

Something she had said at the airport returned to Jeremy. "What was the deal my father was here to do?"

"That is a highly confidential matter, Mr. Bornstein."

"And you mentioned millions of dollars being at stake."

"Which is all I know," she replied smoothly.

"Could the deal have anything to do with the car bomb?" Jeremy persisted.

"I am unable to say."

Did that mean she had no idea? Or that she did, but wouldn't tell Jeremy?

"I'd like to speak to the police about what happened to my parents," he said.

"By all means do. I myself shall arrange it for you."

Jeremy had to find out who the culprits were and make

them pay for it! Bessie was only a kid and must be spared the details, but Janis would surely feel as he did, he thought, as the limousine began winding its way through a secluded estate, graced by an abundance of tall trees, and homes so magnificent, this had to be Caracas's "millionaires' row."

"This reminds me of The Bishops Avenue in North London," he remarked, "only more so!"

"And no doubt that is where you live," said Maria with a smile.

"No, as a matter of fact."

"But this estate would be unlikely to impress Jake Bornstein's son," she declared. "Unlike the tourists who are brought here by their guides to see where most of Venezuela's wealth is concentrated."

"Given the shacks on the mountainside, I wouldn't call it something to be proud of," Jeremy replied.

"It is how things are," said Maria with another of her habitual shrugs.

Then the chauffeur turned the car into a broad forecourt and pulled up in front of the high, wrought-iron gates blocking his path. A uniformed guard, with a vicious-looking Doberman tugging on the chain he was gripping, approached the vehicle to check its occupants before they were allowed to proceed.

Damn right the press won't be able to get at me here! thought Jeremy.

He would not forget his first impression of the family into whose presence he was ushered some minutes later, nor the dignity with which they wore their grief. Briefly, it was like looking at a portrait. The stillness and the unrelieved garments of mourning. The proud, high-cheekboned faces.

He did not immediately register that the group was entirely female, and not until Maria had introduced him to them, one by one, did he realize that they were four generations of Mendez women.

He would later learn that the last of the Mendez men had died with Laura and Jake Bornstein. Dazed by shock and sorrow as he was, it was impossible for Jeremy to absorb much of what was said to him that evening. Only that he was made to feel welcome and that it was a relief to be in this airy and peaceful house.

"If you don't feel like joining the family for a meal, nobody will mind. You must be exhausted," said Senor Mendez's eldest daughter, Lola.

"A tray will be prepared and sent to Mr. Bornstein's room if he wishes it," said her stately mother.

"Thanks for the offer, but all I need is a cold shower and some sleep," Jeremy replied.

"Then Lola shall ring for Carlos to show you immediately to your room."

When Jeremy awoke the following morning, he had no idea where he was. Then the nightmare situation that had brought him to Caracas returned full force and his momentary sense of well-being departed.

His wristwatch told him that he had slept for fourteen hours. How could he have slept at all, with what he had on his mind? Telling his hostess that sleep was what he needed had been just an excuse to avoid company until he'd had time to absorb and consider the few facts Maria Santander had carefully filtered to him.

"Filtered" described it. Maria's manner had been as guarded as this house was. What the hell was going on? Jeremy asked himself. And he'd wasted a whole night, instead of trying to find out! Fallen flat on his face on this sumptuous bed, fully-clothed and out for the count.

After showering in an en suite bathroom that, like the bedroom, was his idea of the Ritz, though he had never stayed there, Jeremy made his way down the sweeping, marble staircase, to the cool and plant-adorned hall, where Carlos, the blue jacket he had worn last night swapped for a white one, told him that breakfast was served on the patio and led the way.

Lola was seated at a large, circular table, with four younger girls, their ages ranging from ten to sixteen, Jeremy reckoned.

"My sisters," she said, introducing them. "Carlotta, Isabella, Estrella, and Rosita."

Though they managed to give him a smile, the girls remained silent, their demeanor subdued. But they'd just lost their father and Jeremy was a stranger in their midst.

"Do you have any brothers?" he asked Lola.

She shook her head. "Nor do we have any Mendez uncles, or male cousins. Did you ever hear of an all-female dynasty?" she added wryly. Her expression shadowed. "That's what the Mendez family has become, Mr. Bornstein."

"Could we call each other by our first names?"

"Why not, and you needn't wait for me to invite you to sit down."

Jeremy took the vacant chair opposite her and said, when Carlos brought him a tall glass of orange juice and a portion of fresh fruit salad sufficient for three people, "I couldn't possibly get through all this."

"Just eat what you want and leave the rest," said Lola airily, "like we do."

In a country where undernourishment must be rife, thought Jeremy, recalling the shanties. Despite his father's wealth, Jeremy hadn't been raised in the way Lola and her sisters evidently had.

We weren't allowed to waste food, nor were we overloaded with pocket money. Sheltered though Jeremy had yesterday realized his life had been, compared with those he was having breakfast with . . .

Jake Bornstein, though, wasn't your run-of-the-mill millionaire; his feet had remained on the ground and he'd made sure the same went for his children. *Wasn't* was now the operative word.

When her sisters had left the table – and most of the food served to them – Jeremy said to Lola, "As far as I know, my father had no enemies. Did yours?"

Lola got up to lean on the stone balustrade overlooking the exotic garden, the simple, black dress she was wearing enhancing her shapely figure.

"I didn't notice last night, how tall you are," Jeremy remarked.

"All the Mendez women have long legs," she said with a smile that briefly lit her expression. "Even my grandmother and my great-grandmother, I'm told. But they would not have dreamed of not hiding them under long skirts!"

Jeremy stopped admiring her legs and sipped some coffee. Sex and socializing weren't what he was here for!

"As to what you just asked me," Lola went on, "it'd be naive to suppose that my father didn't have enemies and I'd say the same of yours. Wealth breeds envy, doesn't it?"

"You think envy is a strong enough motive for doing what was done to them?" Jeremy answered. "Well, I don't!"

"And my advice to you is, cool it."

"Easier said than done. Would you mind telling me where you learned to speak English like a Yank?"

"Is my accent that marked?"

"Well, there are certainly transatlantic overtones."

"Transatlantic for you, but not for me," she corrected him. "I'm a Harvard graduate by the way, and three years in the

States is the probable answer to your question. Their intonation is hard *not* to acquire when it's the only one you hear."

"You don't look old enough to be a graduate," Jeremy said as she returned to the table.

"But I'll never see twenty-one again. Your parents mentioned your being at Oxford."

"You met them?"

"They dined here," Lola revealed while topping up his coffee cup. "The night before it happened. I thought them charming people."

Jeremy turned to watch a colorful bird hop along the balustrade, so Lola would not see that tears had sprung to his eyes.

"Do the police have any clues?" he inquired, collecting himself. "About who planted the bomb?"

"If they have, they wouldn't tell *me*," she replied, "nor you, so I shouldn't bother asking them."

"How can you be so calm about it!"

"Finding the perpetrator won't bring my father and your parents back."

"But *I* have to know the whys and wherefores," Jeremy said, simmering down. Lola was right in one respect: telling him to cool it. He must keep a clear head.

"I intend seeing the police today," he told her, "and if they brush me off, I'll do my own investigating."

Lola put down her cup. "That could be very dangerous for you."

"But it isn't going to stop me."

Chapter 6

*M*arianne, who had remained in England to attend the double funeral, saw Janis flinch when Kurt Kohn appeared at the cemetery. But Janis was unlikely ever to forget that she had been pregnant with Kurt's child, though he had not known. Or the equally secret abortion, after breaking their engagement.

Horrified though Marianne was when Janis confided her intentions, she had not tried to dissuade her. If there's one thing I've learned, thought Marianne now, and it took me long enough to learn it, it's that young people must be allowed to steer their own lives, as I did mine.

Enveloped by her own grief for her departed parents, Janis, a protective arm around Bessie, studied the pensive face of the boy whose heart she had broken. In doing so, she had broken her own heart, too. Would I do any differently, she asked herself, if I could turn back the clock?

While the rabbi intoned the burial service under a leaden sky that matched her feelings, Janis averted her gaze from

Kurt, lest he glance up and meet her eyes. The crucial facts upon which she had based her decision hadn't changed. Kurt had a brilliant future ahead of him in Vienna; his family's contacts would ensure it. But Janis could not have raised her children in a city where anti-Semitism was rife. In a country whose citizens had seen fit to elect Waldheim as their president.

Had Kurt known this, he would have sacrificed his career opportunities to remain with her in England, take his chance of making it to the top in psychiatric research without help – by which time he would be old and gray, Janis had thought. She had loved him too much to stand in his way.

Later, standing with her brother and sister to receive the condolences of family and friends, she steeled herself as Kurt approached. With him was a plump and pretty, dark-haired girl.

"We appreciate your coming," Jeremy said to him.

"And I appreciate your letting me know," Kurt answered in the courteous manner that, for Janis, had singled him out from other boys. "Laura and your father could not have been more kind to me when I was a student in London. Though I hadn't envisaged returning," he added, avoiding Janis's eye, "for this tragic occasion I wanted to pay my respects."

"And we are representing Kurt's parents," said the girl, "who are both operating at the hospital today."

"Allow me to introduce my wife," said Kurt, smiling down at her.

Janis felt as if a knife had been plunged into her side, but managed to smile.

"Ursula is the daughter of the professor with whom I'm now studying," Kurt told them.

"I wish you happiness together," said Janis sincerely. But

her letting Kurt go, for unselfish reasons, hadn't encompassed his quick recovery via another girl.

One now linking his arm possessively – and whose looks are the direct opposite of mine, Janis noted.

"Did you know that my sister and your husband were once engaged?" Bessie asked Ursula.

"That is something he did not tell to me," Ursula replied. Too sharply.

"My brother used to call them Romeo and Juliet." Bessie piled on the agony for all three. "And you're welcome to come to our house for tea. A lot of people will be coming."

"Thank you, but we have other arrangements," said Ursula politely.

"Remember when you helped Jeremy blow up the balloons for my tenth birthday party, Kurt?" Bessie said with a forlorn smile.

But Ursula was leading him away, and those waiting to speak to Janis clustered around her, shutting out the receding view of the young man once her lover and the girl he had made his wife.

The following morning, Janis and Jeremy went together to a suite of offices in the City, for the formal reading of Jake's and Laura's wills.

"Since your stepsister is still a minor, there is no necessity for her to be present," said the silver-haired and rotund man into whose sanctum they were ushered.

Coffee was then brought and poured by his secretary, whose departure he awaited before saying another word.

While he tapped his fingers on the mahogany desk and gazed through the window absently, Janis glanced at the tomes lining the high-ceilinged room and Jeremy recalled his interview with a police inspector in Caracas, the outcome of which was: Go home, Mr. Bornstein. Leave the investigating to us.

When the lawyer cleared his throat and rustled some papers, summoning their attention, for both it was as if they were actors in a play, so unreal did their presence in this setting, and its purpose, seem to them.

"I shall deal with the late Mrs. Bornstein's will first."

"Whatever you think suitable, Mr. Adams," said Jeremy.

"It is a good deal more straightforward than your late father's," the lawyer replied.

Janis and Jeremy then learned that the bulk of Laura's assets had been left to her by her maternal grandfather and would now pass to Bessie, under the terms of *his* will.

The residue of her estate was to be divided equally between Janis, Jeremy, and Bessie.

Janis said emotionally, "I hope that my father treated all three of us equally, too, like he did when he was alive."

"Then let me set your mind at rest," said Mr. Adams, "but we shall come to that shortly. There is one further legacy from your stepmother to you, Miss Bornstein," he added, adjusting his spectacles before reading:

"In the event of my husband and I dying together before my daughter, Bessie, comes of age, I entrust responsibility for her to Janis Bornstein, who shall be her legal guardian."

Janis was momentarily stunned.

"Rather you than me!" Jeremy told her fervently.

"You don't mind?"

"I can do without the trouble this will cause with Bessie's grandmother, though you'll always be welcome to my advice, Janis."

Mr. Adams pointedly cleared his throat again. "May we get on with reading your late father's will?"

* * *

When eventually they emerged onto the street, they stood on the pavement, traffic filtering past them, trying to take in the enormity of Jake Bornstein's wealth. They had not realized that their father was a *multi*-millionaire, nor the breadth of his international business dealings.

The parent company, transferred from Johannesburg to London when Jake married Laura, functioned from a small office in Holborn, where Miss Carter, Jake's middle-aged secretary, held the fort during his frequent absences abroad.

Jeremy broke the silence. "How could Dad have made all that money without having a big organization – like the Mendez company in Caracas?"

"I can't say I ever gave much thought to Dad's business," Janis answered, "but we're going to have to, now. There'll be meetings with accountants and all that, Jeremy. And I'm not cut out for it. Are you?"

Jeremy took her arm and steered her toward the pub on the corner. "I could use a drink, Janis, and I think you could, too! But it won't be like this for Lola Mendez – She's the eldest daughter –"

"So you mentioned." Janis turned up her coat collar against the chill wind, wishing she was still in Sydney where it was now spring. "What you mean is that all the sorting out will fall to Lola's mother –"

"If you'd met her mother, you wouldn't think that," Jeremy replied. "That generation of Venezuelan woman knows her place, it's strictly in the home – and you should see their home!"

"Just one of the differences between the Mendezes and us is that we didn't live a millionaire lifestyle by any stretch of the imagination. Though Dad could probably have bought and sold most of our neighbors, nobody would have known it.

"Remember when he and Laura were house-hunting after they got married, how Shirley wanted Dad to buy a mansion?" Jeremy went on.

"I can't say I do," Janis answered as they entered the pub and found a vacant table beside the hearth.

"You were too busy being miserable about Dad's remarrying," said Jeremy with a bleak smile, "and you missed Jo'burg –"

"You weren't overjoyed, yourself –"

"But he did us a favor by marrying Laura."

Jeremy added after a pause, "Well, as Lola Mendez said in a different context, we can't bring them back."

"She seems to've made quite an impression on you."

"And in different circumstances . . ." Jeremy said with a wink.

"No need to tell me. I know you!"

"What would you like to drink?"

"A Four-X if they have it."

"You used to drink lager and lime –"

"With Kurt. But those days are long gone."

While Jeremy fetched their drinks, Janis let herself recall her student days. Celebrating passing an exam, or a friend's birthday, in the pub close to college, she and Kurt always tucked away together in a cozy corner. The University Jewish Society meetings they'd attended and the fight against insidious anti-Semitism on campuses and elsewhere.

A fight still being battled by today's Jewish students, but how remote Janis now felt from all that. There was a time in your life when you fought for causes, that bore no relation to the personal realities of living. To happiness, or the lonely alternative.

Would she ever be happy again? What Jeremy had just said about Laura and Dad: "Well, we can't bring them back," was like shutting a door on the past. As was seeing Kurt with a wife at his side. A cold finality. And how Janis now felt was as though her life had reached a time of new beginnings.

"What are we going to do about Dad's company?" she said when Jeremy returned to the table.

"That's what I meant about it not being like this for Lola," he harked back. "She struck me as a strong character who'll cope with whatever's required of her, now her father is dead. But the Mendez company, as I mentioned, is a big organization, and it seems to run on oiled wheels. I was met at the airport by one of the cogs. And I've yet to tell you my impressions in that respect.

"The point I was making about Lola is that she'll have a team of executives to smooth her path. Dad, though, if you don't count Miss Carter, was a one-man band."

"This beer tastes different from the way it does on the beach in Sydney," Janis remarked irrelevantly, wiping some foam from her lips, after setting down the glass. "We used to picnic and swim on Sundays."

"On Bondi Beach?"

"Not likely," said Janis, "that's where the druggies hang out, you could step on a needle in the sand. And sometimes," she reminisced, "we'd give the beach a miss and spend the day at Bobbin Head – that's part of Kuringai Chase National Park – where you can hire a boat and sail on the river –"

Jeremy surveyed his sister's tanned complexion and her sun-bleached fair hair. "Your coloring's gone back to how it was when we lived in South Africa. And who's the 'we' you keep mentioning?"

"Just the crowd I got involved with. They're a nice bunch."

"But no special guy?"

"I'd have told you. Wouldn't you tell me if you had a special girl?"

"Sure."

Despite their lengthy separation, they still felt close and both were thankful for that.

"Are you sure you're not upset about Laura's making *me* Bessie's guardian?" Janis asked.

"Knowing Laura, she did it because you're a female," Jeremy answered. "On the quiet, she was a feminist, wasn't she?"

"Not always on the quiet. She told me that when what was then called 'Women's Lib' was getting off the ground, a picture of her burning her bra at a demonstration got into the papers and disgraced the family!"

They shared a laugh that leavened the gloom enveloping them since they learned of their loss.

"Do you think Bessie would fancy living in Australia?" said Janis.

Jeremy's reaction was, "Oh boy, are you storing up trouble for yourself with Shirley!"

"If Laura had wanted her mother to have the yeas and nays over Bessie, she'd have made *her* Bessie's guardian," Janis declared. "Just one of the reasons she didn't has to be that Shirley is too old."

"And I'd rather *you* said that to Shirley than me. She's just had a face-lift, hasn't she?"

"But nothing could make her attitudes anything but hidebound," said Janis. "She's the same age as Marianne, but when did Marianne ever lay down the law to us like Shirley always has?

"She'd try to make Bessie a replica of herself," Janis went on, "and Laura couldn't have been unaware of that."

"And what shall *you* try to make her?" asked Jeremy.

"I shall just do what Laura did with us, though she sometimes had to fight Dad about it. Keep my eye on her and let
her get on with being herself."

A thoughtful pause followed and Janis gazed at what was
left of the beer in her glass. "Not that I yet know who *myself*
is . . ."

"Think you'll find out in Australia?"

"Who knows? But it's an easygoing place. I don't feel
pressurized there and I'm giving it a try." Janis emerged from
her self-absorption and looked at her brother. "When are you
returning to Oxford, Jeremy? You mustn't let what's happened get between you and your studies."

"It already has."

Janis then learned, while the lunch hour crowd milled
around them, what Jeremy had not yet told her. That they
could not assume that the car bomb was intended for Senor
Mendez; that Laura and Jake were just in the wrong place at
the wrong time.

"When Dad used to go off to do one of his deals, the only
thing we knew was which country he was headed for,"
Jeremy reminded her, "and not always that. It'd never been
any different for us, had it? We'd grown up with a father who
took off for wherever, like other kids' dads went to the store
they worked in, or whatever their job was.

"I shouldn't think Laura had any idea of what Dad's
business machinations were," Jeremy continued airing his
thoughts. "He'd arrive back with a piece of jewelry, or an
exotic dress length for her and she'd say, 'Very nice.' "

"It was part of our family routine, like it was for our mum,
before she got ill and for a while Dad stopped traveling, to
be with her."

"And doesn't that prove that with Dad the family always
came first?" said Janis with feeling.

"I'm not accusing him of anything."

"Then why do I get the impression that you are?"

"Look – he was a terrific father," Jeremy replied, "if somewhat Victorian at times and I had clashes with him on that account, though you didn't when you looked all set to fulfill his expectations, getting engaged to the only steady boyfriend you'd had –"

"There's no need to go into all that!"

"But it's part of assessing Jake Bornstein, isn't it?"

"Is that what you're doing?" Janis demanded.

"How am I to find out who killed him and why? If I don't face up to the man he might have been."

Chapter 7

A. P. spent Christmas at Kyverdale Hall with his mother and his grandmother, the familiar feudal traditions evoking the feeling that he, now their custodian, was caught in a time warp.

He could not have been more than five when he had first stood beside his grandfather, while his lordship handed the servants their gifts on Christmas Eve and afterwards invited them to partake of refreshments.

Most of those to whom A.P. was now presenting gailywrapped packages qualified to be called "old retainers." And Christmas was the season of goodwill. Why, then, did A.P. feel that he was presenting *largesse*? Playing "Lord Bountiful."

Because he damn well was – and it was getting up his nose! As the Kyverdale tradition of serving lunch to the servants on Christmas Day undoubtedly would, tomorrow.

What was it but a once-a-year concession? – and all concerned knew it.

You're beginning to think like your friend the miner's son,

A.P. said to himself while pouring sherry for the butler who usually poured it for *him*. Oh the jibes, if Gary Potter witnessed all this!

Was A.P. thinking of doing what Mary Lou Dryden had called "a Tony Benn"? Opting out of the privileged class he was born to?

He watched his mother and grandmother handing round mince pies to the gardeners and the maids. This afternoon, the two had made their Christmas rounds in Kyverdale village, dispensing turkeys and plum puddings at every cottage, as generations of Kyverdale ladies had before them.

Grandmother Kyverdale had made a good job of being what she *wasn't* born to be. And nearly twenty years of being the wife of a middle-class Jew hadn't eroded A.P.'s mother's aristocratic conditioning. Moira Dean had never doubted for a moment who and what she was.

Which isn't to say Mum's a snob, A.P. reflected, observing her friendly manner while she chatted to a kitchen maid. Nor had being the daughter of a wealthy peer stopped her from leaving home to pursue a career.

A.P. recalled Moira's saying, when he was a schoolboy, that giving birth to him had made her happy on more counts than one. "Because the Kyverdale title can skip a generation to the next direct male heir, I was then able to stop feeling I'd let my father down by being a girl," she had revealed.

"When I gave him you, all came right," she had declared, giving A.P. a hug.

For her, but not for me, thought A.P. now. But things hadn't gone right for his mother in another respect. Would they from now on? For his father, too?

A.P. had not seen much of either since the event he hadn't let them know he had found shattering – their divorce. Since it had coincided with his leaving home for Oxford, distance had removed him from their scene. If he spent a weekend in London with one or the other, it was over in a flash, no time to talk about the things that mattered.

Now, his mother had a boyfriend who worked in publishing, as she did – whom she had invited to spend Christmas at Kyverdale Hall, and who hadn't yet arrived. Would Hugh Bellingham get the ticking-off she used to give A.P.'s dad, when he got here late, on Christmas Eve?

There'd been times when Dad didn't come at all, when Christmas had coincided with Chanukah which he had preferred to spend with his mother.

A.P. recalled a bitter quarrel between his parents, when the Bornsteins were giving a Chanukah party on Christmas Eve, and his father had wanted to take him there.

He was only a kid and had fled from the room. But his mother had won, since it was she whom he had accompanied.

A situation that went on for years, A.P. reflected. Then Mum suddenly stopped fighting Dad and let me spend some of the Jewish festivals with his family, on condition I didn't forget I was a Catholic.

A.P. didn't want to forget it. His religion was part of him and always would be. That didn't mean, though, that he didn't feel Jewish, too, if not in the religious way. He could not have been raised by Martin Dean, grown up feeling one of the close-knit clan his father's family was, without being aware that his was a double identity, and the richer for it.

When after dinner that evening Lady Kyverdale retired to her room to rest before they attended Midnight Mass, A.P. was briefly alone with his mother in the library that was now his.

"Is Hugh Bellingham a Catholic?" he asked while she sipped her brandy.

"I'm unlikely to make the same mistake twice."

"Does that mean you're going to marry him?"

"It's certainly looking that way," she said with a smile.

"I hope it works out for you," said A.P.

"But you don't look too cheerful about it," Moira noted.

"I've only met the man twice. But if you're happy, I'm happy for you, Mum."

"Isn't it time you stopped calling me 'Mum,' and began calling me 'Mother'?"

"If you say so."

"Well, it's hardly the way for Lord Kyverdale to address his mother, is it?"

"If you say not."

"Stop behaving the way your father does!"

"You seem to be forgetting that I'm his son, as well as yours."

"Why else would I be worried about how you'll adapt to your new role?"

A.P. got up from the leather Chesterfield to stand with his back to the fire. "If you'd like the truth, I don't feel comfortable with what being *your* son has landed me with."

Moira straightened her black velvet skirt, stalling for time. "Are you saying that taking over where your grandfather left off is beyond you?"

"What I'm actually saying is I don't fancy it —"

"Be that as it may," Moira cut in, "it isn't for you to choose."

"Tell that to Tony Benn."

"Have you turned into a rabid socialist?" Moira's expression was appalled. "If so, I blame that boy from Newcastle you brought to my flat for dinner. He used his butter knife to cut up his chop."

"But his lack of table manners didn't stop him from getting a place at Oxford," A.P. retorted, "nor should it. And if you can't credit me with having ideas and attitudes of my own, too bad."

"You have certainly turned into a rabid *something*!"

"Kindly stop trying to categorize me. The trouble with our society is everyone has to wear a label."

"And since yours is a privileged one, you should think yourself fortunate." Moira went to fortify herself with more brandy and said, returning to the fray, "There's such a thing as the conscience of the rich, my darling, and you must try not to fall foul of it."

"Don't worry, I'm not thinking of giving the family fortune to the poor, or of selling Kyverdale Hall!"

"But right now, I wouldn't put it past you to do something hasty that you'd afterwards regret. It's that red hair you got from your *other* grandfather!"

The arrival of Hugh Bellingham cut short their altercation.

"Sorry I'm so late, darling," he said, kissing Moira. "If I look somewhat disheveled, I had to deal with a flat tire."

He didn't, but A.P. couldn't imagine him looking other than immaculate.

"Then the traffic got more and more horrendous," Hugh continued his apologizing.

But nobody would believe he had driven from London to Somerset and arrived without a rumple in his jacket, his sleek hair looking as if he had just had it shampooed and set. A.P.'s dad, on the other hand, had never paid much attention to sartorial elegance.

"I forgive you, Hugh," said Moira playfully, and A.P. thought there was more chance of her making a go of it with Hugh, a man of her own class and religion, than there ever was with his father.

Hugh was the younger son of a "gentleman farmer" – an

expression that A.P. found somewhat at odds with a farmer's life. There was, too, that Moira and Hugh had their work in common, A.P. reflected when they began discussing an American novel for which every British publisher was currently bidding.

If they married, they would come home from their separate publishing houses, eat dinner, then probably retire early to their twin beds to read manuscripts.

Why did A.P. think they'd have twin beds? Perhaps because there was something curiously passionless about Hugh, a spiritual quality about his thin, pale face.

Unlike my definitely macho dad, thought A.P. – and some of the lyrics in the songs Martin Dean wrote nowadays were raunchy, a far cry from the tender ballads he and his composer partner had written when A.P. was a schoolboy.

"Did you know Dad's latest album has made the charts?" he asked Moira.

"I could hardly not know, since it blasts my ears whenever I'm subjected to piped music. Where is he spending Christmas, by the way? Or should I say Chanukah?"

"In L.A., where he's currently working," A.P. answered, "but why did you ask, since you don't care?"

"Believe it or not, I bear him no ill will."

"That's damn good of you!"

Moira said to Hugh, who was nursing a whiskey, "My son is in a bolshie mood about his inheritance and it's affecting his manners."

"I seem to recall," said Hugh, "my cousin who inherited *our* family title going through that stage when we were at Balliol together."

"Did he ever get over it?" A.P. inquired.

"He had no option but to."

A.P. didn't agree.

* * *

On Boxing Day, the Drydens came for lunch and Kyverdale Hall resounded with the pealing laughter of Mary Lou's irrepressible mother.

"Sukey hasn't changed since our commune days," Moira told Hugh over dessert. "Anyone who felt down in the dumps would repair to the outhouse where Sukey worked, little knowing that the girl cheering them up with her corny jokes would one day be commissioned to design ceramics for the rich and famous."

"But how I made my bread in those days," Sukey recalled, "was strictly for the tourist trade. Remember those hideous toby jugs, Moira?"

"And that dreadful plonk we imbibed was the best we could afford," said Bill Dryden.

"But it's amazing," said Lady Kyverdale, fingering her rope of pearls, "how easily one learns to take fine wines for granted."

"When you were a girl treading the boards, did any young men ever drink champagne out of your slippers?" A.P. dared to ask her.

The old lady sipped some Château d'Yquem and smiled. "Well, your grandfather never did. Once he'd set eyes on me, it was goodbye to all that and we were married a month later."

"Love at first sight for both of you?" Mary Lou found the nerve to inquire.

Though Lady Kyverdale had never been less than kind to her, there was about her an imposing quality, enhanced by her tightly-corseted figure and her Edwardian hairstyle. Mary Lou couldn't visualize her without that rope of pearls, or with her snowy hair let down.

Now, though, her eyes were twinkling, as if she was enjoying remembering her youth. "It was certainly love at first sight for him," she answered Mary Lou, "or he wouldn't have defied his parents to marry me."

"How did yours react?" asked A.P.

"My mother went out and bought herself a new hat – a feathered one, I seem to recall – and my father said he hoped I knew what I was letting myself in for."

"Did you, Grandmother?"

"No. But I never regretted it, A.P." Lady Kyverdale then returned the conversation whence it had begun, as though she had decided she had revealed enough. "I was never quite sure why that commune broke up –"

"Nor I, at the time," said Bill Dryden, "but it's easy, now, to understand. Those of us who lived there together were close friends, but the commune itself had no common aim. It was just a quiet interlude until each of us found our way in the world," he declared while cracking a walnut.

"Some quiet interlude!" said his wife. "With Andy Frolich banging out compositions on the piano, night and day, and those heated discussions we all used to have. Not to mention the kids that some of the members were already lumbered with –"

"Thanks a bunch!" said Mary Lou.

"That didn't include you, honey, you were still just a gleam in your father's wicked eye."

"Nor me," said A.P.

"But your mom got pregnant with you while we were still living on the commune, and every morning the bathroom reverberated with the sound of her morning sickness," Sukey reminisced. "It was enough to put me off ever letting myself in for it!"

"Does that mean I was an accident?" Mary Lou wanted to know.

"Yes, as a matter of fact," said her father, "but a very happy one."

"That's beside the point," she informed him. "Didn't your lot ever do anything positive? Other than further your own careers?"

"This is turning into an inquisition, and it's hard on Hugh, since he isn't a parent," said Moira.

"I am nevertheless an interested observer and waiting with bated breath to learn how Bill is going to handle it."

"With the truth, of course," said Bill. "I can see how it might seem to Mary Lou and A.P. that we were just a group of educated drifters in those days, but in reality it was a very positive experience that helped us become what we finally became.

"Those heated discussions your mother mentioned, Mary Lou — let's just say that they served to bring us down to earth —"

"Good for you," she interrupted, "but you lived on a commune for selfish reasons, and that isn't what communes are about. If I lived on one, it would have to be useful to society."

"Your motives," A.P. told his mother and Mary Lou's parents, "were typical of your 'I'm-all-right-Jack' generation."

"And that asinine comment," said Hugh Bellingham, "is typical of some of the unsolicited manuscripts sent to me by your own generation. Still wet behind the ears and pontificating about the state of the world.

"Is *your* office slush pile awash with such rubbish?" he asked Moira, who had the wisdom to remain silent.

"I'd like to think my mother has more respect for the hard work that's gone into unsolicited manuscripts than the term 'slush pile' implies," said A.P.

As for Hugh Bellingham! Was this the man A.P. might be

getting for a stepfather? "Instead of damning the young authors you mentioned, why not give what their work is saying a chance?" he demanded. "Or are you one of those who thinks that the young are automatically wrong?"

When eventually A.P. and Mary Lou made their escape from the table, they went for a stroll around the estate.

"Doesn't look very Christmassy, does it?" she remarked, surveying the acres of lush parkland. "We rarely get white Christmases anymore and global warming – the fruits of progress! – has to be responsible, A.P."

"But when I was little, a white Christmas was pretty well guaranteed and I used to help the head gardener build a big snowman on the lawn," he said nostalgically, "in front of the house, and the carol singers from the village stood in a circle around it on Christmas Eve."

"Returning to global warming, you're now in a position to speak on ecological issues in the House," said Mary Lou. "That's if you decide to stay a lord –"

"What we discussed the day I spilled paint on your floor isn't something I can make up my mind about just like that!"

"There's no need to snap at me."

"You'll have to forgive me. I seem to be snapping at everyone, at present."

"So I've noticed."

"If I opt out of the title, Mary Lou, I'll be letting my mother and my grandmother down."

"And if you let that influence your decision," she answered, "it won't be your own life that you're living. It'll just be an extension of the corrupt old way, with you perpetuating it."

"There was nothing corrupt about my grandfather."

"But there is about what he stood for."

"You sound like Gary Potter!"

"Who's he?"

"Never mind!"

They emerged from an avenue of ancient oak trees to the lakeside, and Mary Lou exclaimed, "Huntin', shootin' 'n' fishin' describes it!"

"The Kyverdales have never indulged in blood sports," A.P. informed her.

"But you know what I mean," she persisted, "and in case you don't, I'll give it to you in one word. Privilege. Enjoying the fat of the land, while other folk are working for their living – and some haven't even got jobs."

"I wouldn't call that giving it to me in one word."•

"But hasn't it struck you, A.P., that you could do something worthwhile with all this?" she said, gesturing toward the parkland.

A.P. sat down on the upturned boat beside the lake. "Would you mind telling me what?"

"Produce organically grown vegetables and market them cheaply," she said, "for people who'd like to feed their kids with stuff that hasn't been treated with pesticides, but can't afford to. Look at all that land going to waste," she added pointing into the distance.

"Master of all he surveys," she said when A.P. remained silent, "and he doesn't know what to do with it! There are apple orchards here, aren't there? It could be fun to produce non-alcoholic cider –"

"You're actually prepared to let me have some fun?"

"I'm serious about what I'm suggesting, A.P. And I'd like you to think it over. You could even start a commune, couldn't you? One with a useful purpose."

"If I did, would you join it?"

"Who, me?"

It was then that A.P. fell in love with the girl he had known all his life. As though he had never seen her before, so transformed was she in his eyes, her chestnut hair caught by the breeze blowing from the lake, and her usually confident expression suddenly uncertain.

One moment she was just Mary Lou Dryden, his godfather's daughter, and the next . . . It was as if a bolt of lightning had struck him.

"What I'm asking is, would you have the courage of your own convictions?" A.P. said, trying to recover his equilibrium.

"I would certainly give it some thought," she said as they resumed walking, unaware that A.P. had to stop himself from helping her climb the grassy incline beside the lake.

If he did, she would think his sudden solicitousness highly suspect! How was he to get their relationship on a different footing? Transport Mary Lou to the heavenly heights to which she had just catapulted him?

As for the commune . . . What A.P. wanted right now was to be alone on a desert island with Mary Lou.

"First we'd have to decide on the common aim," she said practically. "If I'm to be in on it from the beginning, I'd feel entitled to a say in that."

"Your ideas are important to me, Mary Lou."

She halted at the top of the incline and gave him a piercing glance. "Since when? Stop trying to flannel me into it, A.P. If I join up with you, it'll be because I want to. And if you decide to do it, it had better be a positive commitment for you, too."

A.P. watched her reach for a blade of grass and chew it pensively. "You used to do that when we were little."

"I also made daisy chains, but I'm grown up now and so are you. Save the looking back for when you get old, A.P.!

And the way things already are on this planet, there could be no grass left for me to chew, by then. None for the cows, either, and that's more important."

"You forgot to mention the fish," said A.P.

"Has the lake been affected by that bloody acid rain?"

"I'm afraid so."

"And you haven't given a thought to trying to save it? *And* the fish?"

"It did enter my head, but the estate manager retired when Grandfather died and I haven't yet engaged a replacement."

Mary Lou clomped in her red wellingtons down the incline and sat down on the boat. "Don't just stand there, A.P. I'm waiting for you to join me and I may as well be comfortable while I lecture you.

"You're not going to like this," she went on when he was seated beside her, "but it has to be said and now is the time to say it. You've never struck me as a very positive person and I'm not sure you've got what it takes to do what we're considering doing —"

A.P. gazed at the expanse of water, as gray as his mood now was.

"I expected a sharp retort," said Mary Lou.

And had anyone but she voiced that criticism of him, they would surely have received one. Instead, he said, "Go on, I'm interested to know what you think of me."

"I've already told you, and it's occurred to me that your home life could be responsible," she replied. "All that being pulled two ways, between your parents."

"Also between their two different backgrounds," A.P. added. "It was like doing a balancing act."

"But it's time to come down from the tightrope," Mary Lou declared, "you're your own person, now."

A.P. laughed humorlessly. "But who is he?"

"In that respect," Mary Lou confessed, "it's the same for me. My mom's suggestion that I spend some time with her parents in the States was a convenient straw I clutched at, but where did it get me?"

"How about the film course?"

"All it did was show me who I'm not – a female replica of my successful father. Dad's blessed with a talent I don't have, though it took him long enough to find out who and what *he* is. He spent years roaming around and writing travel books, didn't he? Like your dad didn't know he was a lyric writer until eventually he tried it."

"And we ought to admit, at least to each other, that in a way we're no different," said A.P.

"Except that their reason for living on a commune wouldn't be ours," Mary Lou countered. "Well, it wouldn't be mine. And it had better not be yours. That's why I lectured you about not being positive in your thinking, A.P."

"I'm pleased you did."

"And you're welcome to lecture me, if and when you think it necessary."

A.P. studied her pensive profile, suddenly beautiful to him, and offered her his parka.

"What on earth's the matter with you, today?" she responded.

"The breeze has turned into a cold wind –"

"I've got my own coat on, haven't I?"

"It isn't a heavy one."

"Pure cashmere is warm without being heavy," Mary Lou told him. "My parents gave it to me for Christmas. What did you get?"

"A tankard with the Kyverdale crest on it from Mum, and a velvet smoking-jacket from Grandmother."

"How very symbolic," said Mary Lou with a giggle.

There was no need to tell A.P. of what.

"What will you do with your grandmother if you turn Kyverdale Hall into a commune?" Mary Lou asked. "Pension her off to the South of France?"

"As it happens, Grandfather willed her the villa he bought for their winter breaks in Menton. But the west wing is where Kyverdale dowagers traditionally live."

"After the new lordship has taken a wife, you mean."

"Or if he already has one."

"But don't get any ideas about a marriage of convenience, A.P.," Mary Lou said with a laugh. "There's a limit to how far I'm prepared to go to get our hypothetical commune off the ground!"

Chapter 8

*E*veryone should have Marianne's luck!" Shirley exclaimed while serving dinner to Janis and Bessie on New Year's Eve. "A successful career and a second husband in Bermuda to rush back to."

"You once had a successful career," Bessie reminded her, "and there's nothing to stop *you* from finding a second husband."

"Only the thing I just mentioned, love. Luck. As for my career, what I was doing was helping my father build his business. Designing rainwear at a factory in Manchester, when the sky could have been the limit for me."

"Didn't my Grandpa Peter use to work in the factory, too?"

"In a manner of speaking, but we won't go into that."

Shirley set plates of roast duckling and vegetables before the girls and sat down opposite them.

"Why aren't you eating?" Janis asked her.

"Who'd have an appetite in my circumstances?" Shirley

replied. "When their own daughter did to them what mine did to me?"

Bessie's expression shadowed with distress. "It isn't Janis's fault that Mummy made her my guardian, Grandma —"

"And I'm not holding it against her. It's your mummy I blame."

"But you shouldn't say bad things about her now she's dead!"

Bessie got up from the table and left the room.

"Laura used to make exits like that when she was Bessie's age," Shirley forlornly recalled. "It was nice of you to bring her to stay with me for New Year," she added, to Janis's surprise. "This can't be much fun for you."

"Nor for you. But the one who matters is Bessie, wouldn't you say?"

Janis's gaze roved the room, once described to her by Marianne as a replica of a Hollywood film set. The last thing this place is, is a home, Janis thought. Shirley patted the cushions into place the minute anyone rose from the sofa. And the furnishings are as coldly elegant as she is. The white carpet and the carefully positioned antique tables and chairs. The lacquered curio cabinet, in it a collection of ivories once treasured by Shirley's father.

Shirley toyed with the diamond brooch adorning her black silk dress. "Did you try to persuade Bessie to live with me, Janis?"

"No, I didn't. Bessie must decide for herself."

"How would a kid of fourteen know what's best for her! Any better than *you* do. You've had no experience of life and it wasn't right of Laura to lumber you with such a responsibility," Shirley declared.

Janis said quietly, "Maybe she thought it would be good

for me, and I don't mind. I'd be happy for Bessie to live with me in Australia —"

Shirley began clearing the table, plonking the plates of uneaten food through the dining-alcove hatch. "Since nobody's interested in the meal I went to such trouble to prepare, I'll stop pretending we're celebrating New Year's Eve! It's your intention to drag that poor child all over the world with you, is it?"

Janis stemmed a sharp retort. "Bessie hasn't yet made up her mind what she wants to do."

"It isn't for her to say."

"I happen to think it is. She has three alternatives and one of them she's adamantly against. She knows what she *doesn't* want to do, and that's live with you."

Janis had intended putting this gently, but it was too late now. She had let herself be provoked.

"I already know that her friend Val's parents have offered to have her till she finishes school," Shirley said frigidly, "but how would that look for me? Strangers giving my granddaughter a home."

"If that's the sort of thing that bothers you," said Janis, "it isn't Bessie you're thinking of."

"And when you're a grandmother yourself, you'll know how I feel," Shirley responded. "What's Bessie's third alternative – or aren't I allowed to know?"

"Her grandpa has told her she's welcome to live with him and Hildegard, in Tel Aviv."

"That would be the finish of me!" Shirley sat down on a handy chair. "Would you mind getting me a brandy, Janis? I think I'm going to collapse —"

Janis poured brandy from one of the cut glass decanters on the sideboard and handed Shirley the glass – though she felt like throwing the liquor in her face!

How could a woman as self-centerd as she expect to inspire affection and respect? Her sort, though, didn't see themselves that way, their vision was blurred by pity directed inward.

Though Shirley had tried to step into the matriarchal role vacated by Marianne's move to Bermuda, her efforts were the interfering kind, resulting in resentment instead of the appreciation she craved.

Marianne had once called Shirley the victim of her own personality, and surveying her downcast posture now, spurned by the grandchild she undoubtedly loved, Janis had to be sorry for her.

"Bessie's grandpa has plotted this to make me suffer," Shirley said after sipping some of the brandy.

"Why would he be so vindictive?"

"All right," Shirley conceded, "so maybe he didn't plot it, but you can bet that his wife did! Hildegard is a schemer. How else did she manage to take Peter from me? We weren't exactly happy together, but there was never a word about divorce till Peter went to Israel on holiday without me and met up with her again."

Shirley stared pensively into her glass. "They knew each other in Vienna, when they were kids . . . Did you know that, Janis?"

Janis shook her head.

"Well, you couldn't know all the family history, could you? A lot of murky water had already flowed under the bridge before your dad married my daughter. Like Marianne's brother Arnold marrying-out," Shirley went on. "He was the first of the family to do that, and Marianne the second. It finished their father."

"But it wouldn't nowadays, would it?"

"Nowadays, what parents and grandparents think and feel

doesn't enter into *anything*," Shirley said bitterly, "or Laura wouldn't have made you Bessie's guardian."

They had returned full circle whence Shirley's digression began. But she had not yet finished digressing, her expression still pensive, the brandy glass cupped in her red-taloned hands.

"Peter and Hildegard escaped from Vienna together the day Hitler marched in," she resumed, "and never saw their parents again. By then, Manchester was full of refugees and my parents adopted Peter.

"I only met Hildegard a few times before she went out of our lives – and she looked as if butter wouldn't melt in her mouth!" Shirley added with an upsurge of anger. "You never can tell."

Janis's impression of Hildegard, though she had been in her company only twice, was of a warm and kindly woman. But Shirley would always think of her as the vamp she wasn't.

As ridiculous as for me to put Kurt's wife in that category, Janis reflected. A person must accept the consequences of their own actions, but Shirley never would, in any respect.

"How shall you keep an eye on Bessie if she doesn't go with you to Australia?" Shirley demanded.

"Laura appointed me her legal guardian, not her keeper, and I'd say that anyone who tried to be Bessie's keeper would be in for a rough time."

Chapter 9

*H*ow was it in Manchester?" Bessie's friend inquired on the way to school.

It was the first day of the spring term. And a new year, thought Bessie, but where shall I be this time *next* year? It isn't fair of Janis to let me make up my own mind!

Such was Bessie's confusion, she would have preferred being told what to do – so long as it wasn't that she must live with her grandmother.

"Manchester is my second home," she replied when she and Val were seated side by side aboard a bus. "It's where my mummy came from and I don't feel like a stranger there. The people are nice and friendly, and my gran has a beautiful flat –"

"You sound like you're trying to sell Manchester to me," Val cut in with a laugh, "or is it to yourself?"

"After what I just said, how can you think that?" Bessie answered, adjusting the rucksack, heavy with books, on her lap.

"I was joking," said Val.

"This isn't a joke to me."

Bessie returned the smile of one of the schoolboys standing in the aisle. But if he wasn't bespectacled and pimply, he wouldn't be trying to get off with *me*, she thought. He knew he wouldn't stand a chance with Val, who could get any boy she wanted, with her big blue eyes and auburn hair.

Like Janis could and if I went with her to Sydney – well, what would I be but a nuisance? Janis wouldn't dream of leaving me on my own while she went out on dates.

At present, the two of them were living in the family house, which couldn't be sold until something called "probate" happened. Though Janis had plenty of friends in London, she stayed at home with Bessie, refusing invitations to go out.

Bessie had heard her on the phone, saying things like, "It's nice of you to ask me, but I'm not in the mood. Too much on my mind."

And what was on her mind but Bessie?

"All right, I'm coming!" she snapped when Val prodded her.

"You were so deep in thought, you'd have missed our stop," said Val when they had alighted and joined the girls thronging toward the school. "And when I asked you how Manchester was, I meant how did it go with you and your gran?"

"Well, it didn't change my mind about not living with her."

"You know you'd be welcome at our house."

"And I really appreciate the offer, Val."

"Then why not say yes? I should miss you terribly, Bessie, if you went away."

"I'd miss you, too, Val. But you'd soon get a new best friend. The girls'd be queuing up to take my place."

Val did not deny what she knew was true. But it wouldn't be like that for Bessie, if she chose to live with her grandfather and had to begin all over again, at a new school in Tel Aviv. And even worse for her if she decided to stay with her big sister, who seemed to chop and change all the time about which country she wanted to live in.

As they trudged along the main road, rush hour traffic crawling past them, Val's tender heart was breaking for Bessie, to whom she had felt protective since their first week at school, when nobody had wanted to play with the girl they called "Fatty."

Val had seen Bessie standing alone in a corner of the schoolyard, munching chocolate biscuits and watching her classmates form the alliances that for many would last throughout their school lives.

Val recalled impulsively taking Bessie's hand and bringing her to join the other little girls. But despite me, they treated her cruelly when she had anorexia, Val thought now – for which the worst offenders had lost Val's friendship and the heck with them!

Bessie glanced at a young couple pushing a pram, on the other side of the street, and said flatly, "It was never like that for me, Val. Like it is for that baby, I mean. A mummy *and* a daddy."

"But one-parent families aren't uncommon now."

"And a lot of good that will do the kids," Bessie said with feeling.

"You got a super dad in the end, though."

"That doesn't make up for not knowing who my real dad is. Wouldn't you say I'm entitled to know, Val?"

Val side-stepped the question. "Your mother must have had a good reason for not telling you."

"And that makes me wonder if he was a horrible man who

raped her," Bessie answered. "Even if I never find out his name, it'd be a relief to know he was a nice person."

"How long have you been thinking about this?" Val asked as they entered the school.

"Since I had to decide what to do now my mother's gone and the man I thought of as my father, too. But I didn't get angry about it till I saw that baby being pushed in its pram by its parents!"

"For all we know, they could be its auntie and uncle," said Val, "and you'd better calm down, Bessie –"

"What have I to be calm about!" Bessie responded, aware of other girls on the corridor eyeing her. When they reached the cloakroom, she dumped her rucksack on the floor, took off her coat and threw it on a hook. "And to tell you the truth, Val, I'm sick of this school! Like I am of everything else.

"My whole life is in pieces," she went on, "and Janis says I must pull myself together and make a new beginning, but I don't think I can."

Chapter 10

*J*eremy sat in an air-conditioned office in Caracas Police Headquarters, his expression dogged.

"It's now three months since my parents and Senor Mendez were assassinated," he reminded the inspector in charge of the investigation, "and you still have no idea of who did it?"

Inspector Iglesias spread his hands eloquently. "The mills of justice grind slow, Senor Bornstein."

"But that isn't good enough for *me*. Nor can I accept that you don't have your suspicions."

"Without proof, what use are they to you, or to me? There are terrorist organizations and there are also individuals who, for one reason or another, might have planted the bomb."

"But you don't intend telling me who they are, or what the reasons could be."

The inspector ground out the stub of an acrid-smelling cheroot in the overflowing ashtray on his desk. "So that you could yourself confront them? As your father's heir, your position is already hazardous enough."

"I share the inheritance with my two sisters," Jeremy told him.

"Then I advise you to take good care of them, Mr. Bornstein. Instead of hanging around in Caracas wasting my valuable time."

Jeremy prickled with apprehension on Janis's and Bessie's behalf. "Are you saying we could now be the target my father was?"

"I have issued the same warning to the family of Senor Mendez, though they are well accustomed to having to protect themselves. Senorita Lola Mendez was kidnapped when she was a child," the inspector revealed, "after which she and her sisters went nowhere without a guard.

"Everything has its price, Mr. Bornstein, including immense wealth."

Jeremy left the office without saying another word and again suffering from shock. Why couldn't his father have been just an ordinary businessman, instead of — instead of what?

Greed could account for a kidnapping, but not for assassination. There was no ransom involved. Assassinations were born of hatred, personal, or political. Someone, somewhere, had wanted Luis Mendez and Jake Bornstein removed from the face of the earth. Why?

Though Jeremy hadn't stopped hoping that his father just happened to be in the car at the time, that nobody hated him enough to kill him, he couldn't assume what he didn't know for sure. And even if Jake wasn't the target, Jeremy meant to find out who did it. The hell with the mills of justice grinding slow!

So immersed was he in his thoughts, he was almost run

over by a car while crossing the main street, perspiration beading his brow and his shirt collar sticking to his neck; the humidity of the climate contrasting with the chill air-conditioning in the inspector's office.

Affected, too, by the petrol fumes mingling with dust rising from the pavement, where groups of men lolled against shop windows, some clustered in cafe doorways, their appearance as unkempt as that of the mountainside dwellers, though they were dressed for the city.

Since it wasn't lunchtime, those men were probably unemployed, Jeremy reckoned, yet some were laughing and joking together. Maybe they thought it better to laugh than to cry, to make the best of the only life available to them, he reflected, passing by a group who were wolf-whistling at a pretty girl.

The girl, though, was carrying a briefcase, perhaps a young executive on her way to a meeting, clad in a tailored skirt and a crisp, white blouse. One of those who, like Senor Mendez's press secretary, wasn't at the bottom of the heap.

But there was still a yawning gap between their sort and the affluence epitomized by where Lola Mendez lived her privileged life. Did Lola ever give a thought to what Jeremy was observing? Or did she glide past the evidence, cocooned in the family limousine, oblivious to the shacks on the mountainside and all the rest of it?

Jeremy was again staying with the Mendezes, and finding himself increasingly attracted to her.

"You ought not to have gone off without telling me," she rebuked him when eventually he returned to the house, "nor should you have gone under your own steam."

"You weren't up yet and I decided to go downtown and have another go at Inspector Iglesias," he told her.

"How did you get there?"

"The same way I got back. I picked up a cab."

"But it isn't safe for you to wander around Caracas alone, Jeremy, and the cab drivers could've turned out to be not what they seemed."

"So the inspector more than implied," Jeremy said with forced lightness, "and he wasn't just referring to Caracas. His warning included my sisters. But I don't intend telling them. Janis and Bessie live ordinary lives and I'd like them to go on doing so."

"I must hope you won't regret that decision," said Lola.

"Well, you've always lived an *extra*ordinary life, haven't you?" Jeremy replied. "All this grandeur you're accustomed to," he said glancing around.

"But no peace of mind."

They were seated on the vast patio, Jeremy sipping the planter's punch that Carlos had just set before him. "What was it like to be kidnapped?" he asked Lola.

"Inspector Iglesias ought not to have told you."

"But he wanted to bring home to me that it's risky to be rich, which I have to say I hadn't realized," said Jeremy. "Not that I think my sisters are likely to be kidnapped –"

Lola said with a shudder, "It was a horrible experience for me, Jeremy, in addition to being frightening. The men who grabbed me were smelly and filthy, like the people who live on the mountainside –"

"Poverty-stricken, you mean."

"I don't want to talk about it."

"Did you have a bodyguard by your side while you were at Harvard?"

"Sure."

"What a miserable time you must have had there."

"It's better than ending up dead," Lola answered, "and in

case you thought otherwise, if there was someone I wanted to be alone with, my bodyguard stayed outside the door."

But who'd want to make love to a girl, in that set-up? thought Jeremy. It was a turn-off if ever he'd heard of one.

"Where's your bodyguard now? Watching us from behind a tree?"

"Don't be ridiculous, Jeremy! At home I'm safe and since my father's assassination, I haven't been out."

She rose to pace restlessly, her long hair tossed over one shoulder and her full skirt swirling as she moved.

"My family's still in mourning — but I see you're not wearing a black tie for your father," she remarked.

"At home, I wouldn't be wearing a tie."

"Then why are you wearing one here?"

"Not to would seem disrespectful to your mother."

"My mother isn't *so* formal, or I wouldn't now be wearing purple, instead of black." Lola returned to sit at the table. "What I'm looking forward to, though, is wearing jeans again."

"Designer ones, no doubt."

"What sort of crack is that?"

"It wasn't a crack, just speaking my thoughts aloud."

"And your thoughts seem to center upon the difference between your way of life and mine! Right now, though, we have a common tragedy, and I'm doing my best to come to terms with it. You, however, seem unable to put it into perspective —"

"Perhaps because my perspective is different from yours."

"There you go again, Jeremy!"

"How is your mother bearing up?" he inquired.

"She hasn't put in an appearance to welcome you, has she? That should tell you how. She's devastated, Jeremy, and seems the more so every day. But if you'd known my father, how considerate and kind he was —"

"Yet somebody hated him."

"Why must you remind me of that!"

"It's the only starting point we've got," Jeremy declared.

"Please don't ally me with your own intention," Lola answered, "and you yourself are a babe-in-arms, trying to pit your wits against the unknown. Did you know that your father had a bodyguard?"

Jeremy put down his glass. "What are you talking about?"

"The man who came with him to Caracas, though he wasn't what I meant when I referred to the unknown. Whom I heard telling *my* father's bodyguard that he was looking forward to going on a Caribbean cruise."

"Dad must have thought he needed one in this part of the world," said Jeremy, "and he wasn't wrong. Where is the man now?"

"Do you really expect me to know?"

Lola eyed with disinterest the buffet lunch awaiting them on a side table. "All I'm able to tell you, Jeremy, is that the man was British and the sort you wouldn't notice in a crowd."

"Maybe he was injured in the explosion," Jeremy said thoughtfully.

"Well, that certainly was Pedro's fate."

"Your father's bodyguard?"

"No, his chauffeur. A man with a wife and children, whom my family are, of course, taking care of."

"Where is Pedro, now?"

"He lost both legs and is still in intensive care —"

"Where?"

Lola gave Jeremy the name of the hospital and said when

he rose from his chair and strode away, "Where are you going?"

"The man who came to Caracas with my father could be in that hospital, too," he called over his shoulder. "You've just provided me with a possible clue."

"I wouldn't call it a clue," said Lola, "and hold on a minute, Jeremy – Inspector Iglesias happens to speak English," she went on, when he had halted, "but the hospital administrator probably doesn't."

"Then would you mind telling me where I could hire an interpreter?"

Lola finished her iced lemonade and said calmly, "We don't want your activities known all over Caracas. Reluctant though I am, it had better be me."

Half an hour later, Jeremy was again seated in an air-conditioned office, Lola at his side and opposite them the middle-aged, hospital administrator.

"Ask him to look at his records and see if an Englishman was brought here for treatment after the explosion," he instructed Lola tersely.

"I'm not a moron, Jeremy. I know what to say," she answered before addressing the man – who couldn't take his eyes off her shapely bosom, Jeremy noticed.

A lengthy conversation in Spanish then took place between them, while Jeremy impatiently drummed his fingers on the desk.

"The hospital records are confidential, but I told him you're looking for a missing relative," Lola said when the administrator rose to look in a filing cabinet, the cigarette clamped between his lips meanwhile filling the room with malodorous smoke.

He returned with a red folder and began hunting inside it.

"Haven't they heard of computers in Caracas?" Jeremy said to Lola.

"If you'd visited my father's offices, you wouldn't ask that. But in a small, public hospital . . ."

Jeremy noted a crucifix on the wall. "Is this place staffed by nuns?"

"Sure and that means the nursing is both dedicated and good."

The administrator then found what he was seeking, perused it and gabbled non-stop to Lola for several minutes.

"Senor Ortega says there *was* an Englishman," she eventually told Jeremy, "treated for severe burns, but he discharged himself against doctors' orders."

"What was his name?"

"Perry – and they still have his passport here. It seems he left in a hurry."

"Tell him that Mr. Perry is my cousin," said Jeremy.

"I don't like telling lies and I've already told him one – you didn't come here to look for a missing relative, did you?"

"This isn't a game of truth or dare," Jeremy answered grimly, "and I need to see that passport."

Since Senor Ortega was now mesmerized by Lola's legs, this was not too difficult to arrange.

"They hadn't yet got around to sending the passport to the British Consulate," Lola translated from the reedy little man's Spanish, while Jeremy perused the singed document.

"He says the passport was in Perry's pocket," Lola went on interpreting, "but the clothes he had on when he was admitted weren't fit to wear again and the nuns threw them away."

"Hm," said Jeremy thoughtfully.

"Would you mind sharing whatever you're now thinking with me?" Lola requested.

"Perry wouldn't have left hospital clad in pajamas, would he? So where did he get his new clothing from?"

"Maybe the nuns provided it —"

"If he left in such a hurry? And that's another thing," said Jeremy, "why would he have done that, when he still required treatment? Ask the administrator which ward he was in, Lola."

"Why?"

"Someone must have brought Perry some clothes to wear, and the sister in charge of that ward may know who it was."

They eventually left the hospital with some thought-provoking information for both. The ward sister's description of the woman who had collected Perry, after visiting him the previous day, left them in no doubt that she was Maria Santander. The Mendez company's up-fronter! thought Jeremy.

"Why do I have the feeling — which I've had from the start — that a wall of secrecy is shutting me out?" he said to Lola when they were back inside the family limousine. "What is being kept from me? From you, too."

"How many times must I say that I prefer to leave the investigating to the professionals?" she replied. "And if you think that's because I'm scared for my own safety, you're wrong, Jeremy."

"Then why are you so reluctant to help me?"

Lola leaned her head wearily against the leather upholstery and closed her eyes. When she opened them, her expression was unreadable.

"If you want to be a man with a mission, go ahead and be one," she said, "but don't say you weren't warned if along the way you learn things about your father you would rather not have known."

Chapter 11

*B*essie had finally chosen to live with her grandfather in Tel Aviv, and said to Janis on the eve of her departure, "Please don't take my not going with you to Australia the wrong way."

"Whatever makes you happy is fine with me, love," Janis replied.

Bessie, who had never in her life known true happiness, felt like bursting into tears. But what good would crying do? She'd made her decision and must make the best of it.

"As a matter of fact, I think what you've decided will help you learn to stand on your own feet," Janis said. "Your granddad and Hildegard are busy running their restaurant, aren't they? They won't have time to watch over you like your big sister does," she added with a laugh.

"Like asking me if I've cleaned my shoes for school!"

"And if you've done your homework, which you'll have more of in Israel, since you'll have to learn Hebrew. But it will be all up to you, Bessie, and that's what I actually meant.

The brand new beginning we talked about, including a new country – and don't get downhearted if you don't find it easy."

"I'm not expecting to, Janis." And having to learn a new language was for Bessie the least of it.

"Then you won't be disappointed."

It was difficult for Janis to believe that almost six months had slipped by since Laura and Jake were killed. She had not noticed winter take over from autumn and now it was spring, and the Passover Eve.

People come and go, they're born and eventually they die, but our Jewish traditions continue regardless, she reflected while she and Bessie laid the table for the Seder night meal.

It has to be tradition that's making me do this, Janis thought. The way I headed for a synagogue in Sydney like a homing pigeon, on Rosh Hashanah, though I'm not religious.

There was, though, to *this* Seder night a special poignancy. Janis and Bessie carrying on what Laura had raised them to do.

"Remember the first Seder held in this house?" she asked Bessie.

"I can't say I do."

"Well, you were only about six, and I was a schoolgirl, like you are now. Laura let you and me lay the table and your grandma stood over us, in case we didn't do it properly –"

The scene suddenly returned to Bessie. "You had on a new blouse and skirt. And I was wearing a blue velvet frock that made me look even fatter than I was. I wasn't sure where to put the dish of bitter herbs and Mummy told me to put it beside where Daddy would sit."

"Tonight," said Janis, "it will be beside Jeremy."

They fell silent, continuing to set silverware and glasses on the white damask tablecloth, each with her own private thoughts.

Bessie's were centered upon her frightening new future. Supposing her grandpa and Hildegard found having her a nuisance? How would she make friends at school? It was hard enough for Bessie with people who spoke the same language . . .

Janis's reflections remained briefly with the past. Once, it was necessary to bring folding chairs and to extend the table for the family Seder, so large was the gathering. But not anymore. Nor would there be any elders present and how weird that would seem. A Seder with Jeremy at the head of the table and Janis at the foot. Without Shirley there, to instruct them about the rituals, though they knew them off by heart. And no Marianne, who had once kept the peace between warring members of the clan unwilling to call a truce even for one night.

Well, thought Janis, those days are over and none of the people who'll be at *this* Seder are at war with each other. There would just be her brother and sister, herself, and A.P.

In the event, it was necessary to lay an extra place. A.P. rang up to ask if he could bring Mary Lou.

"Lucky he didn't want to bring all his other communards!" said Janis. "There wouldn't be enough food."

"What's a communard?" Bessie wanted to know.

"A member of a commune," said Jeremy, who had taken A.P.'s call before joining his sisters in the dining room. "And whenever he uses that word, I think of the Paris Commune that was formed after the Franco-Prussian war."

"Does that mean you haven't *quite* forgotten you're supposed to be reading history at Oxford?" said Janis. "Or have you decided to pack it in and become a second Sherlock Holmes?"

"Right now, I wish I'd done a business course," he answered crisply, "like Lola Mendez did at Harvard."

"Who's she?" asked Bessie.

"She lost her father in the explosion that turned us three into orphans," Jeremy added to the little that Bessie had been told.

"But why do you wish you'd done a business course, Jeremy? Are you going to be the new boss of Daddy's business?"

"That's a question I can't answer yet," Jeremy heard himself say.

Janis was taken aback. Her unworldly brother considering becoming an entrepreneur?

Jeremy hid his confusion with a laugh. "All I can say at the moment is, you never know! As for what I said about a business course, it would help me delve into Dad's dealings without the assistance of people I'm not sure are trustworthy."

Jeremy added after pausing, "When I met with Dad's accountants, yesterday – and they're not the people I don't trust – I learned he was in the process of setting up a Charity Fund which he intended calling the Bornstein Foundation."

"I'm glad Mummy changed my name to Bornstein when she married him," Bessie declared.

"And we must certainly continue that project where Dad left off," said Janis. "But if you keep taking off for Caracas, Jeremy, we shall never get all the legal and financial stuff tied up."

"That's going to take ages, Janis, and meanwhile you may as well return to Sydney, no need to hang on here once Bessie's gone to Tel Aviv. I, though, well, I've asked for a year off from college."

"To do what?"

"Something I have to do."

"Waste a year of your life, you mean, but I suppose that's preferable to dropping out of college, like A.P. has."

"You sound just like Dad."

"I'm his daughter, aren't I?"

"It's because I'm his son that I'm doing what I think necessary."

Jeremy refrained from saying that if it were not the Seder night, he would now be in Milan, that stopping over in London was just a brief hiatus in his hunt for more clues.

Janis divined his thoughts if not quite accurately. "You've got involved with that girl in Caracas, haven't you?"

"Why shouldn't Jeremy have a girlfriend in Caracas?" Bessie intervened. "He wouldn't mind you having a boyfriend in Sydney."

Jeremy managed to smile. "And I wouldn't mind *you* having one in Tel Aviv, Bessie."

"I should get that lucky!"

"As for my relationship with Lola Mendez," Jeremy told Janis, "she sometimes acts as my interpreter and treats me like the brother she never had."

The arrival of the Seder night guests ended the conversation, and Mary Lou said after the introductions, "It's nice to meet people I've heard so much about, at last! And I can't wait to taste the special Passover food A.P.'s told me about," she added, glancing at the table.

Janis laughed. "Didn't he also tell you that we don't get to eat it until we've read through most of the Haggadah and completed the rituals – which includes eating bitter herbs."

"The Haggadah is the little book everyone has beside their plate," Bessie supplied, "and I'd better warn you, before we get to the food, that my sister's cooking isn't like my Mummy's was.

"When I stuck a fork into the matzo balls, to test them, I had to force it in," she informed Jeremy and A.P.

"It has to be better cooking than mine," said Mary Lou. "When it's my turn to be the commune chef, everyone hot-foots it to the village store to arm themselves with indigestion tablets. I hate cooking!"

"But on the commune, we all have to do jobs we don't necessarily enjoy," said A.P. ruefully.

"And it wouldn't be the life for me," said Jeremy.

He was smoothing back his hair, before putting on a *yarmulke* and Mary Lou turned to appraise him. "What *would* be the life for you?"

"I'm still in the process of finding out."

"The same goes for me," she replied, "but in the meantime I'm doing something constructive."

Jeremy said to A.P., "That sounds like a recipe for the early disintegration of your dream – if everyone on the commune is seeing it as a fill-in."

"He hasn't got a dream," said Mary Lou before A.P. had time to utter, "but if *you* have, I'm sorry for you," she informed Jeremy.

"Since I haven't, you needn't be," he retorted. "Shall we get cracking with the Seder, Janis?"

While the reading from the Haggadah proceeded and the ancient rituals were performed, Janis was aware of the hostility flowing between her brother and the girl who was their guest. And of A.P. surreptitiously eyeing Mary Lou's set expression.

When eventually it was time to serve the meal, Mary Lou went with Janis and Bessie to the kitchen and said without preamble, "I seem to've got on the wrong side of your brother."

"He'll get over it," said Janis while pouring salt water over hard-boiled eggs.

"That's what we start the Seder meal with," Bessie explained to Mary Lou, "but you don't have to eat it if you'd rather not."

Mary Lou, right now, could not have cared less what she ate and was wishing she had swallowed the words she had said to Jeremy.

In the dining room, A.P. and Jeremy were engaged in a heated exchange.

"How dare you behave the way you are doing, with Mary Lou?" A.P. demanded.

"Why not ask her why she was so snotty with me?"

"I won't have you using words like that with relation to her."

"What are you? Her protector? She strikes me as well able to stand up for herself," said Jeremy.

"That doesn't mean I have to let you insult her."

Jeremy scanned A.P.'s expression. "You're in love with her, aren't you?"

A.P. gazed at the flickering candles in the silver candelabra and made no reply.

"Does she know?"

He shook his head.

"Mary Lou Dryden isn't the girl for you, A.P."

"It isn't for you to say that."

"We've always been honest with each other and I have to speak my mind now —"

"Because you've taken a dislike to her," A.P. interrupted.

"I'm not going to deny that, but it isn't the point, A.P. What is, is that you're already putty in her hands. Doing the things that *she* believes in —"

"That I believe in, too."

"Whose idea was the commune?"

"We more or less arrived at it together."

"But would you have gone ahead with it without her spurring you on?"

"It's hard for me to say."

"But not for *me* to say," declared Jeremy. "I've known you too long and too well, and you wouldn't have turned Kyverdale Hall into what you have if Mary Lou hadn't persuaded you to make better use of your inheritance than your ancestors did.

"I'm not saying you weren't ripe for some sort of change," Jeremy continued, after finishing the wine that Bessie had left in her glass, "but you were always the sort who liked your privacy. Not the commune sort by any stretch of the imagination."

A.P.'s reply was, "If you tell Mary Lou I'm in love with her, I'll never forgive you."

"Why would I tell her? And what are you scared of?"

"If she knew, she might leave the commune. I'm hoping she'll wake up one morning and realize that *she's* in love with *me*."

But Mary Lou, though she told herself it was impossible, had fallen in love with Jeremy.

On the way back to Somerset, A.P. noted that Mary Lou was unduly silent.

"So you and Jeremy didn't hit it off," he said with feigned lightness. "You will when you get to know each other.

"First impressions don't necessarily last," he went on when she made no reply. "My Grandma Marianne took an instant dislike to the man who eventually became her second husband – though my dad's theory about that is it was love at first sight and she was fighting it off."

All Mary Lou needed to hear! Why else had she spoken so cuttingly to Jeremy? Because he wasn't her type and something she had never felt before happened the minute she set eyes on him.

"Jeremy is a cocky bastard and I never want to see him again," she declared, closing her eyes as if it was her intention to take a nap.

But to A.P., it was as if she had shut him out, leaving him to tussle with his painful thoughts. There was more than a grain of truth in what Jeremy had said about Mary Lou's influencing him.

When A.P. first confided his uncertainties, Mary Lou had listed his three options: "Either 'do a Tony Benn,' carry on the old way, or do things *your* way," she had said.

But transforming Kyverdale Hall into a commune was Mary Lou's way, not A.P.'s. Jeremy was right about that. A.P. had grasped at the idea like the floundering man he then was, gaining not just Mary Lou's constant companionship, but the sense of purpose he had lacked.

They had selected carefully when, in response to advertisements in the quality press, applications to join poured in, indicating just how widespread was their generation's disenchantment with living solely for themselves.

While some members were couples, most were unattached and at odds, as Mary Lou was, with the society that had bred them. Scientists and bank clerks, a male model and two librarians, were among the thirty assorted young people now occupying what was once a stately home. Ploughing the land where organically grown vegetables would replace the idle lawns, building a barn to house a dairy herd, heedless of their callused hands.

Did it matter that A.P. was lending himself, and the money

he had inherited, to the pursuit of Mary Lou's idealism? He glanced at the sleeping figure by his side, after driving through Bridgewater – had she been awake, she'd have been delivering a diatribe about the River Parrett, which flowed through the town, probably being polluted, like the lake on the Kyverdale estate, A.P. thought.

Mary Lou would like to save the earth with her own small hands. Patience had never been one of her virtues. And in repose, she reminded A.P. of how she had looked as a child, her unruly curls haloing her head as they had then, enhancing the angelic appearance that had made him think her a sweet little girl.

How could that tiny person exert the power she did upon him? he mused later, while steering the car along a winding, country lane. Since it wasn't like that before he fell in love with her, the power had to be love itself.

When eventually he reached Kyverdale village, the store shuttered for the night, the row of thatched cottages a dark bulk in the moonlight, the ancient church and the graveyard where his ancestors lay combined to prick A.P.'s conscience.

What right had he to tinker with his heritage? To thumb his nose at the way things had been for centuries?

If A.P. wanted no part of that, he ought to have "done a Tony Benn," handed over tradition and what went with it to the distant relative who wouldn't question it.

Come what may, though, there was something in A.P. that wouldn't let him do so. And with, or without Mary Lou he would somehow have made better use of his inheritance than those who had gone before him had. If for no other reason than that he couldn't live as if there wasn't a world outside his own privileged existence.

* * *

When the following Sunday A.P.'s friend, Gary Potter, paid his first visit to the commune, A.P. was surprised to find himself the recipient of Gary's genuine congratulations.

"The lads at New College were laying bets that you wouldn't bring yourself to actually do it," Gary revealed.

"Who was the bookie?"

"Me," said Gary with his cheeky grin, "and the punters lost a packet on a dark horse! When I tell 'em what you've already achieved here —"

"I didn't do it alone," A.P. cut in, "and if you fancy joining us —"

"You and the other dropouts, you mean."

"As it happens there are only two others."

"But I shall stay the course to the bitter end if it kills me and it probably will," said Gary.

"To prove a miner's son has what it takes?"

"If that's how you care to put it," Gary replied. "How I'd put it myself though, is that until this is a country that doesn't have classes, you won't catch me letting mine down.

"Who's that beddable-looking creature?" Gary added, watching a shapely brunette get into a Land Rover parked outside the house.

"The only bed Nina is interested in is the one at the bottom of the estate lake," A.P. informed him, "and her sole interest is to combat the effects of acid rain."

"I wouldn't mind broadening her horizon."

"I bet you wouldn't!"

"Shall I be meeting her at lunch?"

A.P. smiled. "If you're prepared to forego a hot meal and eat a sandwich with her by the lake."

"Now that would be really cozy," said Gary, watching the Land Rover zoom away. "Does she always drive that fast?"

"Why don't you ask her?"

"I will."

"And if you can get cozy with Nina," A.P. told him, "the chaps will be lining up to learn the secret of your success."

That evening, A.P. was invited to the west wing to take coffee with his grandmother.

He wouldn't have required an invitation to visit his Grandma Marianne, he reflected while making his way along the gallery from his own quarters, but would no more have thought of dropping-in on Lady Kyverdale than of addressing her as "Gran."

Her ladyship had always seemed to A.P. a little intimidating – and still does, he thought when eventually he was in her presence, she seated in the ornate gilt chair she had asked to be brought for her from the drawing room of the main house, and he on the brocade love seat placed opposite it.

"What you need, my dear, is someone to share that seat with you," Lady Kyverdale said without preamble. "When are you going to pop the question to that delightful little girl?"

A.P. fidgeted with the tie he had put on because he was visiting her. "There's more than one delightful girl living here. Which do you mean, Grandmother?" he stalled.

"Since we both know whom we are discussing, no need to mention her name," she replied, "and you certainly don't take after your grandfather in *any* respect. No need, either, to tell you he rushed me off my feet."

If nobody else at the Hall had tumbled to where A.P.'s heart lay, this wily old lady had! He watched her pour coffee into the fragile cups that, like the silver pot, were family heirlooms, trying to collect himself.

"How are you managing with only Lizzie to take care of you?" he inquired.

With the exception of her ladyship's personal maid, the staff had been pensioned-off.

"Lizzie has turned out to be an excellent cook," she replied, "who also enjoys polishing silver – which I never did in my girlhood, when my mother, once a month, would take her few bits of Sheffield plate out of the parlor cabinet and present me with that task!

"But kindly don't lead my thoughts astray. At my age I spend too much time dwelling upon the past and it's the present and future that you and I must discuss. Hence my asking you when you intend popping the question, A.P."

"Is that why you invited me for coffee?" he said mustering a smile.

"One of the reasons. And the other is relevant." Lady Kyverdale paused to sip some coffee and A.P. asked if she would like him to pour a glass of her favorite liqueur.

"No, thank you, my dear, but help yourself to whatever you wish," she said glancing toward the decanters that had lived in the library, before A.P. transferred such valuable items to where they would not be damaged in the everyday life of the commune.

"I'm no longer allowed alcohol," his grandmother went on, "and I'm obeying doctors' orders, though it seems I haven't too long to live, whether I do, or not."

A.P. was surprised at the depth of his distress. Until then, he hadn't realized just how fond of her he was. Despite his mother's misguided efforts to prevent it, he had grown up feeling one of his father's family, his visits to Kyverdale Hall seeming more of an ordeal than a pleasure.

Had there been cousins to romp around this echoing old house with me, it might've been different, he reflected now – though he couldn't envisage Grandfather having allowed the rough and tumble of kids at play.

As things were, A.P.'s childhood memories of being here were of a lonely little boy, tiptoeing around as if this were a hallowed place, careful not to disturb his grandparents and counting the hours until it was time to return to London.

"I oughtn't even to be drinking coffee," said her ladyship with a chuckle, "but they can't have it *all* their own way!"

"How long have you known what you've just told me?" A.P. inquired. And how could she laugh, when she knew she was doomed?

"Long enough not to try to dissuade you from making the drastic change you have."

"If you'd told me –"

"You wouldn't have done it, and I forbade your mother to tell you, for that reason. Instead of relegating me to the west wing, you'd have waited for me to die," she said, studying A.P. with her piercing blue gaze, "and I couldn't have that. You putting off what you wanted to do, so your grandmother could breathe her last in her own bedchamber.

"Besides," she continued, "since you'd have eventually gone ahead in my absence, I thought I may as well see your project get off the ground."

Her ladyship had become a familiar figure to the commune's members, clad in her sturdy tweeds, wellingtons on her feet and leaning on her stick, observing with interest the metamorphosis visible all around her.

Even when we dug up the flower beds, she didn't protest, A.P. recalled with chagrin. But if he had known what he now knew, he would at least have preserved the gardens, once her pride and joy.

He had taken her silence for tacit consent which, in a way, it was, relieved that she hadn't kicked up the fuss his mother had.

A.P. appraised the old lady's still upright posture, her head slightly tilted when she looked at him, the smallest suggestion of a blue tint to her hair, the evening dress that had remained *de rigueur* for her, though she invariably dined alone, and the items of Kyverdale jewelery that one day would be worn by A.P.'s wife.

The girl he wanted for his wife, though, wouldn't bedeck herself with those diamonds and pearls. They would be stored in the bank, with the other precious heirlooms already secured there, the silver and the porcelain for which there was not space in the west wing.

But for what and for whom? There was no place for any of it in the times A.P. was living in, he reflected. Like hereditary peerages, it was part of a bygone era.

"You can't possibly approve of what I've done, can you, Grandmother?" he crystallized his thoughts.

"My approval, or disapproval, doesn't enter into it, my dear. The inheritance is yours, to use as you see fit."

"It was Mary Lou who helped me realize that," A.P. found himself confiding.

"Unlike me," said Lady Kyverdale with a smile, "in *my* time, that girl has no hesitation about putting her mark upon what she wasn't born to. But the aristocracy is no longer revered as it was then."

"Do you think it should be?"

She evaded the question and said, with twinkling eyes, "I ran into someone, while taking my afternoon stroll, who makes no bones about what *he* thinks in that respect. Or should I say he almost ran into *me*!"

"Gary Potter?"

"Whose conversation, when I gave lunch to you and your friends the one time I visited you at Oxford, I am unlikely to have forgotten. Today, though, he was hurrying away from the lakeside as if he'd just seen the Loch Ness monster. And if I'd had a beefsteak handy, I'd have offered it to him for his black eye. How on earth did he get it?"

A.P. grinned. "Let's just say that the irresistible force met the immovable object. Exactly how isn't for me to reveal."

"And returning to the subject we were discussing," said Lady Kyverdale, "I think it might be kinder not to tell your grandfather what you're up to, when I see him on the other side. Don't you?"

Reminding A.P. that she hadn't long to live. "Have you been attending seances?" he made himself banter.

"As I did after my brother was killed in the war," she revealed to A.P.'s surprise, "and maintaining spiritual contact was for me a great comfort. Like knowing I'm going to die soon is much less alarming because your grandfather is there waiting for me."

She collected herself and refilled the coffee cups. "What I *should* like to be able to tell him, my dear, is that you are all set to provide the title with an heir. If Mary Lou agreed to a short engagement, I might still be here for your wedding."

Since in the circumstances total honesty was called for, A.P. answered, "I'd like nothing better, Grandmother, and not just because I'd like you to be there. Mary Lou, though, doesn't see me in a romantic light."

"Then you'd better get a move on, hadn't you?" the old lady responded. "Whoever coined the phrase 'faint heart never won fair maiden' wasn't wrong.

"A great deal has changed since I was young, but some things never will and they include a chap sweeping a girl off her feet. I wasn't the gold-digger people must have thought me."

She paused only for breath. "Do you suppose I'd have given up being the toast of the town if your grandfather had allowed me time to think? I was Lady Kyverdale before I knew it. So would you kindly get on with it, A.P.?"

Chapter
12

While A.P. was contemplating Lady Kyverdale's advice and wishing himself endowed with Jeremy's sex appeal and chutzpah, Jeremy continued his hunt for clues.

He had begun by confronting Maria Santander in her office, but she had maintained her initial stance, which equated with a brick wall.

"Then I'd better talk with the Mendez company's chief executive," Jeremy had responded.

"Senor Vargas is out of the country and you would learn no more from him than you have from me."

But this was a brick wall that Jeremy must surmount if he was to follow the trail on the other side. Without hesitation, he had turned on the charm, he recalled with distaste while waiting in Milan for the man he had arranged to meet there – nor had charm alone sufficed.

"Look – I'd like to show my appreciation for the way you saved me from that pack of journalists," he had said, bathing

Maria with the smile that had always worked wonders with women. "May I take you to lunch?"

Afterwards, they had strolled in a park and some cash had eventually changed hands. Jeremy's first lesson that money was power, though this is peanuts, he had thought, compared with how his father must have wielded it.

Jeremy had not viewed being wealthy in that light until money bought him the information he required: the where-abouts of the man who was Jake Bornstein's bodyguard on foreign business trips. For whom Mendez money had ac-quired a new passport in a new name, increasing Jeremy's apprehension about the web of intrigue surrounding his fa-ther's activities.

Nor did Jeremy doubt that a good deal more money would change hands before he knew all he needed to know. Lola, he thought now, was right to call me a babe-in-arms!

Pacing beside Milan Cathedral, Jeremy briefly ruminated upon the world in which he lived, its extremes and its para-doxes.

A nun was shepherding a party of schoolgirls inside, where the devout would be at prayer in the hallowed atmosphere. But outside were stalls offering crucifixes and all the rest, no different from what went on with holy souvenirs beside Jerusalem's Christian and Jewish shrines.

And *outside*, Jeremy reflected, is the real world. Everyone self-orientated and on the make. The porn and the garbage epitomizes it, he thought, evading the shifty men trying to sell him dirty postcards and noting an empty Pepsi can on the cathedral steps. The pollution poisoning the earth. How long would the pigeons he was now eyeing survive the traffic fumes in cities like this one? And never mind the pigeons, how long could the human race survive the effects of its own short sightedness?

One of Mary Lou Dryden's contributions to the Seder night conversation returned to Jeremy: "There's never been a generation faced with the responsibility of rescuing the earth, but we're it."

Jeremy, though, had other things to think about and other fish to fry. Where the hell was Perry? he was fuming to himself when he felt his sleeve being plucked.

"Apologies for keeping you waiting, Mr. Bornstein. My landlady waylaid me, wanting to know when she's going to get her rent."

A broad hint, had Jeremy required one, that anything he learned from Perry would not be for free. "How did you recognize me?" he inquired. "Since I'd seen your picture in your old passport, I expected it to be me approaching you."

"You're the image of your father."

"My *late* father."

"Allow me to offer my condolences."

"I shall need a good deal more from you than that," said Jeremy tersely. "Shall we have our chat in a cafe?"

"I'd rather we just did some window shopping," Perry answered, indicating the elegant arcade lining one side of the square. "A cafe would be more comfortable, but you never know —" he added, glancing over his shoulder.

Did Perry fear that he was being followed? Well, that jelled with his wearing dark glasses, though it wasn't a sunny day.

"Whatever you say, Mr. Perry," Jeremy said, aware of his own nervous tension. *What* did you never know?

"For the present, it's Mr. Peters," said his companion as they strolled toward the arcade.

"You won't have to change the initial on your handkerchieves!"

"I can't afford initialed handkerchieves, I'm not in your

bracket," Perry retorted, "and there's no use in you being sarcastic. You want something from me, don't you?"

"True. But if I get it, you'll get what *you* want from me."

"And I was about to mention," said Perry, "that Peters just happened to be the name on the passport *she* got for me."

They had joined the people thronging onto the pavement and Jeremy halted to gaze into a shop window. "Senorita Santander?"

"She didn't tell me her name and I didn't give a sod what it was. I just upped and did as she said."

"Were you given a reason for their changing your passport and hustling you out of Venezuela?"

"Just that it was for my own safety and I'd be well advised to lie low for a while. She even fixed me up with the place I'm staying at and paid some advance rent.

"As for my safety," Perry went on, "I can hold my own with the best of 'em, or your father wouldn't have employed me.

"I'm talking about handling a gun, as well as fisticuffs," he added when Jeremy turned to appraise his burly figure. "But when I don't know who the enemy is, or where he's coming from — well, it's a different matter."

"You're taking a risk doing what we're now doing then, aren't you?" Jeremy said as they moved on.

"But I'm not a sitting duck, am I? — like I'd be in a cafe," Perry replied, "and you're going to make the risk worth my while."

Jeremy glanced around at the carefree tourists bustling beside him, catching snatches of their conversation, British and Americans intoxicated by the continental atmosphere, as Jeremy and A.P. were when they toured Europe on a shoestring, before going up to Oxford.

Would Jeremy ever again feel carefree? Well, not till the

mystery of his parents' violent deaths was solved and there could be a long way to go before then.

"Did you carry a gun when you worked for my father?" he asked Perry.

"What use would I've been to him without one? Then, though, it was him I was protecting, not myself, and it beats me why they'd now be after *me* – like that woman left me in no doubt of."

Had the Mendez company employed fear for his own safety as a tactic for getting Perry out of the way? So Jeremy would be unable to question him about his father's other life?

"If I'd been in the car," Perry said with a shudder, "well, say no more! But your father'd given me the afternoon off. He and Mr. Mendez were taking your mother out for lunch, you see. I was standing waiting for the chauffeur to drive away and the next thing I knew –!"

"Have you any idea what the deal was that my father was doing with Mr. Mendez?"

They had again halted beside a shop window and Perry turned to look at Jeremy. "Mr. Bornstein, you'd better accept that I never knew a thing about your father's deals and I didn't want to. Okay?"

While Perry told how he had sat playing cards with the bodyguards of men with whom his employer was meeting, it was hard for Jeremy to relate what he was hearing to the uncomplicated family man Jake had been.

As though, Jeremy thought, he was two separate people. The one we knew at home, and another whom we didn't know, whose business ventures had entailed being guarded by a man with a gun.

"Did the police visit you in hospital?" Jeremy inquired as he and Perry retraced their footsteps along the arcade.

"Very briefly, but I was too ill to be interviewed and it sent my temperature up. The doctors said they'd let the police know when they could come again, but *she* had me out of there the next day.

"I'm going to need plastic surgery, which I might have got in that hospital – this is a bit of what the bomb blast did," he said, fingering the deep scars on his blue-jowled face, "but it'll have to wait till I'm back in England and can have it done on the National Health.

"You must discharge yourself and lie low, she instructed me, like I said!"

The Mendez company didn't want Perry questioned by the police, *or* by me, Jeremy registered.

"And I'd like to get back under cover as soon as possible," Perry declared, once again glancing over his shoulder.

"All you've given me, so far, though," said Jeremy, "is a general picture and that isn't enough. What I'd like is some names attached to the places you went to with my father. You must surely know whose bodyguards you were playing cards with."

"That's as may be," Perry said cagily, "but we never talked about our bosses, and the meetings always went on behind closed doors."

A reminder for Jeremy of Lola once describing her home life, so different from his own. Her father closeted in his library with male guests, after dinner, while their wives and her mother yawned their heads off in the salon.

"I remember one time in Haiti," said Perry, "when Mr. Mendez was there, as well, and him and your father were stopping at the same hotel – if that's any use to you, you can have it for nothing. But I shall have to scratch my head, to give you a list of some other names, and that's going to cost you. When are you leaving Milan?"

"When I get what I came for," Jeremy answered. "Shall we

meet again tomorrow and hopefully you'll have made that list?"

"I'll do my best," said Perry, "but venues might have to do. I'm not that good on foreign names I can't even pronounce."

He glanced furtively over his shoulder yet again – it was beginning to give Jeremy the creeps – and said hurriedly, "Let's meet outside the railway station, I'm not chancing my luck in the same spot twice!"

Jeremy watched him walk quickly across the square, as though he felt more vulnerable in open spaces, then made his way back to the Excelsior Hotel, where despite the luxurious comfort of his bed he would probably spend a sleepless night, Lola's voice echoing in his ears:

"If you want to be a man with a mission, go ahead and be one. But don't say you weren't warned if along the way you find out things about your father you would rather not have known."

Would she have said that if she didn't already have her suspicions about her own father's dealings?

What Jeremy had learned from Perry lent strength to the warning, but when he reached the Piazza Duca D'Aosta, where the hotel was situated, he briefly let himself imagine himself and Lola strolling here hand-in-hand, with nothing sinister on their minds.

The fantasy was still with him when he entered the ornate lobby and rode upward in the lift, remembrance of Lola's perfume returning to him as he traversed the corridor to his room.

Her perfume, though, was less elusive than she was! And once inside the room, Jeremy was again enveloped by the living nightmare that allowed him no peace. He wouldn't rest until it was resolved, but the task he had set himself had only just begun.

Assailed, too, by loneliness, he called Janis.

"How nice to hear from you!" she said somewhat sarcastically. "And what are you actually *doing* in Milan?"

"There's someone here I had to see."

"Is Lola Mendez having herself an Italian shopping spree?"

"Why have you taken a dislike to a girl you've never met!"

"*Is* she in Milan?"

"I'm here on business, Janis."

"Dad's business?"

"Well, that's one way of putting it."

"Is that all you intend telling me?"

"For the moment."

"I see," Janis said crisply, "and talking of taking a dislike to someone," she harked back, "you made no secret of yours for Mary Lou Dryden."

"Or she of hers for me."

"And between you, you ruined our Seder night! How long shall you stay in Milan? And where will you be off to next?"

"That remains to be seen, but I'll stay in touch with you, Janis. Meanwhile, as I've already suggested, you may as well go back to Australia, if that's what you fancy doing. While I get on with what I have to do."

"How trite you make my life sound!"

"That wasn't my intention."

"But I have no sense of direction at present," said Janis, "and I can do without you rubbing it in. As for what *you* are doing – and with that girl's encouragement, no doubt."

"Lola did her best to dissuade me," Jeremy revealed.

"Then maybe I should revise my impression of her and hope she might manage to talk you out of the bee in your bonnet."

"Bee in my bonnet? Whoever planted that bomb has to be paid back!"

Janis said after pausing, "I knew you weren't going to leave it to the police, Jeremy. But I didn't know you were on a vengeance trip and that scares me stiff."

Me, too, Jeremy thought. "Call it what you like," he said. "For me, though, it's a task I inherited along with the wealth."

Chapter 13

Bessie arrived in Israel still beset by uncertainties. Did she really want to live with an elderly couple, kind though they were? she asked herself after passing through passport control at Ben Gurion airport.

And who had they asked to meet her, since they couldn't leave their restaurant to be here themselves? Supposing that person didn't recognize her from the snapshot Grandpa had said he would show them?

You'll get a taxi and go to the flat, she instructed herself. No, to the restaurant, there'd be nobody at the flat to let her in, Bessie was thinking as she emerged into the Arrivals hall, thronged with people who seemed to be gabbling in what sounded like Russian.

But Bessie's first lesson in the need for self-sufficiency had done little to reassure her. If she'd stayed in London, with Val and her family – or chosen to go to Sydney, with Janis, she wouldn't have had to quell the panic now gripping her.

It was as though she had leapt into the unknown. Like the

first time she'd jumped into the deep end of a swimming pool, scared that she may not bob up again. But it was too late now, she was reflecting, when a tall, thin youth approached her.

They'd sent a *boy* to meet her! And what a mess Bessie must look, her shirt tugged sideways by the weight of her flight bag and stained, too. Nor had she bothered combing her hair before the plane landed.

Thus was Bessie's first meeting with Sim Levi affected by her own inadequacies, her behavior too.

"You don't look strong enough to lift my big suitcase," she said ungraciously, when he had introduced himself and went with her to the baggage carousel.

"But you can't always judge by appearances," Sim answered with a grin. "Did you have a good flight?"

"When the man sitting next to me wasn't spilling coffee on my clothes. If he'd been drinking beer, I'd smell like a pub!"

"You smell very nice."

"Thanks, it's just some perfume I took from my mother's dressing table. She won't be needing it anymore."

"I was sorry to hear you'd lost your parents."

"Thanks again."

"But pleased to be getting you for a neighbor," Sim added.

"You live in the same block as my grandfather?"

"Next door – which you might be pleased about, as well," he told her, "since there aren't any other young people living in our building –"

"There's my suitcase –" Bessie interrupted. "The one with the red ribbon tied to the handle, so it's easy to pick it out –"

"That's a smart idea," said Sim, hauling the case off the carousel.

"But my sister's idea," said Bessie. "She does a lot of

traveling. And I'm not particularly smart!" she added, raising her voice to be heard above the surrounding babble. "Won't you need a luggage trolley, Sim?" she asked while they fought their way through the crush by the carousel.

"If you go on like this, I'll put the case down and show you my bulging biceps!"

Bessie felt herself blush. "Don't be daft."

"And by the way, I'm invited to eat at your place tonight, when your grandparents get home from work," he said as they left the terminal building, Bessie quickening her pace to keep up with his long stride.

"But I'm not exactly in the mood for company," she replied.

"Then you've come to the wrong country," Sim informed her. "Israel is a very gregarious place."

"And how come you speak English with a Lancashire accent?" she inquired.

"Yorkshire, if you don't mind! I was born in Leeds. My family emigrated here when I was ten – and I didn't want to come," he revealed.

"How long did it take you to settle down?"

"The answer is I didn't notice it happening," Sim said, heading past the taxis and minibuses to where his vehicle was parked. "It just did and sooner or later, it'll be that way for you, Bessie."

She said grudgingly while he was hoisting her suitcase into the boot, "All right. I take back what I said about you not being strong."

"Well, that's something!"

"But did anyone ever tell you that you have a lopsided grin and you look like a beanpole?"

"Insults will get you nowhere!"

"Then I'll have to try something else," said Bessie, "after I've mentioned your wobbling Adam's apple."

Sim turned to look at her and saw in the lamplight a forlorn and disheveled girl doing her best to be defiant. Losing her parents had uprooted her – and she's taking it out on me!

"Look – if you don't want my company, I'll just deliver you to your new home," he said.

"I'm not a parcel!"

"What I meant was, I don't have to stay with you till your grandparents get home from work – that's why they asked me for supper –"

"Hildegard is my *step*grandparent."

Was there nothing she wouldn't split hairs about?

They got into the car and Sim tried again. "This is my mother's car, but I usually only get to borrow my dad's van," he said with a smile, "and it reeks of onions, he's a green-grocer. You're in luck, Bessie!"

"That'll be the day," she responded gloomily. "It was nice of you to meet me, though – and what I said about not being in the mood for company – well, don't take it personally, Sim. What I mean is – it isn't you."

"Then what is it, Bessie? Homesickness? You'll get over that."

"Maybe I will, but it isn't just that. It's everything . . ."

A moment later, Bessie was weeping on Sim Levi's bony shoulder and he was stroking her hair.

Chapter 14

Janis's flight to Sydney was no less fraught than Bessie's to Tel Aviv. Since her father's secretary, whom she had called to tell she was leaving London, had made the reservation, she was again traveling first class. Forcibly reminded that she was now an immensely wealthy young woman. And that money could not buy happiness.

"Are you by any chance related to Jake Bornstein?" inquired the man seated beside her, after a stewardess had addressed Janis by her name.

"Jake Bornstein was my father," Janis said frostily. And what's it to you! she felt like adding.

"Was? I'm sorry to hear that. Did he die of the heart attack I once warned him he'd have if he didn't let up?"

"I beg your pardon?" she said turning to look at him.

"Look – I didn't mean to upset you –"

"Well, you damn well have! And I'd like an explanation for what you just said. For your information my father was assassinated. Someone he was doing a business deal with was in the car with him when the bomb exploded."

"Another arms dealer, probably."

Janis almost choked on the orange juice she was drinking. Who the hell was this guy? How did he know things about her father that she hadn't known, or even suspected?

A short hiatus when they were handed menus to scan allowed her to surreptitiously study him. In his late twenties, she reckoned, and dressed like a Yuppie, complete with striped shirt and discreet tie. His accent told Janis he was Australian – but he wasn't the sort she'd mixed with, nor would she want to.

"I gather you knew my father," she said eventually, "or think you did."

"I can only claim to have met him, but I shouldn't think he was an easy man to know."

"His family would tell you otherwise." A more straightforward man than Jake Bornstein had never lived, Janis thought poignantly.

"That's often the case," her companion answered, "with men like him."

Janis was briefly tongue-tied.

"My name is Jesse Cohen, by the way."

"You don't look Jewish," she remarked, trying to pull herself together.

"Nor do you."

Like Janis, Jesse was fair-haired and blue-eyed.

"But returning to your father," he said, "I happen to be the doctor who was called in when he collapsed in Haiti, a couple of years ago. I was in practice there at the time."

It was news to Janis that her father had been to Haiti, let alone that he had ever collapsed. "Would you mind telling me the circumstances?"

"All I recall is that there were three men with him in the hotel suite. A Frenchman, an Italian, and a Latin American."

"What makes you think they were dealing in arms? My father and those other men?" Janis demanded.

"They might not have been, on that occasion, but one of them was Luis Mendez and it's no secret that he's into the arms scene in that part of the world.

"I recognized him from seeing his picture in a magazine," Jesse went on, "he and his wife standing beside his yacht at some fancy marina – you know the kind of thing."

"He was in the car with my father," Janis supplied.

"And many would say he got what was coming to him," Jesse declared.

"All the more reason to believe he was the sole target."

"If it helps you to believe that, go ahead."

Janis wanted to spit in his eye. "Since you only met my father once, you have no right to slander him!"

"Look – I'm simply facing facts, which you evidently don't."

"Nothing is a fact without proof," Janis replied, "and for your information, my stepmother too died in the explosion. Unlike you, I am emotionally involved and none of this is your business, Dr. Cohen."

Janis pointedly gave her attention to the *Guardian* crossword puzzle.

"I used to do crosswords, myself," said Jesse, "but I got out of the habit when I was where we never saw a newspaper."

"Where was that?" Janis inquired, curiosity getting the better of her.

"Ethiopia, with a relief unit."

"Really?" said Janis. "I didn't know relief workers traveled first class – and you're not dressed like my idea of one."

"As it happens, the flight was overbooked," Jesse informed her, "and I'm one of those whose tickets were upgraded to first – which I'm told only happens *if* you're respectably dressed!

"For the past few months I've been a collar-and-tie doc again," he continued explaining. "Another of the useful ways I've filled in time since my marriage broke up was working with AIDS patients, in London. That's what I intend doing when I get home," he added, "which means I again have a purpose in my life – Why am I telling you this!"

"They say it's easy to talk to strangers."

"But you're the first person to whom I've revealed all – Well, not *quite* all. The rest, in a nutshell, is my wife and I worked together in Sydney. We'd studied medicine together. And had everything planned!"

Janis said after a silence, "I too have learned my lesson in the latter respect, but I can't even talk to a stranger about it."

"That has to mean you're still hurting," said Jesse.

"Does your wife still live in Sydney?"

"I don't know and I don't care. When I found out she was two-timing me and she said it didn't mean anything, I realized I'd never really known her and made my escape."

"What I've also learned," said Janis, "is you can't run away from yourself and your experiences."

Jesse studied her profile. "How long have you been running?"

"I didn't say I was."

"You didn't have to. But what you did say is something it took me three years to find out. And I reckon I'm now as ready as I'm likely to be to get on with my life. How about you?"

Janis replied pensively, "There's still too much that's unresolved in mine – including the mystery surrounding my parents' deaths – though you don't deserve to have me admit that to you, Dr. Cohen!"

"I'm not your enemy," he said, meeting her accusing gaze, "nor was I your father's, and I'd like to be your friend."

"I'm not short of friends in Sydney," Janis continued to rebuff him. Attractive though he was, he represented for her that her father had kept secrets from his family.

Chapter 15

When Lady Kyverdale's condition suddenly worsened and it was necessary for her to enter a nursing home, A.P. asked Mary Lou if she would do him the favor of marrying him.

They were together in the area outside the kitchen now dominated by hen coops and Mary Lou almost dropped the bowl of grain she was clutching.

"Say that again, A.P."

"You heard me the first time."

" 'Do me the honor' was what they said in your ancestors' time, I believe – but 'do me the favor' goes with this unromantic setting, I suppose! And I find what you said, and where you said it, highly suspect, A.P."

"All right, I'll level with you, Mary Lou. Grandmother wants to see me married before she dies."

"And I happen to be a handy candidate? How could you be so despicable! Prepared to use me so your gran will die happy – and why does she want to see you married if not to ensure the continuance of the bloody line!"

A reply A.P. ought to have expected. Why didn't he have the magic touch Jeremy had with girls? he thought for the umpteenth time. Or the cheeky persistence of Gary Potter, who despite the black eye his initial overture had won him, was by now a regular weekend visitor to the commune to share Nina's bed.

You're too much the gentleman by far! A.P. privately lashed himself, while Mary Lou, stiff-backed, went on scattering grain outside the henhouses. What he should do now was *literally* sweep her off her feet, carry her to the barn and prove himself the red-blooded chap he really was.

Did he have the nerve? The answer was no. Nor would he want their first coming together to be more like rape than making love.

Without tenderness, what would it be worth? A.P. was thinking bitterly when Mary Lou asked if he had heard from his "dreadful cousin" lately. As if she had decided to pretend what had just passed between them was unimportant.

To Mary Lou, it probably was . . .

"Not since he sent me a postcard from Haiti," A.P. told her.

"What on earth was he doing there?"

"Since you dislike him, why would you be interested?"

"We have to chat about something."

"Not necessarily."

"In that case, you may as well get on with transferring that pile of cartons you're carrying to the outhouse! And you'd better check that the words 'free range' haven't been omitted, under the picture of Kyverdale Hall, which happened with the last delivery of egg cartons," Mary Lou called as A.P. traversed the yard to the improvised packing house.

"Are you going to turn against me," she demanded when he emerged, "just because I won't aid and abet you to do what aristocrats think they're obliged to do? If so, I shall regret throwing in my lot with you, A.P."

"If you'd like the truth," he heard himself say, "it was more a case of me throwing in mine with you."

Mary Lou stopped feeding the chickens and glared at him. "What the heck do you mean by that?"

"I didn't know where I was going, Mary Lou, and I let you lead me by the hand."

"Are you saying you regret starting the commune and all we've achieved and are still achieving here?"

"No."

"Then what *are* you saying?"

"That I don't find what I'm doing satisfying."

"But the commune is our contribution to rescuing the earth, isn't it? And yours is a selfish bloody attitude if ever I heard one!" Mary Lou flashed. "If you think I enjoy feeding hens and all the rest of it, I don't, but every egg we pack in the cartons and sell at reasonable prices is a nail in the coffin of the battery-produced market that epitomizes our society and –"

"I'm well aware of that," A.P. cut her short.

"Are you also aware how important those speeches on ecology are, that you've been making in the House? Don't you find even *that* satisfying?"

"But it isn't enough."

Mary Lou said while appraising him, "You still don't know what you really want, do you?"

"Only in one respect and that's you for my wife."

Mary Lou could not have failed to see that what he had kept hidden was now in his eyes.

"Why did you have to spoil things!" she cried before fleeing.

"Don't just stand there with the hens clucking and fluttering around your feet! Go after her," Lady Kyverdale would have advised. But A.P. was ill-cast for the role of the masterful lover and the heroine's parting words all wrong for a romantic scenario.

Was Mary Lou now packing her bags to leave the commune?

Had A.P. known where Jeremy was, he would have called him, as they had turned to each other for comfort and support in the old days.

Now, though, they were traversing vastly different paths, propelled there by events, and the same went for Janis and for Bessie. The close-knit family atmosphere that had nurtured all four was just something to look back on, while they made their way forward into their separate futures.

PART TWO

CONSEQUENCES

Chapter 1

*L*ady Kyverdale's funeral was also a reunion for A.P. and Jeremy.

"I really appreciate your coming," said A.P. when eventually the two were alone in his room at Kyverdale Hall.

"When Janis let me know, I just got on a plane, as you would have, for me."

"But let's not get sentimental!"

"The person I'm sentimental about," said Jeremy, "is female and isn't sentimental about *me*."

"Lola Mendez?"

"I don't recall telling you her name."

"But Janis did."

"Did she also tell you that Bessie has a boyfriend?" Jeremy asked with a smile.

"I heard that from Grandma Marianne. Our family grapevine remains highly efficient!"

"One of the reasons for me staying tight-lipped about my current activities," said Jeremy.

A.P. observed his grim expression. "Am I included in that?"

Jeremy shook his head. "And it isn't that I don't trust Janis to keep *her* lips buttoned when I ask her to. Just that I don't want to burden her. If she knew I was rubbing shoulders with men who carry revolvers, she wouldn't sleep at night."

"I can't say I like the idea of that myself, Jeremy."

"Me, neither, but I have to go where the trail leads me, A.P. It's now nine months since Dad and Laura were killed – time enough for a woman to conceive and give birth, for you to've turned your ancestral home into what you have, but that bloody police inspector is still saying he has nothing to tell me."

"And you don't believe him?"

"The answer to that is that I've met with caginess and evasions from the word go, on all sides. For all I know, governments could be involved in this. What I've established for sure, though, is there's big money at stake – a multimillion dollar deal – and that could be the reason for all the secrecy."

"Did you learn that from your father's files?"

Again Jeremy shook his head, his demeanor suddenly weary as he ran a hand through his hair.

"Dad's very respectable London accountants couldn't have been more co-operative, A.P., his lawyer, too. They have nothing to hide and according to their records, nor had he. But it's begun to look as if Dad was involved in an international network they knew nothing about.

"There's such a thing as a Swiss bank account, isn't there?" Jeremy added, recalling yet again Lola's calling him the babe-in-arms he then was, "and deals that are done behind locked doors, in faraway places, at the dead of night –"

A.P. gazed through the window at a scene far removed

from the sinister undercurrents evoked by Jeremy's words. The sunlight of a perfect July evening gilding the meadows and the lake. The dairy herd peacefully grazing and a clump of tall trees silhouetted atop a hillock. Gary Potter and Nina, still clad in the sober garments they had worn for Lady Kyverdale's burial service, strolling down the drive, their arms linked.

It wasn't love that Gary was seeking when he set his cap at Nina, but love had found *him* – with happier consequences than *my* lot, A.P. was reflecting when Jeremy returned him to the topic from which his mind had briefly strayed.

"I'm still not prepared to believe, though, that my dad's business dealings were such that someone thought the world would be a better place minus his presence."

A.P. turned to look at him and noticed that he seemed to have aged. Was nine months long enough for that, too? Given Jeremy's experience, probably, and the same could be said of A.P. Experience could age a person faster than the years.

"If you'd like my opinion of what you're doing, Jeremy, I'd call it a crusade."

Jeremy mustered a smile. "But my sister sees it as a vendetta. And Lola says I'm a man with a mission!"

"May I suggest you leave the vendetta aspect out of it?"

"Could *you*? If someone had blown your parents to smithereens?"

The conversation was abruptly ended by Mary Lou's entering with a tray.

"We thought you may not feel like eating with the rest of us, this evening," she said to A.P.

"I had no idea communes provided such service!" said Jeremy. "Did you have to take a vote?"

"We don't find that necessary in compassionate circumstances," Mary Lou informed him. "Being communards doesn't mean we're not human beings. Since I'm on supper duty, it fell to me to bring some food for A.P."

"But you seem to've forgotten *me*," said Jeremy, eyeing the tray.

Mary Lou set it down on a table beside the sofa. "Why on earth would I wait on *you*?"

"I'm keeping the bereaved company, aren't I?"

"Another reason for offering A.P. my sympathy."

"Will you two kindly stop this?" A.P. intervened. "And Jeremy is welcome to eat my egg salad and strawberries. I'm not hungry."

Mary Lou said accusingly to Jeremy, "See what you've done? A.P. hasn't eaten all day and he ought to now. He should also have an early night, he's making a speech in the House, tomorrow."

"What are you?" Jeremy retorted. "His political secretary, as well as his general adviser and overseer of his bodily welfare?"

"I should like to think," said Mary Lou, "that he looks upon me as his best friend."

"That position," said Jeremy, "was filled long before you re-entered his life. By me."

A.P. stormed to the window, his feelings matching his fiery hair. "If you must squabble, leave me out of it!"

"You're all we have in common," said Jeremy.

"Then do your squabbling somewhere else, I'm sick of the pair of you!" said A.P.

"One of your troubles," Mary Lou said to his stiff back, "is you don't know who your real friends are —"

"But you're going to tell him," Jeremy cut in.

"And you're welcome to hear it. Who do you suppose lends A.P. the everyday support he needs, while you're doing your globe-trotting? When occasionally he receives a picture postcard from you and his face lights up, I feel like saying to him what I'm going to now – that it's time he appreciated the true friendship he's surrounded by on the commune," Mary Lou declared before departing and slamming the door behind her.

A.P. said after a silence, "One of my *other* troubles is I'm still in love with her. Though there are times, and this is one of them, when I don't even like her!"

"Since when was love logical?" said Jeremy. "Despite Lola's liberated education, at heart she's what her mother is, conventional and without an adventurous bone in her beautiful body, conditioned to woman's place being in the home and all that.

"In other words, not the girl for Jeremy Bornstein! I fell for her nevertheless."

"Does she know?"

"Not unless she's caught me looking at her the way I wish she'd look at me. As for the harridan *you've* fallen for –"

"Mary Lou has her shortcomings," A.P. interrupted, "who doesn't? But I've never known her behave with anyone as she does with you – and I could say the same in reverse. What the heck is it with you two?"

"Could be we both think we know what's best for *you*!"

Jeremy sat down on the sofa and glanced around A.P.'s private sanctum. The four-poster bed, in an alcove, the leather-topped desk by the window, the framed cartoons from old copies of *Punch* on the walls, and the crammed bookshelves. And the slippers on the hearth!

"Did Mary Lou put those there?" Jeremy asked with a grin.

A.P. emerged from his own thoughts. "Put what where?"

Jeremy pointed to the slippers.

"I keep them where they're within easy reach when my

feet are killing me after a hard day," said A.P., "and I flop into that wing chair. Mary Lou's solicitousness doesn't go that far!"

"Management is what I'd call it."

"If you're going to be snide with me, I'd rather you left," A.P. replied.

"But at least your fellow-communards didn't vote you out of your own room," Jeremy continued.

"It was a matter of first come, first served," A.P. informed him. "People didn't join all on the same day and, needless to say, I didn't have to arrive, I was already here."

"But if they had voted about accommodation and you'd been voted out of here, would you have taken it lying down?" Jeremy wanted to know.

"Probably not."

"Didn't I say you weren't the commune type?"

"Nor is Mary Lou."

"Selfless-Sarah, you mean! Prepared to sacrifice herself for the cause –"

"So much so," A.P. interrupted, "that she stayed put even though I asked her to marry me and she turned me down. I expected her to remove herself from my scene. Instead of which she told me, half an hour later, that she was going to forget it happened."

"What a strain living under the same roof with her must be for you!"

"Also for her and I admire her for not putting personal feelings first."

"But one day," said Jeremy, "you'll come down to earth and be thankful she refused to marry you. You've had a lucky escape, A.P."

"In your opinion."

Chapter 2

*T*he girl whom Jeremy had assumed did not have an adventurous bone in her body was endeavoring not to think of him while she attended a meeting in the Mendez company board room.

The first time she had been summoned here was when the directors learned that she had accompanied Jeremy Bornstein to the hospital.

Was there nothing that these closed-faced men *didn't* know? Lola thought, appraising them while they waited for the secretary pouring coffee to hand around the cups and return to her own office.

Her gaze came to rest on Senor Vargas, seated at the head of the table in the chair once occupied by her father, his silver hair and mild gray eyes lending him a benign appearance.

But those eyes had briefly seemed twin points of steel, Lola recollected, when she had initially refused to do what was required of her. Then the friendly mask had again descended, matching his plea for Lola's loyalty to the company founded by Luis Mendez.

Only remembrance of the man himself, of how dear he was to her, had allowed Lola to lend herself to a "cover up," she thought now. Unlike Jake Bornstein's son, she had divined from the first that her father and his might have engaged in activities they would not wish known to their families, or to the world.

Jeremy, however, hadn't heeded her warning in that respect. He wasn't the sort to let what might prove to be personally painful stand between him and the truth, and seemed not to have the concern for his sisters that Lola had for hers, and for her mother. Who wouldn't want to go on living if the husband she had idolized turned out to have had feet of clay.

It was for this reason that Lola had agreed to keep the directors informed of Jeremy's progress, while letting him continue thinking her his ally, if a passive one.

Senor Vargas sipped some coffee and said to her without preamble, "What we require you to do now is employ your friendship with Mr. Bornstein to put him off the scent."

"Would you like to tell me how?" Lola flared.

"When you have calmed yourself."

She transferred her gaze from his avuncular smile to an oil painting of her father that had pride of place on the wood-paneled walls. How long would it hang there, now that Vargas was ruling the empire Luis Mendez had arduously built? Diamonds and oil, fertilizers and paint, were among the vast range of holdings accrued by the company whose offices and staff Lola's father had kept relatively small and under his personal control.

"We cannot be sure that this young man has told you everything," Senor Vargas interrupted her conjecturing, "but it's plain from what he *has* divulged that this investigation of his is becoming dangerous."

"Dangerous for him? Or for you?"

"I would've preferred it," Vargas answered, "if you had said for 'us.' The answer to your question however, is that what he is doing is hazardous for his own well-being and for the future of a certain contract of ours."

"I would like to know what that contract is, Senor Vargas."

"There's no need for you to bother your pretty head with business matters," he said smoothly.

No need to bother my *pretty* head! Though Lola had graduated top of her class at Harvard. But that was the attitude of men like the four around this table. Women of their own class were raised to be just adornments and appendages, and even if you stepped briefly out of line, as Lola had by doing a business course, you were expected to *toe* the line ever after.

Nor had Lola's own expectations changed from those she was conditioned to. Her college roommate, Elizabeth Pinkerton, who came from Boston, was nothing if not a feminist – but Lola hadn't envisaged ever emulating Elizabeth even in her private thoughts.

And if Senor Vargas got his wish, Lola's mental mutiny continued, she would end up married to his son Juan, who had recently switched his attentions from his long-time girlfriend to Lola.

Suddenly, Lola felt that she was being subjected to a two-pronged, father and son attack. That the Vargases would stop at nothing to entrench themselves still further in the Mendez company; that the web of intrigue following her father's assassination wasn't all that was going on.

At the same time, she was sickened by the knowledge that she could no longer trust Juan. But Jeremy can't trust me, she bleakly thought, though he still believes that he can. I'm as treacherous as Juan.

Just how treacherous she would now be expected to be was then put to her by Senor Vargas.

"I have here the disinformation for you to feed to young Bornstein."

Lola eyed the sheet of paper in his hand. How she was to "put Jeremy off the scent," all carefully worked out. "May I take it with me?" she asked with distaste.

"Certainly not."

"Kindly don't speak to me as you doubtless did to that press secretary you sacked!"

"She proved herself open to a bribe."

"But you wouldn't be above *offering* bribes, would you?" said Lola.

"What else do you suppose the young man you have so much respect for is doing?" Vargas answered. "Who but he was the cause of Senorita Santander's dismissal?"

"The way I'd put it," said Lola, "is he has to play *your* game in *your* world and *his* motive is an honorable one. As mine is," she added, "though the same can't be said of what I'm lending myself to.

"If this meeting is now over," she went on, "kindly leave me alone with that piece of paper and I'll try to memorize what's written on it."

"After which it must be handed directly to me, for shredding," said Vargas, unruffled, "and I must trust you to carry the plan through."

Vargas waited until the others at the table had left, before rising to hand Lola the sheet of paper. "Juan was hoping to take you to lunch today," he said with a smile, "but something cropped up in Istanbul."

"Is the Topkapi Museum up for sale and you're thinking of acquiring it for the company?" Lola said with sarcasm.

"First I'd have to call a board meeting," he chuckled.

"But the other directors are your yes-men, aren't they?" They hadn't uttered a word.

"They're my valued colleagues," Vargas answered, "and I trust them. As your father did. Now is there anything else I can do for you?" he inquired too solicitously.

"You can stop talking to me about trust. Coming from you, it reminds me of the old saying, 'Honor among thieves'!"

"I'll construe that as the outburst of an overemotional young woman."

"Then perhaps I should remind you that you are still only the *acting* chairman of the Mendez company, and that I and my family are now the major shareholders," said Lola, watching the smile disappear from his face.

Chapter 3

*B*essie's having a boyfriend was an exaggeration initiated by her grandmother, and which Bessie found embarrassing when Shirley visited her in Tel Aviv.

"So when's the wedding, love?" Shirley teased her while they were sunbathing on the beach.

"Will you pack it in, Gran! And if you say things like that in front of Sim, you'll ruin my friendship with him."

"Hasn't he kissed you yet?"

"If he had, you'd be the last person I'd tell."

"Meanwhile," said Shirley, "you'll get burnt if you don't put some more sun lotion on. Let me do it for you –"

"I'll do it myself!"

"You can't put it on your back."

"Then I'll put my shirt on. Anything for peace!"

"You shouldn't expose yourself at all," Shirley continued nagging. "You have my mother's milky skin."

Also her beaky nose and her currant eyes, Bessie recalled

from the photographs of her namesake in Shirley's family gallery.

"Did my great-grandmother have a birthmark like mine on her arm?" she inquired.

Shirley's anxious response was, "You're not having trouble with that, are you? Itching, or anything? If so, you must let the doctor look at it."

"Why are you always warning me about things, Grandma!" Bessie exclaimed. "It's impossible to talk to you about *anything*, without you doing your best to put the fear of God into me – and when I was little you succeeded."

"I love you very much, Bessie. And you're now all I have in the world."

"But if I heeded you, I'd wrap myself in cottonwool and never cross the road!"

"If I promise to be different, will you come home and live with me?"

So pathetic did Shirley briefly seem, Bessie could not but be sorry for her. One way and another, Grandma had lost everyone dear to her. Including me, Bessie thought. But she was incapable of being different, or she wouldn't have alienated all the people she had.

"It wouldn't work," Bessie said, hardening her heart, "and I've already made more friends here than I had in London, though I still miss Val. I thought I'd be the only one at school who's from England, but there're plenty of others whose families emigrated like Sim's did, who remember what it was like for them when they first got here."

"But Sim is your *best* friend," Shirley said with a wink.

"And the way you're behaving about him," said Bessie, "is just one of the reasons why me living with you wouldn't work. If a boy asked me the time in the street, you'd think it was because he fancied me. But I'm not the sort boys fancy, Grandma."

"That's what my mother thought, before my dad asked her to marry him, she told me."

"But family history is he married her for her money," said Bessie.

"The hell with family history!" Shirley flashed. "Whoever you got that from should be shot. But you'd better beware of it happening to *you*," she added, simmering down. "With what your stepfather left you, you're worth a fortune, love."

Bessie watched a bronzed, bikini-clad girl, beautiful enough to be Miss World, flirting with a crowd of admiring boys, and turned on her grandmother.

"I'm not like you, money mad, and I never shall be! The fortune you just mentioned doesn't mean a thing to me and I'd swap it for knowing who my real father is."

"Is that why you're suddenly so interested in your birthmark?" Shirley divined.

"Well, it wasn't passed down to me from your family, was it? And Grandpa Peter says it isn't from his."

"Birthmarks aren't necessarily hereditary, love."

"You don't want me to find my father, do you?" Bessie accused her.

"I believe in leaving well alone."

"But I've found out that distinctive birthmarks often *are* hereditary."

"And I'll now have sleepless nights worrying about you accosting strange middle-aged men who happen to have a star-shaped blemish on their forearm!" Shirley exclaimed.

"I must be thankful," she added, "that not every man walks around in a short-sleeved shirt, not even in Israel –"

"Will you stop it, Grandma!"

"If you'll give me your word to put what we've been discussing from your mind."

"I'll do no such thing," Bessie replied, watching Shirley transfer herself from her beach towel to a deckchair shaded by a parasol, pausing only to adjust her black lycra swimsuit.

"When I was little, you didn't want me to learn how to swim, did you?" Bessie's mind swooped backward. "In case I got drowned."

"What has that to do with this?"

"You're now trying to stop me from doing something else that could be good for me."

"Who told you that distinctive birthmarks are often hereditary?" Shirley demanded.

"Naomi Bloch, who's in my class, said her dad and her granddad have the same one she has on her shoulder, and it made me think. That's when I asked Grandpa Peter if mine came from his family."

"And if he's encouraging you, I'll –"

"He isn't."

"For once, we agree!"

Bessie was sprawled on the sand, gazing pensively at the sea lapping the shore, oblivious to the ball games and carefree frolicking all around her.

Shirley eyed her with increasing trepidation. "What would you do if you *did* manage to find your real father?"

"I shan't know that till it happens."

Chapter 4

Who was the man who answered your phone?" Shirley inquired when she called Janis.

"It's me who's Bessie's guardian, not you who's mine!" Janis said more jocularly than she felt.

"That doesn't mean I've stopped taking the interest in you I always have," Shirley replied, "and I'd be obliged if you wouldn't make such hurtful remarks. I've just returned from Israel full of anxiety about Bessie – though, as you enjoy reminding me, Laura was foolish enough to put *you* in charge of her."

"What are you anxious about this time?" Janis asked, exchanging a glance with Jesse Cohen, who was beside her in her kitchen preparing a salad dressing.

"Before we get into that, is everything all right with you, Janis?"

Irritating though Shirley was, Janis could not deny that her concern was genuine. She had tried to be as grandmotherly with Janis and Jeremy as she was with Bessie and that hadn't ended when Laura and Jake died.

"I'm fine," Janis said.

"That wasn't my impression when Kurt turned up for the funeral with his wife. I'm sure Marianne saw the look on your face, too, though she brushed me off when I mentioned it to her."

Janis would have been amazed if Marianne hadn't. "Since I didn't know Kurt had married, it was a bit of a surprise," she answered, keeping her tone light.

"Just as long as that's *all* it was," said Shirley, "that you haven't realized the mistake you made in jilting him and are now crying over spilt milk. I've spilt plenty in *my* time, Janis," she continued her homily, "and wasted too many years shedding tears over what might have been – or I might not have ended up all alone.

"Believe it or not, I haven't gone short of proposals."

Janis did believe it. Shirley was still an attractive woman, helped to remain so by all the artifices money could buy.

"But my heart wasn't in it," Shirley went on, "and letting that matter, comparing every man I met with Peter, was *my* big mistake. People – including Bessie! – think all I'm interested in is money when what I really am is incurably romantic."

Though it was possible that Shirley was both, the romantic side of her had escaped Janis!

"You still haven't told me who your visitor is," Shirley quizzed.

And Janis was thankful that he couldn't hear Shirley's contribution to the conversation. "Would you mind if I called you back later?"

"What I want to tell you is very important."

"Then could you make it brief? I smell something burning in the oven," Janis said desperately.

"I rang up to let Bessie's legal guardian know that she's determined to find her real father."

Janis could not stop herself from saying, "Only you could make that seem a crime. To me, it seems natural."

Shirley replied coldly, "Would Laura and your dad have wanted it?"

"Probably not. But now they're both in their graves, it can't hurt them. And if it helps Bessie, I'm all for it."

"Does that mean you'll let her squander her inheritance on a search that could come to nothing? And on the subject of inheritances, Janis, I'd better give you the warning I gave to Bessie: Beware of fortune hunters. Who *is* the man you've got with you?"

Jesse said after Janis had slammed down the receiver, "*I* don't smell anything burning in the oven."

"Because there's nothing in it! We're having a cold meal, aren't we?"

"And the classic question from me, right now, would be: what was all that about? – Only I'm not going to ask it."

Janis stopped glaring at the telephone and managed to smile. "You're the soul of discretion, Jesse, but it'll do me good to tell you. And would you believe that woman got up in the middle of the night in England to ruin my appetite for lunch in Australia?"

"Or maybe she just couldn't sleep."

"Given her mental machinations, that's more than likely," Janis said caustically. "At present, they're concentrated on my sister and me. She's never going to accept that young people are capable of finding their own salvation."

"But I've found mine," said Jesse.

"Working with AIDS patients, you mean?"

"You know darn well what I mean."

"But I think it's too soon for you to know," said Janis.

"In personal matters, I'm a decisive guy."

"Like the way you upped and left when you found out your wife was two-timing you?" Janis said, resuming the task Shirley's call had interrupted.

Jesse watched her sprinkle some chopped chives on the potato salad. "That wasn't a decision, Janis, it was an instinct. I'm strong on instinct, too. And I knew you were special the minute we met," he said, dispelling the moment of tension with his warm smile.

"When we got off the plane in Sydney, I thought I was never going to see you again – But for once, I got lucky. Running into you at a synagogue social I went to just to please my parents, and there you were, helping to serve the refreshments!"

"My dad used to say that for Jews, it's a small world," Janis recalled, "and that one way of us finding company in a strange place was to do what he sometimes did when he couldn't get home for the weekend – head for a synagogue."

"That doesn't match my impression of him," said Jesse.

"But as you mentioned on the plane, you only met him once." And what you told me made me feel I never wanted to be with you again, thought Janis. "It certainly worked for me," she said, "finding company that way, I mean."

"I noticed your popularity," said Jesse. "Was there a special guy?"

"I wasn't ready for that."

"And now?"

"Kindly stop fishing!"

But Jesse has inserted himself into my life and I've let him, she thought, fetching a platter of cold cuts from the refrigerator. Last Sunday they had driven to Crowdy Bay National

Park, Janis's first visit to the beauty spot that Australians took for granted and she'd considered it well worth the four hour journey, though for Jesse, who'd lived in this free and easy country all his life, distance and the infinite variety of the terrain, the waterfalls and the colorful foliage, and the tang of eucalyptus seeming to hover in the air, were nothing to get excited about.

While Janis's childhood memories of South Africa included the scenic beauty through which she had traveled on trips with her parents, the apartheid laws imposed on beaches and parks had marred the Bornsteins' family outings, as they had for other white families who were their friends.

Many of whom emigrated because they couldn't bear it, Janis reflected, while garnishing the cold cuts with sprigs of parsley.

"Is it worth all that dressing the food up, when all we're going to do is eat it!" Jesse said with a smile.

"I do things the way Laura did."

"And I've gathered she was very artistic."

Janis had a vision of Laura piping a mayonnaise design on a cold salmon, and surrounded by the debris that always accumulated around her when she cooked. "She wasn't too tidy, though!"

"I shouldn't think the two usually go together," said Jesse, "but in you, they do."

Janis glanced around her tiny, but immaculate kitchen and had another vision: her mum preparing food for a dinner party and the kitchen seeming immaculate nevertheless. "I must have got my tidy streak from my birth-mother –"

"I never heard that expression before."

"I saw it in the dedication in an American novel. The author had paid a joint tribute to the two women who had raised her. And my two," Janis went on, "well, each in her way was a remarkable person and I have a lot to thank each of them for, though I didn't realize it when they were alive. If I were to have twin daughters, I'd call one Laura and the other Julia," Janis said poignantly.

"Meanwhile," said Jesse, "you get the glasses and I'll open our Sunday bottle of wine."

A twosome is what we've become, Janis registered. But while they ate their meal in the spring sunlight, the table on the verandah flanked by the potted shrubs Janis called her garden, she found herself beset by unreality.

What was she doing, growing ever closer to a man whose very presence reminded her of the shady circumstances in which he had met her father? Who'd sowed in her mind seeds of doubt that her heart continued to deny.

Even when they had a night out together downtown, strolling with other couples in the Village Center and along William Street, glamorized by the neon lights, then on to a disco where the throbbing music was enough to blank out your thoughts, for Janis her dad's shadow continued to hover between them.

Why does Jesse have to be the only man I've met since Kurt who makes me feel whole again? she thought, watching him top up their wine glasses. Strong enough to make the new beginning Janis hadn't thought possible.

"Heard from your brother recently?" Jesse inquired.

"Why do you want to know?"

"It was just a casual question."

"Like hell it was! You're hoping to be proved right about my dad. I'm sorry I confided to you what Jeremy is doing."

"On the contrary," said Jesse, "for your sake I'm hoping to be proved wrong."

Then the telephone summoned Janis inside.

When eventually she returned she said, looking dazed, "Jeremy's been injured. In another incident in Caracas."

"Was the call from a hospital?"

Janis shook her head.

"Let's get you out of the sunlight and I'll make you some tea," Jesse said briskly.

"I don't want any tea."

"Doctor's orders," he declared, leading her into the living room and settling her on the sofa.

While Jesse put the kettle on to boil and a teabag into a mug, keeping an eye on her over the counter top, Janis tried to collect her thoughts, anxiety about Jeremy causing her stomach to churn.

"The call was from Senor Mendez's daughter," she eventually told Jesse, "and I didn't think my first contact with the lovely Lola would be her telling me what she did. You're not the only one with strong instincts, Jesse, and I've felt from the first time he mentioned her that that girl is trouble for my headstrong brother."

"Did she give you the details of the incident?"

"Only that again it involved a car and Jeremy is lucky to be alive," Janis said with a shudder.

Jesse brought her the mug of tea, into which he had heaped three spoonfuls of sugar.

"This tastes terrible!"

"Then pretend it's medicine, which it is, for shock, and swallow it down," he instructed.

He then went to fetch a blanket and said while wrapping it around her, "This is the rest of the treatment, which I forgot till I saw you shiver. But I'm not usually emotionally involved with my patients – and I see that you keep your bedroom tidy, too."

Fetching the blanket was the first time Jesse had crossed

that threshold, though not for the want of trying. For Janis, taking that step would put a seal on their relationship that she wasn't yet ready for. She had never slept around, as some of her friends did. For her there had to be love along with the sex.

Did she love Jesse? Janis asked herself, surveying the tall, broad-shouldered figure now watching over her and noticing there was a button missing from his plaid shirt.

"Feeling better?" he asked her.

"Yes, thank you, Doctor! But I wouldn't mind you making my plane reservations, while I pack a case yet again. I told Lola Mendez I'd be in Caracas as soon as I could get there."

"And I'm not letting you go alone."

Chapter
5

*S*uch was the efficiency – if not the accuracy – of the family grapevine, A.P. learned from a relative in Munich that Jeremy was in hospital in Caracas, and Janis on her way to be with him.

"I hate to be the one to have to tell you," his cousin, Howard Klein, had prefaced the news. "Especially when you're here for a break. It was Shirley who rang up to tell me about the accident."

"Accident?" said A.P.

"I prefer to think it wasn't another incident."

"Since when were you an ostrich, Howard?"

"Jeremy wouldn't be the first person to find his brakes failing on a hill. He'd hired a car, Shirley told me."

"And who told her?"

"Bessie, who got it from Janis. Janis had called her to say she was going away and didn't know for how long. When the kid asked why, Janis told her the truth."

A palatable version of the truth, thought A.P. "How badly

injured is Jeremy?" he asked. "And why did you wait till now to tell me?"

"I didn't want you badgering me with questions till I felt ready to answer them," said Howard.

"No matter where you lived, you'd still be a blunt Mancunian," said A.P.

Howard smiled. "Like my aunt Marianne?"

"Well, I can't say that living in Bermuda has changed Gran."

"When Karin and I stayed with Marianne," said Howard, "the Sabbath dinner she gave us included 'tsimmes,' like your great-grandmother, Sarah Sandberg, used to make.

"Has becoming Lord Kyverdale changed *you*, A.P.?"

"Yes, as a matter of fact."

They were seated at the kitchen table and Howard rose to fetch the coffee pot from the stove. "And except for the way you mentioned, I'm not the same chap I used to be," he said refilling their mugs.

Howard's hair, once as fiery as A.P.'s, was dulled by gray. And the lines etched beside his mouth reminded A.P. of his dad's appearance, nowadays.

The two were the same age and both had suffered broken marriages, but A.P. sensed that with Howard there was more to it.

"Being part of West Germany's postwar Jewish community isn't easy," Howard said, as though he had divined A.P.'s thoughts.

"The neo-Nazis, you mean?"

"That scourge isn't confined to Germany! And it isn't just that, A.P. It's the conscience-thing about living here, though some who do have very personal reasons."

"Like your father-in-law returned to rebuild his dead father's business," said A.P., "not letting what Hitler did get the better of him."

"And there are plenty here who, like him, believe that if no Jews had returned to Germany, Hitler would have in effect achieved what he set out to do. That doesn't stop Karin and me from worrying about raising our kids here, though, letting them in for the inner conflict that a lot of the teenagers we know are living with."

"Jeremy and I had that illustrated for us, when I was last here," said A.P., recalling a buxom girl in a clingy sweater, livid with indignation because her family's return had made German her mother tongue. Jeremy had remarked, later, "That girl has to be a tiger in bed."

"You still haven't told me how badly Jeremy was injured," he prodded Howard.

"According to Shirley, it could be touch and go, but you know what an exaggerator she is."

A reminder that allowed A.P. to hope and he blotted out a mental picture of the cheeky grin he might never see again. "If you're worried about raising your children here, Howard, why don't you just leave?"

"Choices are rarely that simple, A.P."

Given his own experience, A.P. had to agree.

"Even if my wife weren't indispensable to her father's business," Howard went on, "I have my son from my first marriage here, don't I?"

"How is Ben doing?"

"He's the one I worry about most, since he doesn't live with me. He thinks the world of *you*, by the way."

A.P. said with a smile, "I can't imagine why."

"Ben's never forgotten that long chat you had with him, when you were here for the visit you just mentioned. Since then, modeling himself on his hero has been his ambition."

Then heaven help him, thought A.P. "Including my dropping out of Oxford?" he said wryly.

Howard helped himself to a biscuit and bit into it. "Don't tell Karin I've been noshing, she wants me to slim down to how I looked before she married me!

"About Ben, well, I don't think anything you did would shake his loyalty, A.P., and it's good for a lad to have someone to look up to."

"Provided they're worthy of it," A.P. countered, "and I've yet to prove I am. As a kid, I looked up to Jeremy – and see how he's turned out! Why didn't that damned crusading fool give up before he was stopped?" A.P.'s feelings poured out.

Howard said after a silence, "I tried to persuade him to when I last saw him."

"Jeremy came to stay with you?"

"Stay with me? If I hadn't run into him outside the Bayerischer Hof Hotel, I wouldn't have known he was in Munich! – And I didn't mention it to Karin, she'd have been as hurt as I was."

"But in fairness to Jeremy," said A.P. "I have to say he kept away from you and your family for your sake. He must have come here to meet someone he didn't trust, and if he was followed to your home –"

"Stop being so bloody melodramatic," Howard cut in, "he just didn't have time to see us, or couldn't be bothered. And when I think what a close-knit clan we once were . . ."

"In my view, we still are," A.P. declared, "or you wouldn't be anxious on Jeremy's behalf. Nor would I have come to stay with *you*, when I need a break."

A.P. took his mug of coffee and stood gazing through the window at the rose garden, at this time of year a treat for the eyes, blooms of a breathtaking beauty and of a rich variety of hue bordering a narrow pathway to the rustic summerhouse in which he and Ben had sat talking, just a couple of summers ago.

A.P. and Jeremy were then looking forward to going up to Oxford, euphoric about the student life that lay ahead, unaware that events would so soon conspire to bring them down to earth.

"What I actually need is some breathing space," A.P. said to Howard.

"Who's been giving you claustrophobia?"

"Let's just say there are things I have to sort out." Including myself.

"That you can't talk to your father about?"

"He's still working in L.A."

"What a glitzy life my cousin Martin leads!"

"You wouldn't think so if you saw him laboring night and day when he can't get his lyrics right," A.P. replied. "When I spent a weekend with him – before he left for the States – I barely saw him. Dad works extremely hard."

"But I heard he now has an American girlfriend," said Howard as though that were compensation.

"Whom I haven't yet met," said A.P., "but I'm hoping to like her more than I do my mother's obnoxious boyfriend!"

Howard said after pausing, "Wouldn't you say that what matters is for your parents to be happy?"

"Sure. But if whoever they remarried proved to be another mistake, I'd be sorry I told them to get a divorce."

Howard was astonished. "It was your idea? And you had the chutzpah to tell them to do it?"

"If you'd had the parent trouble I had while I was growing up, you might have done the same."

"That was once Ben's lot," Howard said quietly.

"But he was too young, before your marriage broke up, to

realize that you and Christina were unhappy. It wasn't just myself I was sorry for," A.P. recalled.

"And to set the record straight," said Howard, "only Christina was unhappy, she was homesick for her parents and fled with Ben back to Munich. But Ben now has plenty of reason to feel sorry for himself, A.P. How would you like to be a half-Jewish kid growing up in a German-gentile family?"

That evening, so many children were present at supper Howard joked that his wife resembled "the old woman who lived in a shoe."

"To me, Karin looks as young as when I last saw her," A.P. remarked, watching her ladling soup. "And as beautiful, if I may say so."

"You certainly may!" said Karin with a laugh. "Though I was pregnant at the time and feeling far from beautiful. With that little monster," she added, when her youngest child threw a chunk of bread on the floor.

Ben, seated beside A.P., was glancing around the table. "My mother wouldn't let me invite friends for a meal without asking her and she would never let me invite this many."

"But she doesn't have a housekeeper, does she?" said Howard.

"Only this time," said Karin, "my kids did it on Frau Schwartz's day off! Also, I'm sorry for A.P. who can't hear himself speak above the chatter and it isn't even in his own language."

Ben then replied to Howard, "*My* mother doesn't need a housekeeper, she doesn't go to work, like Karin does."

It's as if, for some reason, he has a down on his mum, thought A.P. Was that why Howard had defended Christina? The opposite of how some men in his position behaved, losing no opportunity to poison the child's mind against the ex-wife.

Howard, though, was concerned only with Ben's welfare. Rather than subject Ben to a tug-o'war between his parents, he had refrained from fighting a custody battle.

A.P., like the other younger members of the family, knew more of his elders' personal histories than they supposed. Including that it was love of a different kind than the paternal that had eventually transplanted Howard from Manchester to German soil, after meeting the green-eyed brunette now offering A.P. more dumplings for his soup.

"It's as well that we have an outsize freezer, to cope with emergencies!" said Howard.

"But what you're calling an emergency and apologizing about, I'm rather enjoying," said A.P.

"You actually like kids?"

"I haven't had much opportunity to find out. But being among them, like this, gives me some hope for the future."

"A profound statement if ever I heard one."

"What I meant," said A.P., "is when my generation's done all we can ecologically, it'll be kids like those now gobbling Karin's delicious soup who'll reap the benefit and continue the good work."

"That," said Howard, "minus the soup, sounds like an excerpt from the speeches I'm told you've been making in the House of Lords – and I forgot to tell you that Ben's become a junior Green."

"Please don't make fun of me, Dad," said Ben, "and I wanted to tell A.P., myself."

Howard's eleven-year-old stepdaughter, Magda, then switched her attention from her friends and her language to English. "Ben is right to say not to make fun of this," she told

Howard severely. "It is a matter of life and death for the earth."

She then asked A.P. if British children engaged in ecological projects at school and was delighted to hear that they did.

"I and my classmates," said her brother, Rudy, "are writing compositions about what is happening to the rainforest and they will be sent to our parents."

"Don't bother having yours sent to us," said Howard, "we already know."

"But do you care?" asked Magda, riveting Howard with accusing, blue eyes. "I have asked you to stop buying products harmful to the ecology, but you go on doing so."

Karin brought two huge bowls of sauerkraut to the table and told Magda and Rudy to clear away the soup plates. "When I tried using an ozone-friendly hair spray, it spurted out in globs and I had to rewash my hair!"

"Is your hair more important than the earth's atmosphere?" asked Magda. "And I have decided to be a vegetarian —"

"Starting from now?" Karin cut in. "If so, there'd be more bratwurst for the rest of us."

"Starting from now," Magda said determinedly.

"And I shall join you," said Rudy.

Karin's reaction was, "When Frau Schwartz hears about this, she'll hand in her notice!"

"Why?" asked Ben.

"Frau Schwartz is a good, old-fashioned Bavarian cook," said Howard. "Without meat her cuisine wouldn't exist, as it wouldn't without potatoes."

"Rudy and I will be content with just potatoes," Magda declared stoically.

"And when I grow up," said Ben, "I'm going to live on a commune, and save the earth, just like A.P."

A.P. had to laugh. "I wouldn't say we were exactly doing that. Just making our small contribution to an immense task, and if everyone did —"

"The earth could be saved?" Ben interrupted.

"There would certainly be a much better chance."

Karin had begun serving the sauerkraut and Rudy wanted to know if the cabbage was organically grown.

"If you ask Frau Schwartz questions like that, she'll think you're accusing her of poisoning you, and you haven't been poisoned yet, have you?"

"But perhaps with humans it takes longer," the little boy answered.

"For the pesticides to kill us off," said his sister.

"These kids," Howard said to A.P., "are ruining my appetite!"

"And I would not eat that sausage if I were you," said Magda, "the meat may be infected."

"So speaks the five-minute vegetarian! But I did warn you, didn't I, A.P., before they got home from school, that our kids are ecology-mad."

"Which sounded like good news to me and I'm having an interesting evening in their company," A.P. answered.

"So might I, if I didn't have to put up with it all the time."

Not just interesting, exciting, thought A.P., surveying the animated young faces around the table, while Magda translated the adults' conversation into German. And the attitudes so evident here had to be a reflection of how kids were beginning to think throughout the Western world.

A far cry from my lot at their age *and* in our teens, A.P. reflected. Duped by the ever-escalating consumer society that today's kids were rejecting.

If Mary Lou were here, she'd jump for joy and who but she was the catalyst for A.P.'s reshaping his life? On the afternoon he'd fallen in love with her, anything she might then have suggested would have seemed to him like a candle lighting his way, and so it had continued until she finally snuffed the candle out.

Hope was its name, and without the hope that she could love him, A.P. was again as if stumbling in the dark.

Later, escorting Ben home through leafy avenues of picturesque houses, passing by a white steepled church seeming ghostly in the moonlight, A.P. found himself as drawn to the boy now as he was when they first met.

"You didn't have to do this," said Ben. "My dad would have taken me in his car, like he always does."

"Are you finding it too long a walk?" A.P. asked, glancing down at the small figure trying to keep up with him and slowing his own pace.

"Not in the least, but –"

"No buts," said A.P. with a smile, "I'm only here for a couple of days and I wanted the opportunity to chat with you."

"I'm honored," said Ben.

"Don't be ridiculous!"

"But you are now a lord, aren't you?"

"And that changes nothing between you and me."

They fell silent and A.P. noted Ben's pensive expression. "What's on your busy mind now, Ben?"

"Well – I'm never going to see much of you, am I? You have too much to do, to come to Munich often – and I'm afraid you'll forget me."

"That," said A.P. adamantly, "is never going to happen." He saw Ben's expression brighten and added, "In your school holiday, would you be too busy to come and visit *me*?"

"You're inviting me to Kyverdale Hall?" Ben said incredulously.

"You would have to pull your weight, of course, now it's a commune."

"Help with the farming, you mean?"

"And take your turn peeling spuds and washing dishes!"

"I would happily scrub the floors," said Ben.

"That, too," said A.P. with a laugh.

Then the animation in Ben's eyes clouded. "But my mother wouldn't allow me to come. I haven't been back to England since . . ."

. . . Your parents split up, A.P. silently completed the sentence. A scarring experience for any child, but, as Howard had pointed out, in Ben's case the consequences could be more damaging.

"I never saw my Jewish grandparents again," Ben resumed speaking, "but I remember how kind they were to me. Though my Grandpa Klein is now dead, my grandma is still alive. And I have an aunt and two cousins, don't I? – Whom I should very much like to meet."

Which is highly unlikely, A.P. reflected, since all those whom Ben had just mentioned now lived in Israel. A place that Howard's ex-wife would never let their child visit.

"My mother isn't anti-Semitic," Ben went on – telepathically, "it's just that –"

"You don't have to explain to me," A.P. cut in, "she and *my* mother were once close friends."

"Does that mean they quarrelled and ended their friendship?"

"On the contrary, they remained close until your mother left England, and I think that what they had in common accounted for the failure of both their marriages, Ben."

How could A.P. be having this conversation with a kid of

ten? But this one was wiser than he ought to be. And closely resembled the grandfather he had mentioned. A more Semitic-looking child would be hard to find.

"What I meant," A.P. continued, "was they fought against you and me being absorbed into our fathers' family."

Ben's response confirmed A.P.'s assessment of him. "Perhaps they were afraid that when we grew up we would want to be Jews."

"Though I feel part of me is Jewish, that hasn't happened to me," A.P. replied.

"But you're a Catholic, aren't you?"

Was there nothing that this kid wasn't clued-up about, with regard to A.P.!

"One of my schoolfriends is your religion," said Ben, "but I'm only a Protestant, aren't I?"

"What do you mean, *only* a Protestant?" A.P. inquired, though he thought he knew.

"Well," said Ben thoughtfully, "I don't have to worry about committing mortal sins, do I?"

A.P. smiled. "Do you know what a mortal sin is?"

"No, but my friend said his priest is always warning him about it and it sent a shiver down my spine."

What Ben meant by being "only a Protestant," but was unable to otherwise express, was that he didn't feel shackled to his religion, A.P. reflected, as Catholics and Jews did.

"Also, like you I feel that part of me is Jewish," the boy declared.

"But you'll realize when you're older, as I did, that what you've just said applies to your identity, not to religion," A.P. told him.

They had halted to cross the street and Ben said, while they waited for a car to pass by, "Would you please explain that to me?"

"Your identity, Ben, is the person you are."

"And he's very mixed up," Ben answered.

"In some ways, the same goes for the person *I* am."

"But you didn't become Jewish, so I shan't, either," said Ben decisively.

"Hold on a minute!" A.P. exclaimed. "Let's get this friendship of ours into perspective, shall we?"

"Perspective?"

"I'll explain that word to you some other time. What I want you to understand now, Ben, is that I'm pleased you have so much respect for me and I'll try to live up to it, but you mustn't model yourself on me."

They crossed the street and continued on their way silently, Ben's expression now crestfallen, but A.P. must allow time for his words to sink in.

"That's where I live," the boy said eventually, pointing to an immaculate-looking house with a blue front door and shutters to match, "and I'm sorry to have upset you."

"I'm not in the least upset," A.P. assured him, "but it had to be said and don't let it upset *you*, Ben. Let me add that should you ever need my help, I'll be there for you."

"Then would you mind starting now, A.P.? If I, or my father, asked my mother to let me visit you, she would refuse. But she enjoys reading in magazines about the Princess of Wales and may not bring herself to say no to an English lord."

"You shrewd little devil!" said A.P. with a laugh. But Ben too was laughing and it was good to know that he could, overly serious child that he was. "All right, we'll give it a go – though I don't entertain the Royal Family at Kyverdale Hall!"

"Would it be possible for Rudy and Magda to come, too?"

"I don't see why not, if your dad and Karin are willing."

Ben exhibited some more of his dry shrewdness. "I should think they'd be pleased to be rid of them for a while. And would there also be space for our friends who want to save the earth, as we do, to come and see how it's done?"

A.P. elaborated on his previous reply in that respect, "The only bit of the earth that I and *my* friends are saving is the Kyverdale estate."

But joining in our project would be a worthwhile experience for kids, he thought, and it didn't have to be limited to just a few.

"You've given me an interesting idea," he told Ben, envisaging a field full of tents and hordes of youngsters lining up to be served with their meals in the banqueting room that was no longer used, their lively voices filling an ancestral home that, despite the communards' presence, echoed with emptiness, and their faces glowing beside the campfire that A.P. would light for them at night.

"May I know what it is?"

"If I carry it through, you'll find out. But first things first," said A.P., giving his young companion a conspiratorial grin. "I must do my best to behave in a lordly manner when your mum opens the door!"

"It could be my stepfather," said Ben, "but he is usually on my side. I once heard him telling my mother, when they were arguing in their bedroom and raised their voices, that she is wrong not to let Dad take me to England to visit my relatives there.

"Uncle Hans – that's what I call him – also shouted that she was being very stupid, because one day I might pay her back for it."

In the event, it was Christina who came to let her son in, a tirade issuing from her lips which, since it was in German, A.P. was unable to comprehend.

"My mother was reminding me it was a special favor for me to be allowed to visit Dad on a weeknight," Ben translated, "and she's angry with me for getting home late."

Christina calmed herself and added in English, "It was kind of his lordship to see my son home. And difficult," she said appraising A.P., "for me to believe that this tall young man is the child of dear Moira. The little boy I once held on my lap.

"But why am I keeping his lordship standing in the porch?" she said, sounding flustered. "Would he care to come in for a schnapps?"

"I'd be delighted to join you, though I'd prefer something nonalcoholic," A.P. answered, wishing she would stop addressing him as if through a third party.

By the time they were drinking coffee – in a living room as immaculate as the house's exterior – A.P. was mentally grinding his teeth, such was Christina's deference.

Under other circumstances, he'd have tried to put her at her ease. But he was here for one purpose only, to get her permission for Ben to visit him, and the kid was probably right about how that could be achieved.

"My husband works hard, he has retired early to bed," said Christina apologetically. "He is now head of the printing business that was my late father's. And of course, it will one day be for Ben, my eldest son, to continue what his Grandfather Schmidt began."

Inheritance again, thought A.P.

"I don't want to be a printer."

"You are still only a little boy," said Christina, "but will change your mind when you grow up."

Christina could be in for a disappointment in that respect, A.P. reflected while noting how matronly the flaxen-haired beauty Howard had married now looked. As stolid as her attitudes so evidently were, and oh what a struggle it would be for Ben to maintain his individuality.

"Would his lordship care to hear Ben play the piano?"

"I didn't know you were a pianist," A.P. said with a smile to Ben, who was beside him on the blue sofa that matched the carpet and the curtains, drinking the milk his mother had insisted he have.

"He plays very nicely," said Christina, while A.P. was wondering if, for her, the only color in the rainbow was blue, since even her frock was that shade.

"But he does not practice as often as he should," Christina went on. "All he seems interested in is what he calls 'saving the earth' – as if a child like him could make an impression upon the damage that has been done to it!"

"I'd love to hear you play, Ben," said A.P., steering the conversation away from a subject that could decide Christina against Ben's visiting Kyverdale Hall.

Ben put down the glass of milk, went to seat himself at the piano beside the window, and began playing a Chopin nocturne, immediately losing himself in the music he was creating, and rendering A.P. spellbound.

Plays very nicely? thought A.P. in the moment of silence that followed the unexpected recital. If I'm any judge, Ben has the makings of a concert pianist.

It then struck A.P. that, almost without exception, everyone on the commune was subjecting themselves to the common aim, their individual development halted, and some might consequently go to their graves without fulfilling their true potential.

Mary Lou was as artistic as her mother, but what was she doing with her talent? Granted, she hadn't known how to channel it *before* throwing in her lot with the commune, but the experimenting and exploring she might still have been doing was now over for her.

The same went for Nina, whose pre-commune history included acting with a repertory company and A.P. could imagine her going from strength to strength had she continued along that path.

For both girls, though, it was as if the arts no longer mattered in a world gone to seed, and A.P. didn't agree. The arts were the mirror of society and should go on fulfilling that function as they had through the centuries, serving, too, to uplift the spirit in grim times – and the outlook for the human race had never seemed more grim than now.

With the new man in the Kremlin, it was possible that the hovering threat of a nuclear holocaust might be removed – and how ironic it was that Man, by other methods, had inflicted a slow death upon the planet.

Thus did A.P.'s thoughts sweep back and forth while the silence lengthened, returning finally to the little boy awaiting his pronouncement about the music that had set him thinking.

"You're some pianist, Ben!" he declared.

"And now he will perhaps practice more often," said Christina with satisfaction. "My son has a high regard for his lordship, is that not so, Ben?

"It was why he was allowed to eat supper at his father's table this evening," she explained, "though my husband and I are raising our children not to always expect their own way. Or they will also expect it when they are adults and be disappointed," she added.

A.P. noticed the downward curve of Christina's lips in repose and wondered if her second marriage might not have been the love match her first was, but a settling for the safe thing.

"Is that your husband?" he asked, glancing at a framed photograph that stood with some others atop a china cabinet.

"But when I married Hans, he did not have that double chin. He is too fond of his food —"

"Like my dad," Ben cut in, to A.P.

"But in other respects I have no complaints about Hans," Christina continued, "and he is good to Ben."

"At Kyverdale Hall there's a Bechstein piano," was A.P.'s preamble to the request he had yet to make, "and Ben might enjoy playing it, as my late grandmother did."

Christina seemed overwhelmed. "Did you hear the offer that his lordship has made to you, Ben? To play the piano in his ancestral home?"

Got her! thought A.P., exchanging a smile with the little boy whom now, more than ever, he was determined to take under his wing.

Chapter
6

Jeremy was dreaming of his father, beside him in a crimson Ferrari as he drove along a winding road, the mountainside towering ominously against a sullen sky and a procession of weary pail-bearers gazing down as the car hurtled by.

"Are you trying to get us killed, Jeremy!"

"You're already dead and I can't stop now," Jeremy heard himself reply.

Then Maria Santander appeared before the windscreen and fell beneath the wheels.

"Now look what you've done," his father rebuked him as the vehicle careened even faster.

"I didn't mean to – the brakes aren't working – I'm going to die, too!"

"A possibility you should have considered before starting out."

"I did it for you, Dad," Jeremy cried as the dream disintegrated. "I never told you I loved you and now it's too late . . ."

He became aware of tears running down his face onto the pristine hospital sheet. And of a familiar face. "Janis?"

"I'm here."

"I wasn't sure if you were real —"

"Please don't weep, Jeremy, I can't bear it," she said, gently drying his eyes with one of the lace-edged handkerchieves he recalled Shirley giving her for Chanukah, years ago.

"The expensive handkerchieves Shirley once gave *me* are still in the box unsullied," Jeremy said, trying to be jocular.

"And *I'm* not the fancy hankie sort, but someone helped me pack my case and I didn't pay much attention to the sundries he was tossing into it."

"Got a guy who acts as your general dogsbody, have you?"

"If that's how you care to put it. Jesse is a great one for looking after people, which could be because he's a doctor. As a matter of fact, he's here with me."

"Won't let you out of his sight, eh!" Jeremy said as a nurse bustled into the room.

"If you're thinking of chucking my visitor out, so I can waste more time sitting on a bedpan, forget it," Jeremy said before a thermometer muzzled him.

Despite what he's been through, he still looks like my cheeky kid brother, Janis thought, surveying the dressing on his forehead and his bandaged arm, while the nurse took his pulse.

"You still have a fever," the stringy woman pronounced after reading the thermometer.

"Could be due to your proximity," he said, giving her a wink, "but much as I'll miss you, when are they going to let me out of here? Today would suit me fine."

"It is my misfortune that my speaking English allows me

to understand all that this difficult patient says!" the nurse exclaimed to Janis. "Though I do *not* understand his haste to leave hospital so soon after undergoing –"

"My sister only just got here," Jeremy cut her short, "she doesn't yet know I've had an operation."

"The doctor will speak with her when he arrives to do his rounds."

"I'll tell her myself."

Janis found her voice. "Tell me what?"

"Remember what our favorite bedtime story was, when we were little? Well, from now on you can address me as Captain Hook," Jeremy said with bravado.

Oh dear God . . .

"There's nothing but padding where you're now looking."

Janis averted her eyes from where his hand should be.

By the time she had steeled herself to help him bear the unbearable, the nurse was gone from the room, and again it was Jeremy who set the tone.

"As well I'm left-handed," he said with a nonchalance that tugged at Janis's heartstrings, "but you have to get lucky sometimes!"

"Start being sensible, too."

"Who, me?"

"Yes, Jeremy. You."

His response was, "Lucky, also, it wasn't a foot that had to come off."

"You're telling me you intend going on with what you were doing, aren't you? Didn't you get the message!"

"Too true I did, and it could mean I'm getting too close for *their* comfort. All the more reason for not giving up now."

"You bloody fool!"

"Tell me more about Jesse."

Janis almost lost her temper. "If that's intended to divert

me from what we're discussing, I'm not falling for it, Jeremy. And you'll be meeting him, anyway."

Jeremy answered, after glancing at a basket of flowers that dominated the room, "If there's one thing I've learned since Dad and Laura were killed, Janis, it's that nobody is necessarily what they seem. How long have you known this guy?"

"Long enough."

"I thought I knew Lola Mendez. Was it she who called you?" Jeremy went on, when Janis nodded, "And no doubt she invited you to stay at her home?"

"I thought that a kind gesture."

"And so it could've been," said Jeremy. "On the other hand, though, it could be that the Mendez company wants you under surveillance while you're in Caracas. Like they've probably had me, on all my trips here."

Janis was shocked. "Is that how you construe the hospitality you've received from Lola? Don't you trust her?"

Jeremy said after pausing, "From now on I don't trust *anyone*, and the same should apply to you. Jake Bornstein was your father, too, and something else I've learned is that a deal worth millions is somehow involved in the mystery.

"What I'm up against, Janis, isn't just those who planted the bomb trying to prevent me from finding out who they are. There's also the Mendez company's determination to carry through the deal I mentioned, and they won't have me getting in their way."

While Janis was digesting that alarming information, Jeremy said flatly, "It wouldn't surprise me if, among other things, Luis Mendez was selling arms to military dictators — and Caracas wasn't the only place where Dad had meetings with him."

"I already know that," said Janis, relaying what she had been told by Jesse.

"No need to say why you kept it to yourself," said Jeremy. "You don't want Dad's memory besmirched. Nor do I. But it's odds on he was up to his neck in shady deals."

"I'll believe that when you provide some proof."

"What would you call what you just described? Jake Bornstein closeted with Mendez and whoever the others were – with bodyguards outside the door."

"The last bit is your fertile imagination," Janis replied.

"The hell it is. Dad's bodyguard was hiding in Milan. It was him I was there to see. He was my first clue."

A charged silence followed, Janis assailed by the sense of unreality that had initially dogged Jeremy. But his being in a hospital in Caracas, minus a hand, was all too real.

"As to what I said about trusting *nobody*," he resumed, "didn't it strike you as odd that a guy who encountered Dad in Haiti suddenly entered your life?"

Janis answered more lightly than she felt, "Never heard of coincidence?"

"Another," said Jeremy, "is I came back to Caracas after Lola called me with some interesting information. And only she knew I was coming and that I intended hiring a car.

"Well, only Lola and whoever she may have told," he added brusquely.

"But you can't be certain she told *anyone*, can you? Has it been established that the car brakes *were* tampered with?"

"Not yet, but for me it doesn't have to be, my meeting with an accident in Caracas would be one coincidence too many."

For Lola too, thought Janis, since she'd used the word "incident" when she called.

"Uncertainties, though, have dogged me from the outset," Jeremy continued, "only they weren't attached to Lola. She'd lost her father, as we had our parents, and I assumed she was my ally, if a passive one.

"Now, however, my mind keeps returning to something she said on the evening we met – No, it was the following morning, when I joined Lola and her sisters for breakfast on the patio and she asked me if I'd ever heard of an all-female dynasty."

"I see nothing sinister in that."

"Nor did I, at the time. But when she mentioned recently that she's thinking of getting herself voted chairman of the Mendez company . . ."

"If it can be done, why shouldn't she?"

"Her wanting to doesn't jell with the Lola I know. Or thought I knew! And putting one thing with another," Jeremy went on airing his doubts, "I can no longer take it for granted that Lola is on my side. When the real her could be a female version of her father, using friendship with me to stay abreast of my progress every step of the way, her sole concern that nothing must interfere with that big-bucks deal, not even human lives!"

Janis waited for him to calm down, before saying quietly, "But you're in love with her, aren't you?"

"If I am, that's *my* problem. And yours is whether or not to take Jesse at his face value."

"The only problem I'm having about Jesse is I still associate him with the circumstances in which he met Dad, but I'm working on it. Nor am I so paranoid as to imagine he was planted in my life for some sinister reason."

"If you're now going to tell me I'm being paranoid with regard to Lola –"

"Where would it get me?" Janis cut in. "And where has your vengeance trip got *you*?"

Chapter 7

Bessie had not equated seeking the man who had
fathered her with digging into her mother's past,
nor was she deterred when it was put to her that
way.

The occasion was a visit from one of the family's elders
now living with her married daughter in a West Bank settlement, and Ann Klein's plump and pleasant face had creased
with distress when she learned from Bessie of her intention.

"Haven't we had enough trouble in our family, without
you looking for more?" she demanded.

"You can't blame Bessie for wanting to know who he is,"
said the younger of the two granddaughters who had accompanied Ann to Tel Aviv.

"Anit, like you, Bessie, is another of the family rebels!"
Ann exclaimed. "We haven't gone short of them, and what
young people don't realize is that their selfish actions don't
just affect themselves, everyone who loves them suffers.

"My son Howard's marrying Christina is a good example,"

Ann continued her lecture, "and what a disastrous chain of events that was the cause of. Because of it, I have an only grandson I haven't seen since he was a tiny tot, and my poor husband never saw Ben again."

"You could go to Munich to see him," said Anit.

Ann, momentarily overcome by emotion, stopped dabbing her eyes. "Me set foot on German soil? Never! And don't ever let your father hear you suggest that, Anit. His grandparents died in the Holocaust, didn't they?"

"But how long," said Anit, "can Jews go on living in the past?"

"Didn't I say she was a rebel!" Ann flashed.

"I don't mean we shouldn't remember the Holocaust," said Anit.

"But the Germans would like the rest of the world to forget it," Ann declared, "and they've done a good job of sweeping it under the carpet – as if the swastikas now being daubed on Jewish gravestones, even in England, have nothing to do with their past."

Bessie helped herself to a sandwich from the tea table and returned the conversation to her own obsession. "But you'd like me to sweep my mother's past under the carpet, and I'm not going to."

"Don't let Grandma lead you away from the subject," Anit advised. "She's always doing that with me."

"Because some of *your* subjects are unseemly," said her sister, Chavah.

Though both girls were decorously clad, recognizable as of the ultraorthodox faith by their ankle-length skirts and long-sleeved blouses, despite the heat of the Israeli summer, the aura of piety emanating from Chavah was not present in Anit's demeanor.

"And you," Anit answered, "probably censor even your thoughts."

"My thoughts don't need censoring."

"That's even worse and I'm sorry for you," Anit told her. "And if I were Bessie, I'd employ a private detective to find my father."

"That's what I thought of doing," said Bessie, "but I've only got one clue, and I'm not even sure if it is one," she added glancing down at the birthmark on her forearm.

"And what your mum got up to when she was a girl is none of your business," said Ann.

"She wasn't a girl, she was thirty," Bessie countered, "and I'm the result, aren't I? – Which entitles me to know who she got up to it with."

"Really, Bessie –" Chavah said averting her eyes to her tea cup.

Anit said with a giggle, "My sister and I aren't allowed to think of how babies are made, Bessie. That's what I meant about Chavah censoring her thoughts."

"And I sometimes think *you* are a throwback," Chavah informed her, "to some disgraceful female there once was in our family."

"Like my mum was, you mean?" Bessie challenged her.

"Well, she did cause a scandal, didn't she?"

Ann put down the slice of strudel she was eating. "And I didn't come here to discuss it!" She sipped some tea and added, "I'm thankful, Bessie, that Peter and Hildegard aren't at home to hear what you're trying to dig up that's best left lying."

Bessie managed to smile and summed up her new home life. "To find them here, you'd have to come at the crack of dawn, or after midnight, and that goes for every day of the week."

"They work on the Sabbath?" said Chavah sounding shocked.

"Not everyone," said her sister, "lives to the letter of the laws of Judaism, like you and I have to."

"Have to?"

"I can't help how I feel. To me, how we live is like an imprisonment."

"And if our parents knew that, they'd make haste and marry you off."

"Like they're doing with you," Anit retorted, "but you don't mind. For me it would be like the key turning in the lock, shackling me for the rest of my life. You, though, think everything is God's will, even the way we're expected to dress," Anit added, unfastening the top button of her blouse and fanning herself with a magazine from the pile on the sofa table.

"I'm sorry the air-conditioning isn't working," said Bessie. "The engineer was supposed to come this morning, but he didn't turn up."

"That," said Anit, "isn't the point. You look lovely and cool in your tee-shirt and shorts. Chavah and I, though — Well, say no more!"

"If only you wouldn't," said Chavah.

"But no such luck," said her grandmother, when Anit went on with feeling, "And when we get married, we'll be expected to cut off our hair and wear a wig, or a headscarf. It isn't fair!"

"What was good enough for our mother is good enough for us," Chavah declaimed.

"But she married Dad because she fell in love with him, didn't she?" Anit persisted.

"Head over heels, when she was only seventeen," Ann put in with a sigh, "and it could be her you take after, Anit."

"My mother, a rebel?" said Chavah.

"Well," Ann recalled, "she didn't have her parents' permission to come and help Israel during the '67 war. Nor did your mum's brother, Mark, Bessie. But he was killed in a chance accident and never came back."

"That's one thing my mother *did* tell me."

"Did she also tell you it was my father who supported them? He was the family's most ardent Zionist, but it was still a shock to the rest of us when he did what he did behind our backs. We couldn't believe it when he told us he'd driven them to London, bought their plane tickets and put them on one of the flights taking hundreds of young volunteers to Israel."

"Nor can I, from what I've heard about how strict he was with the kids in the family," said Bessie.

"And the one time he stepped out of character," said Ann, "he lost his only grandson because of it, and in another way I lost my daughter."

"Is that how you felt about my mum meeting Dad and marrying him?" asked Anit.

"Well, she wasn't going to be living around the corner from me, was she? But I remember your great-grandmother, Sarah Sandberg, saying something about being unable to stop a tree from growing new branches and that through Kate there would be a branch of our family in Israel."

"Only I never thought I'd end up living with them," Ann added, munching strudel as if she needed comforting on that account.

Anit harked back to the point from which Ann's lengthy digression had sprung. "But if Mum hadn't met Dad, if she'd lived with you in England, you wouldn't have told her who to marry, would you, Grandma?"

"Matchmaking went out of fashion before *my* time," Ann replied.

"I expect people had more important things to think about," said Anit, "like getting themselves accepted in a gentile country."

"But in Israel, we don't have that problem," said Chavah smugly, "we can live according to God's laws without being ridiculed."

"My sister," said Anit, "seems unaware of how the majority of Israelis view the ultraorthodox way of life, which they consider archaic."

"But our mother wasn't raised that way, was she?" said Chavah. "She must have had a good reason for turning her back on the modern way."

"The reason," Ann informed her, "was your father. My dear daughter," she added quietly, "is a bit like me, willing to bend her own life to fit in with the man she loves and his ideas – though I went on strike when your granddad was a housebound invalid and it turned him into a tyrant."

"Nothing would make my mother go on strike," Chavah replied confidently, "so it *can't* be her Anit takes after. Her coming to help Israel in the '67 war, without your permission, was God's will, since it was in a good cause –"

"Trust *you* to see it that way!" Anit cut in, rising to restlessly pace the stuffy room.

"And how can you refer to religion as ideas?" Chavah rebuked Ann.

"Call it what you like, love," Ann answered, "what I was trying to tell you is there're some women, and your mum is one of them, who end up forgetting how independent they were when they were single. Before they know it, their husband's attitudes become their own."

"But that," Anit vowed, "is never going to happen to me."

"Then heaven help your husband," said Chavah, "and isn't it time we went home?"

"It's been nice seeing Bessie, but I'm beginning to wish we hadn't come!" said Ann.

"And if our parents knew the things Anit's been saying, she'd get it from them good and proper," said Chavah in the Lancashire accent the sisters had acquired from their Mancunian mother.

Bessie surveyed the tea table and remarked that the spread was barely touched.

"Grandma hasn't done too badly," said Anit, "but for Chavah and me, everything has to be ultra-kosher!"

"And the sooner you're married off the better," Chavah told her.

"First they'd have to catch me."

Bessie watched Anit – another of the family's numerous redheads – plonk herself mutinously on the window seat and fold her arms. Reminding Bessie of her mother, who had also refused to do what was expected of her: marry the man who got her pregnant.

In appearance, too, Anit could be taken for Laura's daughter, Bessie thought, but *I* look nothing like my beautiful mum.

Then Anit gave her a wink and for each of them it was as though she had found a friend.

"Could Anit come and spend a weekend with me?" Bessie asked Ann.

It was Chavah who replied. "She wouldn't be able to eat here, would she?"

"Unless I brought a picnic basket," said Anit sarcastically.

"But quite enough damage has been done this afternoon," Chavah opined.

"What my sister means," Anit told Bessie, "is the placid

pond her life is has been ruffled. I, though, have terrible misgivings about Jews settling on Arab land – and last week, I wrote to the Prime Minister about it."

Chavah was horror stricken. "You did what?"

"If I had the courage, I'd move to Tel Aviv and join the Peace Now Movement," Anit capped her inflammatory revelations.

"You and I could share a flat, couldn't we?" said Bessie eagerly.

"How could we afford to rent one?"

"Bessie," said Ann, "is now wealthy enough to buy one! But she'd need her legal guardian's permission and I intend ringing up Janis to talk sense to her in case she requires me to."

It was now Ann's turn to rise and pace back and forth, fan-pleated skirt swirling and heels clacking on the polished wood floor as her agitation escalated.

"The only one capable of dealing with Anit is her father," she declared, "and I must leave it to him, though in many ways she has my sympathy –"

"I won't tell him you said that," Anit cut in.

But Ann had already turned her attention to Bessie. "How could you think of moving out of here? Of upsetting the kind couple who gave you a home when you needed one? And, like Anit, you're still only sixteen –"

"On the settlement, that's old enough to be a married woman," Anit reminded her.

"But you'd then have a husband to take care of you, as I shall soon," said Chavah.

"And before you know it, you'll have kids one after another," Anit answered. "Would you fancy that?" she asked Bessie.

Chavah informed them, after Bessie had shaken her head,

that raising children was what a Jewish marriage was all about, and bearing them the sacred duty of a Jewish wife.

"For those who've turned back the clock as if birth control hadn't been invented," said Anit witheringly, "also as if the world hadn't already got too many mouths to feed.

"It isn't that I don't believe in God," she added, turning to Bessie, "just that there's too much about the ultraortho-dox way that doesn't make sense – and I don't think He'd make some of the Jewish laws He did, if He were making them now."

Bessie said quietly, "When Mummy was taken from me, I wondered if there was a God. And I thought that again when Jeremy lost his hand."

"That's a terrible sin," Chavah pronounced, "and you've committed it twice."

"But if I found my real father, I never would again."

"This," said Ann, picking up her handbag, and the gloves she still wore for town, as she had in England, "is definitely where I came in!"

"What you mean," Bessie accused her, "is you wouldn't provide me with a clue, even if you could."

"And I can't."

The following day, Bessie's gloom was enlivened by a call from Bermuda.

"It's lovely to hear your voice," she told Marianne.

"That's nice to know."

"Finished writing your new book, yet?" Bessie inquired.

"Not quite. And after Ann rang to tell me about her chat with you, I couldn't concentrate."

"I wouldn't call it a chat!"

"And what's all this about you wanting to find your fa-ther?" Marianne asked in her direct fashion.

Bessie's response was, "I'm amazed you hadn't already heard about it from my grandma, who nearly had a fit when I mentioned it while she was here visiting me."

"Shirley wouldn't confide in me except in a crisis," Marianne replied, "and let's hope this won't turn into one, Bessie, for you *or* for her."

Bessie said after pausing, "You were very close to my mother, weren't you?"

"Which didn't help my relationship with your gran," Marianne said dryly, "but if you're now going to ask if Laura told me her secret, she didn't and that's the truth, love."

"But did my mother ever talk to you about him? Even though she didn't mention his name?"

"Only once, Bessie."

"It'd mean a lot to me to know what she told you, however little it was, Marianne."

"And I'm sitting on my verandah gazing down at Elbow Beach and wondering if I have the right to tell you."

"To break Mummy's confidence, you mean? But she's dead and I'm still alive."

Marianne replied, "That's exactly what my husband said, when I discussed my dilemma with him. He hasn't finished writing *his* new book, either. Nowadays, we spend so much time talking about family matters, I ask myself why I was under the illusion that coming to live in Bermuda would allow me to get on with my work!"

"I'm sorry to be one of the family matters that's stopping you from working," said Bessie contritely.

"And how're you getting on with *your* work at school?" Marianne asked.

"I still have trouble with maths."

"So did your mum," Marianne recalled. "Laura wasn't in the least academic."

"A brilliant photographer like her didn't need to be," Bessie answered, "and if I thought I could be one, I'd —"

"What you have to be is yourself," Marianne cut her short. "Trying to follow in one's parents' footsteps can be a big mistake."

"And I couldn't with the one I know nothing about," Bessie returned to the topic from which they had strayed. "Was he someone dreadful, Marianne? I don't mind admitting to you that that's my worst fear —"

"Then set your mind at rest, love."

Bessie had absently removed some wilted leaves from a plant on the hall table and found herself crushing them, while she awaited Marianne's next words.

"From the little your mum told me, I gathered he was a decent man."

"Then why didn't he marry her?" Bessie demanded.

"For two excellent reasons," Marianne said gently. "He already had a wife and children, and your mother didn't bother telling him she had conceived."

"What you've told me isn't *my* idea of a decent man!"

"And may Laura forgive me for doing what I think best," said Marianne. "But you are still too young to understand the situations men sometimes get themselves into," she answered Bessie's outburst. "Your mother was a very attractive woman."

"Are you saying she trapped him?"

"In a way, yes."

"I'd rather not believe that."

"You'd prefer it to have been the other way round?"

Bessie sat down on the chair beside the telephone, the crushed leaves still in her hand. "Wouldn't you, if it were your mother?"

"That would depend on why she did it," Marianne replied,

"and to give it to you straight, Bessie — now I've started, I may as well — at that point in her life, your mum didn't want a man in her life, but she passionately wanted a child."

"And I've lived until now thinking myself an accident she could've done without!"

"Doesn't knowing you weren't make you feel better?"

"But I still need to know who my father was."

"All I can add," said Marianne, "is he was an Israeli."

Bessie's heart leapt with joy. "Then I have to apologize to God for doubting Him, and thank Him for guiding me to the right place."

Marianne's husband watched her replace the receiver and brought her a planter's punch.

"If that doesn't help put the sparkle back into you, I'll make you another," he said.

"But it would be a false sparkle, wouldn't it? My heart's breaking for Bessie —"

Simon fondled her cheek. "Your heart, hon, is always breaking for someone or other in your family! But you told me on our first date that you were a family woman, and you always will be I guess."

Simon adjusted a cushion on the cane sofa and made himself comfortable beside Marianne, a tall, frosted glass in his hand.

"If you'd known the guy's name, would you have told it to Bessie?"

"Since I don't, why present myself with a hypothetical dilemma? The one I was faced with was difficult enough! And if you'd heard what Bessie finally said to me, Simon, you'd be left in no doubt that she's determined to find him."

Simon absently watched a little yellow bird descend briefly on the verandah rail before flying on its way. "But where would Bessie begin her search from? Unlike Jeremy's search —"

Marianne cut in with a shudder, "Don't even mention that to me! When I think of what it's led to, and he hasn't even succeeded in finding the assassins . . . Can you imagine that livewire lad maimed as he now is?"

"That won't stop him from continuing the hunt," said Simon, grimly, "but I've no intention of telling him what I know."

Marianne turned to look at him. "I beg your pardon?"

"Okay, so I haven't even told you."

"Told me what?"

"That I once saw Jake Bornstein in New York – he didn't see me – having a drink with a C.I.A. agent."

Marianne was momentarily speechless. "Since when were you acquainted with C.I.A. agents?"

Simon got up to lean against the railing. "Would you believe me if I told you I was once one, myself?"

Marianne surveyed the man with whom she was sharing her autumn years, his slight figure silhouetted against the dazzling midday light, the shaggy gray hair and the dear, familiar face.

"No, I would not," she replied.

"Then ask yourself if Laura would've believed Jake capable of living a double life."

"We don't know for sure that he did."

"Come off it, Marianne! How many more limbs must Jeremy lose to convince you? And in lesser ways, most people live double lives, even when it's only inside themselves.

"The things we hold back from those who think they know us," Simon went on, "bits of ourselves and our past that could damage a relationship, however slightly, if they were known —"

Marianne cut him short. "You didn't have to tell me what you just did about *yourself* and I wish you hadn't!"

"It makes you see me differently, doesn't it? And that proves what I just said."

Marianne inquired coldly, "How long were you a member of the Company? Isn't that what they call it?"

"I was recruited after the war, but kissed it goodbye when the McCarthy witch hunt made me ashamed of my country."

Marianne listened to the crickets chirping, her gaze fixed upon the shadowy area at the far end of the verandah, where tall treetops had shut out the sun.

As shadowy as her husband's past had proved to be . . . Would she ever feel quite the same toward him?

Simon said with his quizzical smile, "A guy I used to hang out with once remarked that confession is good for the confessor, but not necessarily for the recipient."

"A *C.I.A.* guy? And would I be wrong in supposing that the kiss goodbye you mentioned isn't necessarily a two-way thing? That they could call on you again and you would have to do their bidding?"

"You've seen too many TV spy series," Simon said lightly, "though you seem to have missed the ones when the ex-agent *didn't* do what was required of him. How long will it take you to recover from this, hon?"

"If and when I do, I'll let you know. Meanwhile, I think you *should* tell Jeremy who his father was drinking with in New York."

"Why?"

"I agree with you that losing a hand isn't going to stop him short. If he doesn't yet know of the C.I.A. connection, it could be a good lead for him."

"Look – I hadn't set eyes on that guy since the fifties," said Simon. "For all I know, he's no longer active."

"Then what was he doing with Jake? Who, according to Laura, only rubbed shoulders with the diamond dealers on his business trips to New York."

Marianne went on after pausing, "But it seems she knew as much about her husband as I about mine, or should I say as little? Letting me assume that writing of one sort or another was how you'd always made your bread, till finally your first novel was a bestseller!"

"And since we're having this home truths session, is there anything you'd care to tell *me*?"

"Nothing that could compare with *your* revelation, and I'm thankful Laura went to her grave in blissful ignorance of Jake's machinations. Unfortunately, however, his children are now paying the price."

"As Bessie is for Laura's," Simon pointed out.

"But Laura wasn't motivated by greed, and what but that would've made the multi-millionaire Jake was continue piling it up?"

"Could be what he wanted was power, and once a guy gets hooked on that particular drug . . ."

"He and his innocent wife can end up blown to bits! I think I do need another drink."

Simon fetched the jug of punch, refilled both their glasses, and returned the traumatic conversation whence it had begun.

"The reason I didn't go make my presence known to Jake was I chose not to renew my acquaintance with my ex-colleague."

"But didn't it strike you as odd, his being with Jake?"

"Chatting with the guy beside you at the bar isn't exactly uncommon, Marianne."

"And how does it strike you now?"

"I've had to stop myself from offering Jeremy my assistance."

Marianne said apprehensively, "Supplying him with the information is all I want you to do."

"And I was about to add that Jeremy wouldn't want me – or anyone else – along. Finding out who planted that bomb, and why, is a task he's set himself and his personal need."

"For someone with no kids, your insight on the subject is sometimes better than mine," said Marianne.

"Isn't there an old saying that the onlooker sees more of the game? And wasn't calling your grandson scheduled for next on your agenda?"

Marianne was still seated with the telephone on her lap.

"If that was a crack, Simon, I haven't spoken to A.P. since he got back from Munich and he sounded depressed when I last called him."

"An onlooker you'll never be, Marianne."

Chapter
8

A.P.'s plan for a summer camp on the Kyverdale estate was received enthusiastically by the commune members, if somewhat suspiciously by Mary Lou.

"Why do you want to do it?" she asked while they were making tea, after the weekly meeting was over. "And I'm fed-up with doing kitchen duty, aren't you?" she said irrelevantly, fetching a pitcher of milk from the outsize refrigerator, her boots clomping noisily on the stone-flagged floor. "I feel like telling the others to get off their butts and make their own bloody bedtime beverage!"

"That's hardly the commune spirit," A.P. enjoyed informing her, "and our turn to be waited on will soon come again."

"That doesn't mean I have to like every aspect of commune life!"

"But most of the time, you're the grin-and-bear-it type."

"Unlike you, if I may say so."

GET YOUR FOUR FREE BOOKS TODAY ($20.49 VALUE)

FILL IN THE ORDER FORM BELOW NOW!

YES! *I want to join the Timeless Romance Reader Service. Please send me my 4 FREE HarperMonogram historical romances. Then each month send me 4 new historical romances to preview without obligation for 10 days. I'll pay the low subscription price of $4.00 for every book I choose to keep – a total savings of at least $2.00 each month – and home delivery is free! I understand that I may return any title within 10 days without obligation and I may cancel this subscription at any time without obligation. There is no minimum number of books to purchase.*

NAME_____

ADDRESS _____

CITY_____STATE_____ZIP_____

TELEPHONE_____

SIGNATURE _____

(If under 18 parent or guardian must sign. Program, price, terms, and conditions subject to cancellation and change. Orders subject to acceptance by HarperMonogram.)

"If what you mean is I bear it, but I don't do much grinning, I'm not as good at pretending as you are, Mary Lou. And I've never hidden from you that this isn't exactly the life for me."

A.P. watched her begin plonking mugs on a huge tray. "I'm getting the impression that the same goes for you."

"But the cause is more important," she declared.

"Not to me, Mary Lou, since I only have one life."

"And no doubt you'll soon be opting out and kicking us off your land! As I told you on the occasion I'd prefer to forget, your trouble, A.P., is you don't know what you want."

A.P. went on spooning tea from the biscuit tin that served as a caddy into an earthenware teapot donated by Mary Lou's mother who had fashioned it with her own hands, its size suitable for an army platoon brew-up, and adorned by a winking-eye design that had implied for Mary Lou that her mother was laughing at her.

"And I said I wanted *you*," A.P. answered. "That still goes."

"Why the hell did I rake it up!" she exclaimed, slopping milk into the mugs.

"Well, it wasn't too far below the surface, was it?"

"And it's spoiled our friendship."

"If you say so."

"We can't be alone together anymore," Mary Lou went on, "without the inconvenient undercurrents that weren't there before."

"I'm prepared to continue ignoring them, if you are," said A.P.

Mary Lou's response was, "Other than running out on something I'm deeply committed to, do I have a choice? And you still haven't told me why you suddenly want to surround yourself with kids. Are some of the German ones you mentioned in need of a free holiday?"

"My young relatives certainly aren't and I shouldn't think their pals are – but you've given me an idea," A.P. added thoughtfully.

"Oh yes?"

"As well as organizing an international summer camp to encourage junior Greens, we could also do something for the arts, and on a permanent level –"

"Have kids running wild here all the time?" Mary Lou interrupted. "Oh no, A.P.!"

"Not running wild. What I'm thinking about, Mary Lou, is a music and painting school, for talented youngsters from poor families. There's space for it in the west wing –"

"For which you'd have to engage teachers," Mary Lou pointed out.

"That needn't be a problem."

A.P. was visualizing Ben at the Bechstein in the west wing; though he wasn't from a poor family, there was more than one interpretation of the term "deprived child."

"You could be involved in the painting classes, and as well as music, drama could be included," A.P.'s thoughts raced ahead, "and Nina could have a hand in that –"

Mary Lou returned him to earth vis-à-vis the commune's common aim. "Exciting though it would be for Nina and for me, it isn't what we're here for, A.P. But I've never known you sound so enthusiastic as you did when you put your plan for the camp to the meeting," she added, "or as you seem to be about the idea you just said *I* gave you –"

"That could be because organic farming and all the rest of it leaves me cold," he replied.

"Or is it that you've found out what you want to do with your life?"

A.P. said with a smile, "If you think *you* know, would you mind telling me?"

"Work with children, you clot!"

"You could be right."

Mary Lou returned his smile and A.P. went to fill the teapot from the samovar that was her father's gift to the commune. She couldn't say that her parents had been anything but encouraging – the opposite of how A.P.'s mum had reacted to the transformation of her ancestral home, though his dad had sent a cable from L.A. wishing the project luck.

Mary Lou was filling a basin with brown sugar at the scrub-top table and A.P. thought how lovely she looked in the yellow blouse she had worn for supper, when the girls made an effort with their appearance after their long day's work, though Mary Lou didn't go so far as to wear a skirt and high heels instead of jeans and her favorite boots.

A.P. said gruffly, such was her effect upon him, "If we don't make haste with the tea and biscuits, the others will be singing, 'Why are we waiting?'."

Then the telephone rang distantly and he glanced at the clock.

"Are you expecting a late call? Is someone in your family ill?" Mary Lou asked, noting his anxious expression.

"Yes, but since he is your 'bête noire,' I didn't bother telling you."

"Jeremy?"

"He's in a clinic in Caracas and Janis is there with him. She's keeping me posted."

"A public hospital wouldn't be good enough for him," Mary Lou said, hiding her own anxiety, "and if his Venezuelan girlfriend's been feeding him arsenic, I wouldn't blame her!"

"And I was right not to tell you! You really hate him, don't you?"

Also myself for loving him, she silently added.

"He was making good progress, but suffered a setback and today he had to have more surgery. Would it make you feel more kindly toward him if I told you his hand was amputated?"

Kindly? Mary Lou wanted to rush to Jeremy's side, as his sister had.

Nina then came to tell A.P. the call was for him.

"I'll take it in the library," he said tersely, striding from the room.

"What's the matter with *him*?" Nina asked Mary Lou. "And I could say the same about *you* –"

If Nina's entrance had not distracted him, A.P. would surely have seen Mary Lou's emotion written on her face.

"Nothing is the matter with either of us," she said with unaccustomed crispness.

"Except that you both barked at me."

Mary Lou began filling the mugs. "I didn't mean to, Nina."

"But you told me a bare-faced lie when I asked what was the matter with you and A.P. You've had a row, haven't you? And there were the rest of us, our tongues hanging out for the tea, but we decided that leaving the two of you alone together was more important than our thirst."

Nina eyed the clock. "Do you realize how long you were in here, keeping us waiting?"

"It's time I *did* realize," said Mary Lou, setting down the heavy pot with a thump, "that there's absolutely nothing that doesn't get discussed on this bloody commune!"

"A commune," Nina replied, "is in some ways a microcosm of society."

"Will you please stop parroting Gary Potter? And would you mind carrying the biscuit barrel into the living room, there isn't room for it on the tray."

"The heck with tea and biscuits." Nina sat down in the Windsor chair beside the hearth, swept her abundant, black hair carelessly over one shoulder, and crossed her lovely legs.

"You don't mind keeping the others waiting when *you* feel like chatting," Mary Lou observed.

"And before I gave in to Gary, there must have been plenty of discussions about me – the 'will she, or won't she,' kind."

"Also the chaps laying bets," Mary Lou revealed, "which I thought disgusting."

"Talking of laying –" said Nina.

Mary Lou cut her short. "Is that what they're saying about A.P. and me?"

"Hoping," said Nina, "and not just for your sakes. The atmosphere you two jointly engender is affecting the rest of us."

"Has there been a meeting about it?" asked Mary Lou sarcastically.

"Yes, as a matter of fact."

"Well, I ought not to be surprised," said Mary Lou, "and how smug you sound, Nina."

And how radiant she looks, Mary Lou registered. Not just radiant, fulfilled, and love was responsible. But what had love done to Mary Lou? Deprived her of her self-respect, because she couldn't respect the object of her desire.

"Getting laid is in my opinion what you need," Nina informed her.

But not by A.P. And there were times when Mary Lou let herself believe that desire was all she felt for Jeremy. That once slaked, the fever consuming her would cease to be.

"It did wonders for me," Nina went on, "and look where it led – Gary and I are now thinking of getting married."

"Don't bother tossing your bouquet to me. I've no intention of being the next bride!"

"And I'd rather sound smug than the way you often do, nowadays," Nina answered, " 'shrewish' describes it. But I've told you what the remedy is," she added with a wink, as A.P. returned and she pointedly made her exit.

Mary Lou said, when he glanced at the tea going cold on the table, "We got sidetracked by what you chaps would call 'girl talk' – and you look as if you could use something stronger than what's in those mugs."

"It's Jeremy –"

Mary Lou's heart missed a beat.

"He's – well, the only way to put it is he's disappeared. Janis said the additional surgery was only minor, and she was told she could visit him as usual. When she arrived, he wasn't there."

"Worrying his sister wouldn't worry *him*!" said the part of Mary Lou that despised him.

"That isn't true," said A.P. "but right now, Jeremy is obsessed by only one matter."

"Since I've no idea what it is, I can't comment."

"Would you like me to tell you?"

"If it would make you feel better."

A.P. paced the hearth rug, then slumped into the Windsor chair, his gaze absently fixed upon the copper cauldron used for jam-making, but now hanging from the oak beam beside the hearth.

"Nothing would make me feel better about the risks

Jeremy is taking," he declared, "which doesn't mean I don't admire what he's doing. And so might you."

While A.P. relayed Jeremy's attempts to hunt down the assassins, Mary Lou grew increasingly alarmed.

"And you think his disappearing from the clinic is connected?" she asked when finally A.P. fell silent.

"What I actually think is that if he'd lost a foot, instead of a hand, he would now be hobbling along the trail on crutches."

Chapter 9

fter Jeremy's disappearance, Janis and Jesse visited Lola Mendez.

"Is my brother, by any chance, hiding out here?" Janis inquired without preamble. "Till I've left the country?"

"What are you talking about?" Lola replied. "When I called the hospital, Jeremy wasn't yet back from the theater —"

"But this time he was only given a local anaesthetic, they said. And before I was there to stop him, off he went!"

Lola's response was, "We should consider ourselves lucky he waited this long."

We? thought Janis, as they followed Lola into the library, where the desk was strewn with papers.

"I was occupying my mind while Jeremy had the surgery," Lola said, "and now there's something extra to be concerned about!"

Another indication that she really cared about him. But

given Jeremy's suspicions, was the show of concern genuine, or false?

"Please sit down," Lola invited them, gesturing to a sumptuous leather sofa and seating herself behind the desk. "This room hasn't had much use since my father's death," she added.

"That's a pity," said Jesse, surveying the books lining the walls.

"They're not to my taste," Lola told him, "and I sometimes wonder if my father ordered them by the yard."

"I'm surprised he had time to read," said Janis. "My father didn't."

"Does that mean you're now prepared to link them together?"

"Their deaths did that."

"But when shall you stop believing that only *my* father was the target?"

"If and when I'm proved wrong. And meanwhile my brother is risking *his* life!"

"To clear his father's name."

Janis said coldly, "Jeremy is out for revenge."

"When he started out, that was certainly so," Lola agreed, "but by now, what I warned him about then has to have happened —"

"That he might find out things he'd rather not know?" Janis blotted out what she had already learned from Jesse and from Jeremy, again venting her feelings on Lola. "Presumably you already knew some of your own father's dealings were questionable."

"And like it or not, Janis, the two were involved in joint ventures. One of which resulted in the car bomb being planted. Since the attempt to stop Jeremy short — well, I'm now wondering how he eluded the guard I put at the clinic."

"And nothing you did," said Janis, "would amaze me."

There was then a hiatus in the conversation while the butler, entering with a laden silver tray, served them with iced coffee and a selection of tiny pastries.

Janis watched Lola sink her teeth in a chocolate eclair, though she and Jesse had declined.

"You're wondering how I can, with all that's going on," Lola said when the three were again alone, "but life in this house is a matter of routine.

"Carlos has served my family for so long, I can't remember his not being here. When he brings the coffee and the cakes, I know it's four o'clock, as I know it's seven-thirty when he enters with cocktails and canapés in the evening. I find the routine immensely comforting."

"I," said Janis, "should find it immensely boring and so would my brother. But our background is poles apart from yours, butlers and bodyguards don't feature in it. Did Jeremy know you'd put a guard at the clinic?"

"He wouldn't have agreed to it, but he's wily enough to have somehow found out and evaded him."

With that Janis agreed.

"The other possibility," said Lola, "and it has to be faced, is that Jeremy was snatched from the clinic, and the guard, too."

It was now necessary for Janis to blot out a frightening vision: Jeremy bound and gagged, or worse, in one of the mountainside shacks he had mentioned when describing a recurring dream about himself and their father.

To Janis, as to Jeremy, it was as though she were caught up in an escalating series of events which bore no relation to how the Bornsteins had lived. Assassination wasn't how nice Jewish couples from North London expected to end their days. Nor, in their wildest imagination, could their children have envisaged it, or the consequences for themselves.

How could all this have happened to folk like us? Janis asked herself, while mental pictures of the family life she had known flashed before her eyes. Eating meals at the kitchen table. Her father fixing a washer on a tap. Seated together in the synagogue, with families like themselves.

But if Lola Mendez was right, there was a side of Jake Bornstein that his family and friends had never seen and someone had wanted him dead. She had to be wrong.

Janis stemmed her fears for her brother and told Lola bluntly, "Getting snatched from clinics doesn't happen to ordinary people, and it hasn't yet been established that Jeremy's car crash wasn't an accident."

Lola dabbed her lips with a dainty napkin and said to Jesse, "Thank goodness this determined ostrich has you to watch over her! It saved me the trouble of putting a guard at the hotel she preferred to stay in, rather than be my guest."

The glance the two were now exchanging was for Janis as if the ground had rocked beneath her feet. They weren't the total strangers they'd pretended to be when they met at the clinic.

"You've had me under surveillance, haven't you?" Janis accused Jesse.

"Don't be ridiculous."

"Isn't that what they call it, in *your* world?" Janis sprang to her feet, aflame with fury. "Jeremy cautioned me about you, but I didn't heed him –"

"Jeremy," Lola interrupted, "has learned to think as all three of us must, till the treachery is finally resolved."

"Don't you talk to me about treachery! As for you," Janis said, returning her attention to Jesse, "you should've been an actor, not a doctor. You and Lola are old acquaintances, aren't you? And that puts her on a par with *you*.

"Experts in the art of deceit is what I'd call both of you. And who's paying you to keep an eye on me? Lola, the other side, or both?"   .

"There are *two* other sides," said Lola, "those who planted the car bomb, and the man still running my father's company –"

"And millions of dollars are at stake," said Janis with disgust.

"How wouldn't money be the root cause?" Lola replied.

But Janis was striding from the room.

Janis asked the taxi-driver waiting to transport her and Jesse to their hotel to take her directly to the airport.

If he, too, was on someone's payroll, she might not get there! What had Dad done – if he *had* done it – that had landed Jeremy and now her in this frightening situation?

Not just frightening, sickening, since she had let herself be conned by the handsome Dr. Cohen. As Lola had hood-winked Jeremy, she thought as the uniformed guard and his snarling dog watched the taxi leave the grounds.

"The senorita wishes I should again await her? At the airport?" asked the fleshy-faced driver.

"No, thanks. I'm leaving town."

Janis could do nothing to help her brother by remaining here, and on a personal level, she couldn't get out of Caracas fast enough, nor away from the man she'd been fool enough to trust.

Anger had propelled her from his presence. Pain, too, as though she were a creature escaping from a trap, but not before being injured by its prongs.

As for leaving without her luggage, what were a few

clothes and a suitcase to the wealthy woman Janis now was? And even that was unreal.

Mingling with her bitter reflections was anxiety for Jeremy, while the vehicle sped onward and the man at the wheel practiced his surprisingly good English, delivering a monologue about the tourists who were his main source of a livelihood, pausing only to light cigarettes that polluted the air with acrid fumes.

Hovering at the back of Janis's mind was apprehension that she might somehow be stopped from leaving the country where the nightmare began. When eventually she was inside the airport terminal and a woman accosted her, she found herself trembling.

"Do you know if there's a medical center here, dear? I twisted my ankle, getting off the plane."

"Why didn't you ask one of the crew?" Janis inquired warily, though it was a relief that the woman was British.

"It didn't seem too bad – but look at it now!"

Janis switched her gaze from the pleasant, middle-aged face to the swelling above a sensible brown shoe.

"If I don't get it strapped-up immediately –"

"But I'm afraid I can't help you. I'm not familiar with this airport."

"Why didn't you just say so, instead of keeping me standing here!"

Because I've learned that corruption has many faces, Janis silently answered as the woman hobbled away, and I had to be sure. Jesse, with his warm smile. And the lovely Lola Mendez. Possibly even my dad.

What further proof was required that henceforth Janis must be on the alert? Nor could she any longer disregard Shirley's warning to be on the lookout for fortune hunters. Once you'd opened your mind to the depths of corruption, you had to accept that there was more than one kind and a plethora of motives.

Janis bought a ticket for the only flight on which standby places were still available, which happened to be going to Paris, and went to equip herself with a flight bag and some toiletries.

She was selecting a toothbrush when Jesse appeared at her side. "How dare you follow me!" she lashed him, heedless of heads turning to look at them. "If I required a bodyguard, I'd engage one myself, and it wouldn't be you. You're a liar and I can't abide liars!"

"I've never lied to you, Janis."

"You just didn't tell me the truth."

"Why are you going to Paris?"

"Is there nothing your paymistress can't check-up on? And in double quick time!"

"Don't be ridiculous, Janis. I just did the rounds of the reservation desks, when I got here. And I'm here because I love you."

"Lying again!"

Janis completed her shopping and Jesse went with her to the cash desk. "Why are you still following me?" she said frigidly.

"I don't want this to be the end for us."

"If I'd been less naive, there wouldn't have been a beginning," she replied, "believing we just happened to reencounter each other at that synagogue social.

"Now, though, how do I know if the nice couple you introduced me to there are really your parents? And if they are, they could be in on it too – whatever *it* is!"

"You're being ridiculous again."

"You still don't know what you've done to me, do you,

Jesse? That you've made me as wary – and as cynical – as my brother has become. And God knows where he is . . ."

"Lola called the clinic and found out that someone phoned Jeremy just before he went missing, which implies that he left of his own accord."

"And you waited till now to tell me, when it should've been the first thing you said." Janis paid for her purchases and picked up the carrier bag. "What sort of person are you? Don't bother answering, I know!"

"But my reply to your accusation is you barely allowed me to get a word in," said Jesse as they pushed their way out of the crowded shop. "May I buy you a coffee and do some explaining?"

"What I need," said Janis before striding away to join the motley throng, "is a double-brandy and you out of my sight."

Chapter 10

Bessie opened the apartment door and could not believe her eyes.

"Aren't you going to invite me in?"

"My brother doesn't need an invitation. But you look terrible, Jeremy," she added after they had hugged each other. "I'm sorry about your hand –"

"The one I no longer have, you mean," he said flippantly, following her to the living room, "and I'm afraid the stump's giving me a bit of trouble at the moment."

Bessie eyed the grubby-looking dressing visible beneath his jacket cuff, and watched him lower himself onto the sofa, as if he was in pain.

"They shouldn't have let you out of hospital yet, Jeremy. And if I'd known you were coming, Sim and I would've met your plane."

"Is Sim your boyfriend?"

"I'm not sure."

"You were never sure of anything, Bessie. And I was too sure of everything."

"I'm not sure what you mean."

Bleak though his private thoughts were, Jeremy had to laugh. And it struck him that, each in their own way, Jake and Laura had much to answer for. Bessie's insecurity stemmed from her early childhood experience; and who could feel whole if they didn't know who had fathered them? Jake, though, had given his children a sense of security, and it was now for Jeremy as if his own life had been built on shifting sands.

"What time do your granddad and Hildegard get home from the restaurant?" he asked Bessie.

"They don't close till midnight, and then they have to clear up. But I'll fix the guest room bed for you now, Jeremy. You needn't wait up for them."

"Thanks, but I'm not staying, Bessie."

"You'd be welcome," she assured him. "They love having guests, though they hardly see them, and —"

"I'd rather they didn't know I'd been here," Jeremy interrupted, "and the same goes for Janis. Can I trust you to keep it to yourself?"

"I'm not the family sneak anymore!"

"Is that what I used to call you?"

"That and a lot of other things."

Appraising Bessie, Jeremy recalled the child whose mother had married his father, as plain-looking now as she was then – but a good deal more intelligent than he had once supposed. More sensitive, too.

"The first time you called me a sneak was the day Mummy and Daddy got back from their honeymoon," she reminded him, "and you and Janis had a quarrel that was nothing to do with me.

198 ▼ MAISIE MOSCO

"I was sitting looking at a picture book, when Janis threw a plant at you, and the china pot it was in got smashed. When Mummy came into the room and noticed that the window was broken, too, I told her you'd put your elbow through it, fighting with Janis.

"But I was only a little girl, wasn't I?"

And the teenage one you now are still finds it necessary to justify her childhood behavior, Jeremy thought with compassion. "Becoming a family didn't happen easily for any of us," he said with the benefit of hindsight.

"But we *did* become one," Bessie answered, "and I'm very worried about you, Jeremy. So would Janis be, if she saw how you look."

"I'll be fine when I've had a bit of a rest," he replied, mustering a smile, "and I wouldn't mind a nice cup of tea."

When Bessie returned with the tea, his complexion seemed to her even more ashen, and blood had seeped through his dressing.

"I could ring up the doctor," Bessie said. "In an emergency he wouldn't mind coming late at night –"

"Let's not make a drama out of a crisis," Jeremy joked, "as the TV commercial puts it –"

"But they're only selling something, I'm trying to stop my brother from bleeding to death," she answered as the blood-stain grew larger and Jeremy went on sipping tea. "Will you let me call the doctor?"

"I'd rather you didn't."

"Then I'll go next door and fetch Sim. He has a certificate in first aid."

Bessie was gone before Jeremy could stop her. Only the ominous throb where his hand used to be prevented him from fleeing her sisterly concern, as he had Janis's.

The gawky youth with her when she reappeared proved to be surprisingly deft and gentle.

"Thanks for making me more comfortable," Jeremy said to him when the dressing was changed. "You'd make a good nurse!"

"But I'd rather be a journalist."

"After you've done your army service," said Bessie.

"And if I get sent to Gaza, or the West Bank, my conscience is unlikely to survive it, even if *I* do."

There's more to this lad than first impressions imply, Jeremy was thinking when Sim asked if he was taking antibiotics.

"Not since I left the clinic."

"They didn't give you a supply?"

"They didn't know I was leaving. Nor did Janis," Jeremy added to Bessie.

"How could you have done that to her? After she schlepped from Australia to be with you!"

"She wasn't around at the time – or she'd have chained me to the bed," Jeremy replied with grim humor.

"I feel like doing that now," said Bessie, "and why don't you want Janis to know you're in Israel? She isn't one of your enemies."

"What enemies?"

Bessie gave him a withering glance. "I'm not daft, Jeremy. And I don't intend keeping secrets from Janis, like you and she have from me."

Sim returned to medical matters. "Are you allergic to penicillin, Jeremy? Some people are."

It was Bessie who answered. "He can't be, he was given it for the boils he used to get on his neck."

"What a remarkable memory you have," Jeremy told her affectionately.

"And I sometimes wish I hadn't," she said while Sim rummaged in his first aid box.

"My mum's the sort who never takes what she's prescribed," Sim said handing Jeremy a bottle of tablets, "so you can have the penicillin her dentist thinks got rid of a tooth abscess.

"Mum's remedy for everything from sore throats to bruises is salt water," he added with one of his lop-sided grins.

"Was that why you bathed Jeremy's wound with salt water?" Bessie inquired.

"And boy, did it sting!" said Jeremy.

"But saline solution is a handy sterilizer, as well as the uses my mother puts it to," said Sim, "and I'd suggest you get the next amateur who changes your dressing to do what I did. Everyone keeps salt in their kitchen."

Jeremy swallowed one of the penicillin tablets with the remains of his tea, and rose. "Thanks for the advice, Sim. Meanwhile, I have to get myself to Nazareth."

"At this hour, you'd have to hire a car," Bessie told him.

"*And* a driver," he added, glancing at his bandaged stump.

"I'll take you there in my dad's van," said Sim.

Journeying north, through peaceful countryside he found hard to relate to Israel's inner turmoil, Jeremy regretted involving the lad beside him in his own hazardous activities.

"I shouldn't have let you do this, Sim, but I really appreciate it."

"Thanks aren't necessary," Sim replied, "in Israel we understand too well how it feels when people you love are cut down by terrorists. Also the urge for revenge – though I wouldn't recommend it."

Jeremy's response was, "My elder sister should've had more sense than to worry Bessie on my account."

"She didn't have to. Bessie isn't the simpleton her family seem to take her for. What do you suppose she's been thinking since you suddenly took time off from college to jet-set all over the world?

"And you're still trying to kid her, aren't you?" Sim went on. "Expecting her to accept unquestioningly whatever she's told – including that your car crash in Caracas was an accident."

Jeremy said after a silence, during which they had driven past an Arab village, "What you call kidding Bessie is my way of protecting her, Sim."

"And you mean well, don't tell me, which was probably her mother's trouble, too. But Bessie is out in the world now, isn't she? And beginning to stand on her own feet, which she was never allowed to do."

"You seem to know a lot about our family background!" Jeremy was stung to reply.

"Well, it didn't take me too long to put the pieces together."

"What pieces?"

"I'll leave you to figure it out. But you're too busy, aren't you, doing your own thing? I'm not sure I'd have the guts, even if vengeance was in me, but my reluctant admiration for you is tempered by your attitude to Bessie."

"And I bet you come top of the class for English!" said Jeremy.

"Bessie, though, comes bottom for most subjects, which adds to her sense of inadequacy."

"Maybe you should be a psychologist, as well as a journalist."

"Would you mind taking what I'm saying seriously?" Sim

requested. "Your little sister is a beautiful person and I happen to care about her. Nothing's ever gone right for Bessie, has it? Or so it seems to me."

Jeremy eyed Sim's bespectacled profile – good-looking he wasn't, but what a character! "How it seems to me, Sim, is that Bessie got lucky when she met you."

They fell silent, Jeremy aware of a too familiar tension as he drew nearer to his destination.

How long it now seemed since he had met the nervous bodyguard, Perry, outside Milan Cathedral, and how many leads had he followed-up in the interim? Meeting with one shady individual after another, in this foreign city, or that, each of them supplying, for a price, information that, little by little, had changed Jeremy's perception of his father.

Like the shifty-looking oriental in Hong Kong, who had revealed that Jake had dealt in smuggled jade. Liquor and diamonds, too, had cropped-up in that respect on Jeremy's travels, and a tip-off from a woman in Madrid had led him to Amsterdam where, if the informant he visited was to be believed, his father had been part of a network dealing in fake paintings.

Nothing Jeremy had learned, though, had thrown light upon who might have planted the car bomb. Instead, his father had been spoken of with respect, and if that wasn't a joke, given those who were voicing it . . .

Nor, until Jeremy got the phone call that evoked his speedy departure from the clinic, as fear had hastened Perry's from the hospital, had there been a Middle East connection.

Was he now to learn that Jake Bornstein had sold arms to Israel's enemies and himself paid the price?

The shop to which Jeremy had been instructed to come was shuttered for the night, and only his own shadow and a prowling cat kept him company in the moonlight as he rapped on the door.

"I dozed off, waiting for you," said the obese man who let him in.

"Who was the woman who called me?"

"My wife. I never go out and we don't have a telephone."

"Welcome to my world," he said, switching on a light, and Jeremy found himself in a small space only describable as an Aladdin's cave.

Silver and brass ornaments were crammed cheek-by-jowl, and Chanukah menorahs by the score mingled with statuettes of the Holy Virgin. Jeweled crucifixes adorned the walls, side by side with ornate mezuzahs, the floor was barely visible for copper urns and colorful Arab tapestries were suspended from the ceiling.

"Here's where the tourists like to browse, though they don't always buy," said the man, "and since the Intifada, they don't come to Israel in droves, like they used to – Who can blame them?

"Come, you'll join me for a schnapps, while we talk."

Jeremy followed him to the end of the "cave" and behind a bead curtain, into a cluttered living room.

"Sit down. That dog in the corner won't bite you! My mother loved pottery animals. The dog she gave me and her photograph are now all I have to remind me of her –"

"Could we get down to business?" Jeremy cut in.

"A young man in a hurry is what I've heard you are," said his host, "but take the weight off your feet all the same."

Jeremy put himself in an armchair and forced a smile.

"So was your father, when I first knew him, and nobody could say he slowed down."

Jeremy accepted a glass of kümmel. "May I know your name?"

"My friends who still speak to me call me Izzie – and your father was one of the few."

"What am I supposed to deduce from that?"

"You couldn't tell from how my wife speaks English – when she called you – that she's an Arab woman? And *I'm* a Jew. A recipe for ostracization that we both have to live with."

"I'm sorry about your situation," said Jeremy, "but would you mind explaining why you summoned me here?"

"You're the son of a true friend," said Izzie, "and since he died I've been keeping tabs on you."

Who hasn't! thought Jeremy. And the "friendship" bit could be a lie and probably was. "I'd be interested to know how," he said.

"Listen, I never said who my sources were when I was with Interpol and why would I, now?"

Jeremy eyed him with surprise.

"So I don't jell with your idea of an Interpol agent," Izzie gleaned from his expression. "A Mossad one, either. But I've had time since those days to go to seed, I'm an old man now. Also, for your information, agents come in all shapes and sizes, so don't ever be too sure about who's living next door to you."

"How did you meet my father?"

"It was your mother I met first," Izzie said with a reminiscent smile, "and what a lovely person Julia was. I was on a case in South Africa at the time and I had to make contact with the law firm she worked for.

"While I was there, it was Rosh Hashanah and she invited me home for supper. You and your sister were too young to stay up for the meal, but your mother let you watch her light the candles, after you'd had your baths. The last time I saw you, you were wearing pajamas."

"My mother, like my stepmother, was the hospitable sort." And how different this encounter was from Jeremy's expectations.

"It was in Jo'burg, all those years ago," Izzie continued, "that your father saved my life. And afterwards, we stayed in touch."

"My father saved your life?"

"I collapsed at the supper table, on the evening I just told you about. When I came to, I was in a hospital room. Your father paid for me to have the heart operation I couldn't afford, even though he'd just met me. That's the sort of man he was."

But he was another sort of man, too.

"Eventually," said Izzie, "I was able to repay the money, though he wanted me to forget it. What he did for me, I'm *never* going to forget. The state my heart was in, without that operation I wouldn't have got back to England alive."

"When did you last see my father?" Jeremy asked.

"Not too long before what I feared might happen happened, and –"

"Why did you fear it?"

"You're just like *my* son, always interrupting!"

"And he would probably be asking if a man who had to have heart surgery should be drinking," said Jeremy watching Izzie waddle to the sideboard to refill his glass.

"When he's here, I don't do it, but he isn't here often. His mother doesn't know he works for the Mossad," Izzie added with a malicious chuckle that wobbled his treble-chin. "She thinks he's a traveling salesman, like she thought I was, and I'm pleased he too is getting one over on her!

"Zack is from my first marriage," he explained, "and your father was right when he said, after meeting Netta, that she wasn't for me."

Jeremy heard the rocking chair creak when Izzie lowered himself into it, and squeak protestingly when he began swaying back and forth.

"If I'd listened to him," Izzie resumed his tale, "I wouldn't have married her. But what I listened to was the message from between my legs! She was built like Marilyn Monroe.

"And if your father had listened to *me* –"

"You still haven't said why you feared for him."

"Again you're interrupting! He'd got in the clutches of men like Luis Mendez, hadn't he? Only that wasn't how he saw it –"

"How *did* he see it?"

"I'm trying to tell you, aren't I?"

Izzie's chins were wobbling again, as if he was overcome by emotion, the squeak-squeak of the chair increasing in pace as he strove to assemble his thoughts.

"I loved that man," he said eventually, "and I want his son to understand him. Would I have asked you to come here when you're not yet fit to travel, if it wasn't important?"

And would Jeremy have made the onerous journey, just to hear his father whitewashed?

"When I learned you were hunting his killers," said Izzie, "I thought, that boy doesn't know what he's up against and he's no match for it. Then Zack sent me word that you'd lost your hand, and I said to myself it was time for me to intercede. To put you in the picture.

"I'd seen that car bomb coming," Izzie went on, "that or some other horrific end for the power broker your father had become. He, though, didn't see himself that way – and we're now back to where you last interrupted me.

"Jake wouldn't have bothered using a bodyguard, if I hadn't begged him to. Not even after he got involved with

Mendez. 'Okay,' he said to me, 'but only to set your mind at rest. I don't want you having another heart attack.'

"Set my mind at rest?" Izzie levered himself from the rocker and again went to refill his glass, the ornamental bells trimming the red tablecloth tinkling as he approached. "I used to lie awake nights thinking of him and where my heart was, was in my mouth! Without the bodyguard, though, they might have got him a lot sooner."

Jeremy waited with bated breath.

"I can see from your expression you're expecting me to tell you who *they* are," said Izzie, "and I'm sorry to disappoint you. In the world we're now living in, the list of amoral possibilities knows no bounds. And a man can't use money like chips in a game without making enemies. A game was all it was to Jake."

"Including selling arms to the highest bidder?"

Izzie laughed sardonically. "Like governments do? While their diplomats mouth protests about the same regimes they sell to. But Jake Bornstein wasn't a hypocrite. If he ever did any arms deals, he'd've made sure it was with the right people."

"Wouldn't you call it hypocrisy," said Jeremy, "to live like the pillar of respectability you're not?"

"Listen," said Izzie, returning to rock himself in his chair, "your father was just the middleman, wasn't he? An entrepreneur was what he called himself. He once told me he'd just bought and sold a big factory without even setting eyes on it.

"That could've resulted in a lot of workers losing their jobs, and plenty of his deals could've had a bad effect on people's lives, one way or another. But Jake wouldn't have given that a thought. And he had a finger in so many pies, how could he have kept track of the end results of all his dealings?"

Jeremy forced a smile and rose. "Thanks for your time, Izzie."

"And you think I've wasted yours."

Jeremy was aware of a heaviness in his stump, but suddenly it was as if a fog had been lifted from his mind. "On the contrary," he replied, "if we'd met sooner, I wouldn't have wasted my time seeking clues in the wrong places."

Chapter
11

*J*anis's sole comfort, on arriving in Paris, was that Henry
Moritz was still based there and would welcome her
when she arrived at his flat, as he would any of his
young relatives.

"Two unexpected guests in one day!" Henry said with a
smile when he opened the door.

"Jeremy's here? How is he?" Janis asked anxiously, following Henry between the stacks of books lining the route to his
living room.

"Not your brother, dear, A.P. But Jeremy was fine when
I last saw him."

"When was that?"

"A few weeks ago, he said he was leaving that night for
Tokyo. And you haven't said hello to me!"

Janis dumped her bag on the shabby sofa, kissed Henry,
and received a hug from A.P. "Forgive the oversight, Henry,
I'm punch drunk after flying from Caracas – and that isn't
all!"

"But when I was your age," he replied, "the youngsters in the family didn't go rushing all over the world like your lot do."

"It's a different world," Janis said grimly.

"I was about to add, except for me," said Henry, "and I'm not the best of examples, am I?"

"If I may get a word in," said A.P., "you, Henry, have always done your own thing and it didn't involve selling out to the fleshpots. That doesn't seem a bad example to me."

"What it sometimes involved, though, was not knowing where my next meal was coming from," Henry said reminiscently.

"But you didn't let that stop you from devoting your life to causes," said A.P.

"Which you're now doing a good deal more usefully than I ever did, A.P.," Henry went on after pausing. "As for the joke Jeremy made about himself, when he was briefly here –"

"I'm surprised my brother still has a sense of humor," Janis cut in.

"He was just fobbing me off, dear, when I asked why he'd taken a year off from Oxford – black sheep though I am, that's something I *didn't* do – Jeremy's reply was, 'Now I'm rich, I fancy a bit of jet-setting!'"

"The laugh that went with it couldn't have sounded more forced," Henry added.

Janis exchanged a glance with A.P. "The family grapevine seems to have neglected Henry."

"But I'm capable of putting two and two together about Jeremy's travels and the tension I sensed in him. More strength to his elbow is what I say."

"Since he's just had a hand amputated, that makes me want to puke!" Janis exclaimed.

Henry sat down on the sofa, shock written in his expression. "If I'd known, I wouldn't have said it."

"You'd have expressed the same sentiment in different words! And A.P. no doubt agrees with you. You men and your macho attitudes have brought about too many wars and what is my brother now doing but fighting his own private one?"

"If I could make Jeremy call a halt, I would," A.P. told her.

"But how I see it," said Henry, "is better to live proudly with only one hand, than minus one's self-respect."

Janis gazed through the window at a scene pulsating with life. Students drinking coffee at the pavement cafe across the street; people thronging in and out of the Metro on the corner; a party of Japanese, cameras slung from their shoulders, entering a bistro.

"What good will self-respect do Jeremy if he ends up dead?" she replied.

When after supper Janis took her troubles to bed, A.P. and Henry went for a stroll beside the Seine.

"Paris is my favorite city, in case you hadn't guessed!" Henry said, watching one of the colorful bateaux sail by, packed with passengers as always in the tourist season.

"Then why haven't you made your permanent home here?"

"A permanent home," said Henry, "would ruin my image!"

"Would you mind being serious?"

"Let's just say I'm afflicted with an ongoing restlessness, A.P. Not to mention my interest in international politics – which the family insists on calling 'espousing causes'!"

"Are you sure there isn't a woman in it, Henry?"

"Some more family gossip, A.P.?"

"Just an educated guess."

Henry halted at a flower stall and selected a spray of sweet-smelling freesias, fishing some coins from the pocket of his shabby, tweed jacket and counting them into the elderly flowerseller's gnarled hand.

"Merci, monsieur."

"Au revoir, madame," he replied with his charming smile and remarked to A.P., as they went on their way, that it would take more than flowers to raise Janis's spirits. "No harm in trying, though."

"You're a thoughtful person, Henry."

"Family history wouldn't agree, and I already belong in the archives. I'll never see fifty again!"

A.P. glanced at the slim and upright figure beside him. "You look just as you did when I last saw you, and you're never going to seem old to me, Henry."

"But it's your lot who are now making history, A.P., each in your own way. When I began doing my own thing – as you succinctly put it – instead of settling down, as my twin brother did, it was interpreted as Henry turning his back on the family and on convention.

"Nowadays, though, grandparents and parents consider themselves lucky if *any* of their expectations in that respect materialize."

"It's their fault, for having expectations," A.P. declared.

"With that I agree, though I might not if I were a parent," said Henry with a laugh. "What I *do* seem to be, is a haven for you youngsters to run to! And what was all that about an educated guess and a woman in my life?" he harked back.

"Well, there's one in mine and –"

"I'd be surprised if there weren't," Henry interrupted, "you're a good looking chap. The image of your great-grand-dad, Abraham Sandberg."

"I'm told I inherited his temperament, too."

"Like the other redheads in the clan. Including my sister-in-law, Leona," Henry added quietly, and A.P. recalled hearing another snippet of family history: that Leona had married the wrong twin.

"I'm sorry I couldn't be there for your maiden speech," Henry said after a silence, "I was in Hungary.

"People in the West tend to forget the sense of isolation those behind the Iron Curtain have to live with – that's why I keep regular contact with my friends there."

"But 1989 has been a good year for Hungarians," said A.P., "what with the barbed wire fence between Hungary and Austria coming down in May."

"Poland is leading the way, though," Henry declared. "I couldn't have envisaged less than a decade ago, an even *partly* free election taking place there. But I was in Warsaw in June, when it happened and the communists were crushed."

"How do you get by financially, Henry? With all the traveling you do, and you still have to eat –"

"Some capital prudently invested by my twin, willed by our grandfather, continues to provide me with an income supplemented by the articles I write.

"My needs are few, A.P., and *my* educated guess, as I was about to say, is that the groundswell pushing for democracy in Eastern Europe won't be too long in bursting through the fetters."

"I wouldn't bet on it," said A.P. Talking politics is the price of staying with Henry, he thought with a smile as they sat down on a bench beneath the trees, on the Quai d'Orsay.

Henry then returned to personal matters. "You mentioned a woman in your life, A.P. Is she giving you a bad time?"

"You could say that!"

"And it takes me back. My first affair was with a woman of thirty-five, I recall, and I still an undergrad."

"Mary Lou is my age and we're not having an affair."

"But don't be discouraged. Some take longer to let you bed them."

"I haven't tried to, Henry. And nowadays it isn't done that way. Sex is had by agreement and it's as likely to be the girl, as the chap, who puts the proposition."

"How very unromantic."

"Romance," said A.P. "has gone out of fashion, and that makes me an anachronism. And how I feel about Mary Lou isn't just sex. I'm in love with her, but she turned me down."

"There'll be other girls, A.P."

"I didn't expect that pat reply from you."

"But it's nonetheless true."

"Why I didn't expect it, Henry, is it's occurred to me that something of the kind might have happened to you, when you were young. That it could be why you took off as you did and have never settled down."

"Something of the kind, but not quite," said Henry brusquely, "and if you don't want to end up a rolling stone complete with the rest of the proverb, again I'm not the best of examples, A.P."

"I happen to think you've done some terrific things in your time. Like helping your Chilean friends escape after the Pinochet coup, and that's just one instance among the many. You even took part in the student uprising in the sixties, didn't you? Here in Paris, and you got clapped in jail."

"Me and Danny the Red! But he has other things to do with his life now. And I'd be obliged if you'd stop listing the right things *I've* spent my life doing for the wrong reasons.

"You were absolutely right about me, of course, and how very perceptive you are."

"Where shall you be off to next, Henry?"

"The world has no shortage of good causes! Have you heard of the Deep Greens? How they're forcing the ecology issue wide open in the States?"

"But I don't approve of their tactics," said A.P., "they're far too militant for me."

"They're making themselves felt, though, aren't they?" Henry replied. "Whole families are now getting in on it, lying down in the path of trucks transporting men to chop down trees is the least of it. I'm considering joining them."

A.P. got a mental picture of Henry sprawled on a country lane, a truck trundling toward him. Were there no lengths this remarkable man wouldn't go to, in support of a worthy cause?

Well, A.P. now had one of his own. "Since you're still only considering it," he said carefully, "why not come back to England and be *peacefully* green, with me and my friends?"

Henry was astounded. "You're asking me to join your commune?"

"And to help me with my personal equivalent of your taking off, years ago, to do your own thing. I now know what mine is, and if Mary Lou never marries me, I'll still have that."

While Henry gazed absently down at the evidence that someone had picnicked on the bench, A.P. outlined his plan for an international summer camp for children, and for the arts project that had also sprung from his visiting Ben.

"You can't say it isn't a cause worth supporting," he capped it.

"But I wouldn't know one end of a child from another, my dear chap."

A.P. had to laugh. "Children are individuals, Henry, but many never get the chance to fulfill their potential and that's what the arts aspect of my idea is about. Nor do they get the chance to know kids from other countries – and children are the future, aren't they?

"Wouldn't you say there'd be more hope for the world if nations were able to understand each other? Instead of us always seeing the Germans in Hitler's shadow, the Yanks thinking we're just stiff upper lip Limeys, and all the rest of the misconceptions that contribute to strife."

"Just how international is this scheme of yours going to get?"

"Initially it will have to be limited to Europe, since the first camp is scheduled for later this month. It hasn't been easy to arrange, Henry, and we still haven't fixed up for a French group to come. That's why I'm now in France and hoping to enlist your aid."

"What sort of French children would you like?"

Again A.P. had to laugh. "We're not talking about chocolates, Henry! A child is a child."

"I could have a word with a priest I know."

"Have a word with whoever you like, just get me the kids. Meanwhile, Mary Lou will be frantic until I get back, there's so much to do and Kyverdale Hall is overflowing with camp beds and not yet erected tents."

"Though I've never been camping, I think 'pitched' is the word," said Henry, "and this girl who's daft enough not to want you lives on the commune, does she? I look forward to meeting her."

"Does that mean you've decided to join us?"

"As long as I don't have to sign a contract never to leave!"

The following day, Janis went to buy some essential clothing and encountered a former classmate.

"It's terrific to see you!" said Claudia Forsythe.

"But I blinked when I saw *you*." The school snob selling the *Herald Tribune* on the Rue de Rivoli?"

"You won't tell my parents, will you?"

"Since I no longer live in London, I'm unlikely to see them."

"I was awfully sorry to hear you'd lost yours, and in that absolutely horrendous way," said Claudia. "Where are you living now, Janis?"

"A good question."

"You don't have a home?"

"I wouldn't call my flat in Sydney that."

"But how stupendous! All those fabulous beaches."

"You always did talk in superlatives," said Janis with a smile. "Do you still want to be an actress?"

"I didn't get into RADA, did I?" said Claudia, adjusting the sack of newspapers slung from her shoulder.

"The Royal Academy isn't the only drama school."

"But I'd set my heart on training there, Janis, and it hadn't entered my head that I wasn't good enough. For a while I was in the absolute depths of despair, then I met a chap who said he could get me a part in a film."

"Oh yes?" Janis said dryly.

"Needless to say, it turned out to be a porno movie! Which I ought to have guessed, since he didn't ask me to audition."

Janis eyed the skin-tight *Herald Tribune* tee-shirt that Claudia was wearing. "He probably thought you a natural, but you always did make the most of yourself."

"That's the second crack you've made about what I was like at school, Janis, but in some ways I'm no longer the same person."

"Me, neither."

"And you look too dreadful even for my superlatives."

"Thanks! Do you have time for a coffee?"

"I have time for lunch, if *you're* buying."

Janis found herself liking the new Claudia and linked her arm as they went to find a table at a pavement cafe.

"When I refused to live at home, like my sister did till she got married, my parents stopped my allowance," Claudia explained, "so I moved into a 'squat' with some other out of work theatricals. I'd still be there, if another chap with a proposition hadn't come along and I hadn't been a gullible idiot yet again!"

They fell silent until they had ordered their food, the thrum of the vibrant city all around them enhancing Janis's feeling that the loneliest place could be in the midst of a crowd.

Until she'd let Jesse into her life, loneliness had dogged her wherever she went. Now, she must live with it again, and with the bitter aftertaste of how he had duped her.

"I'm glad I ran into you," she said warmly, watching Claudia's silky dark hair tumble to her shoulders when she took off her red peaked cap.

"Same here, but you must have loathed me at school, you and the rest of our class! But that's down to my dear parents for raising me as if we're top drawer, which we're not."

Oh, the things parents are responsible for, thought Janis, bleakly. Directly and indirectly. Whether or not Jake Bornstein was an innocent victim, the reverberations of the car bomb had, one way and another, damaged his children.

"I remember inviting you to one of my birthday parties," Claudia reminisced, "but you couldn't – or was it wouldn't – come. Or you'd have seen me press the bell for the maid, and heard her address me as 'Miss Claudia.'

"Who the heck did I think I was!" Claudia added with a laugh, as a platter of steak and chips was placed before her. "And it's just too marvelous of you to treat me to lunch,

Janis. I haven't had a square meal since I don't know when."

"How long have you been in Paris?"

"Since the lying sod I mentioned engaged me to appear in a show here, that turned out to be a nude revue with unmentionable trimmings. I've had it with men, Janis!"

"Me, too."

"I remember hearing you'd got engaged while you were at college –"

"I broke it off, but he isn't the cause of my disillusion, Claudia. Like you, I afterwards got involved with a liar and I'm still in pieces because of him."

"You, though, can be in pieces in comfort," said Claudia, sloshing ketchup on her steak. "Your millionaire father won't have left you penniless. I, however, can't even afford the plane fare back to England."

"Is that why you're selling newspapers?"

"It's preferable to being exploited by the opposite sex."

Janis stopped picking at the omelette she had ordered though she wasn't hungry and studied Claudia's determined expression. "Does that mean you've become a feminist?"

"I've had reason to, haven't I?"

"My own experience was a good deal more personal," Janis said, as remembrance painfully returned to her. In Caracas she had tossed caution to the winds; slept with Jesse. And how much more vulnerable that had rendered her when presented with his deceit.

"I didn't say my relationship with the chap who brought me here was entirely business," Claudia answered. "He calls himself an impresario, but what he is, is an effing pimp!"

She drank some Perrier to help her cool down, but her hazel eyes continued to blaze with wrath. "If a man so much as asked me the time, right now, I'd hit him with that bottle!"

"And I'd say, 'Good for you,' but it wouldn't change a thing."

"If there were such a thing as a Protestant nunnery, I'd put myself in one," Claudia declared.

"But not for long."

"And what are *your* immediate plans, Janis?"

"I don't have any."

"Meanwhile, if you're not going to eat your salad, I will," said Claudia. "In my present position I can't bear to see food wasted."

"It's really as bad as that?"

"And Mummy and Daddy would say they told me so, if they knew, but they never will. Believe it or not, Janis, I want them to be proud of me –"

"Where are you living?" Janis interrupted.

"In Montmartre. With three girls who haven't yet accepted that they are being exploited! – But their day will come. They're letting me owe them my share of the rent."

"And how do you intend paying it?"

Claudia drank some more Perrier and put down the glass. "Since I'm never going to play Joan of Arc, I'm thinking of emulating Florence Nightingale. D'you think a nurse's uniform would suit me?"

"Never mind the uniform, think of the bedpans."

"You're trying to put me off."

"Because it isn't for you."

"That remains to be seen," said Claudia, "and I wouldn't mind doing my training in Canada, I've always wanted to see Niagara Falls."

"That's why you chose Canada?"

"It beats sticking a pin in an atlas."

"Right now," said Janis, "I couldn't even be bothered to do that."

Claudia crumbled a bit of bread beside her on the paper tablecloth, her show of bravado gone. "They say that when you reach rock bottom, there's nowhere to go but up, Janis."

"And I wish I could believe that."

"There's only one way to find out."

"But why nursing, Claudia?"

"It would be an absolutely and utterly new beginning for me, a cleansing for my bruised soul."

"But heaven help the patients!"

Claudia retorted, "You couldn't possibly make a worse nurse than you think I shall, so why not join me?"

Janis said after a silence, "If the lying sod in *my* life weren't a doctor, I would probably clutch at that suggestion as though it were a lifebelt in a sea of despondency. But the last place to forget him is in a hospital."

"And if you let that stop you from doing something worthwhile you might otherwise have done, he's got one over you again," Claudia replied.

"Something that wouldn't have entered my head, if I hadn't run into *you*!"

"Call it fate," Claudia said with her pert grin, "and since you're not going to *let* him get one over you again, when are we leaving for Canada?"

They looked at each other and burst out laughing.

"What the heck have we got to laugh about?" Janis said through her mirth.

"It's better than crying," Claudia answered, as unable to control herself as Janis was, "and a step in the right direction, wouldn't you say?"

Janis said when the laughter had petered out, "All right, I'll go with you to Canada."

"It's going to be fun working together."

"I didn't say I'd decided to become a nurse."

"Then why are you bothering to come?"

"You're good company, Claudia. And I have to move on somewhere."

When Janis returned to the flat, Henry and A.P. were out. A note by the telephone requested her to call Bessie.

"How did you know I was here, Bessie?"

"*You* didn't bother telling me, did you? When I rang your hotel in Caracas, you'd left. So I called the commune to see if A.P. had heard from you.

"They said he was in Paris, and when he told me you'd arrived *yesterday* – it isn't fair of you, Janis, and my granddad will kill me when he gets his phone bill!"

"I'll arrange for your calls to be paid for, Bessie."

"That isn't my biggest worry! Jeremy was here and he didn't want me to tell you, Janis. If you'd seen how ill he looked – I had to tell you, didn't I?"

"Where is he now?"

"My friend, Sim, drove him to Nazareth and –"

"I've changed my mind," Janis cut in. "I don't want to know. Jeremy has something to get out of his system."

"And I've guessed what it is," said Bessie.

"But don't let it get to you like it did to me."

"It already has."

"Then you must harden yourself, as I finally have," Janis replied. "I'll be off to Canada shortly. If Jeremy wants to see me, he'll have to come where I am. If I'm working, I shan't let his fleeting presence interfere with my job."

"This doesn't sound like you, Janis."

"But you'd better believe it, Bessie. What I'm saying is, if our brother wants to go on risking his life, that's his decision and you and I must get on with ours."

"I've found out my real father is an Israeli."

Janis bit back the cautioning words she wanted to say and said instead, "I hope you find him."

Bessie could be heading for yet another painful experience, but there was no way Janis could save her. As she couldn't save Jeremy from the hazards of doing what he felt he must. It was time to disentangle their separate lives. For Janis to put their mutual tragedy behind her and truly begin again.

PART THREE

REPARATIONS

Chapter 1

Jeremy's talk with Izzie had caused him to see his hunt for clues as the threshing in the dark it was. All he had gained was a chipped image of his father.

What would Laura have done if she had learned that her husband was well-known at a San Juan brothel? – Though the "madam" had said Jake and the men he met with in a private room weren't there for the usual reason.

Why that house had featured as a business rendezvous Jeremy had not established, and it no longer mattered to him. It was as if a dizzying kaleidoscope of faces and places, gathering momentum as one informant passed him to the next, had stopped shimmering painfully, allowing him a new clarity of vision.

These were Jeremy's ruminations after emerging from Izzie's claustrophobic quarters into the dawn of a new day. Time to get his act together and that had better include ensuring he was physically fit to resume what A.P. called his "crusade."

He had flown to London that evening and was now a patient in the Humana Wellington Hospital, using the hiatus to plan a strategy. As Lola had planned hers from the outset, he thought while a physiotherapist exercised his limbs.

Who but Lola could have set him up for the car crash that maimed him? And that had to mean her initially urging him not to risk his life was a ploy to halt him before he began.

Side by side with Jeremy's cold conjecture was remembrance of Lola's warm smile – and if what he felt for her was love, more fool him! He'd refrained from so much as holding her hand. Treated her with the respect she didn't deserve.

She, though, was privately aiding and abetting the Mendez directors to protect the deal that was somehow connected to the assassinations. If it weren't, would the press secretary, Maria Santander, have mentioned it before hustling Jeremy away from the waiting journalists, on his first trip to Caracas?

Put that together with Izzie's remark that Jake Bornstein hadn't given a thought to the final outcome of his middleman dealings . . . It was then that Jeremy's vision had cleared.

What was there about that big bucks deal that necessitated such secrecy? Jeremy intended to find out. There had to be evidence locked away in the Mendez company offices – and Lola was the key.

"We'll soon have you back in circulation," said the physiotherapist before departing.

But not soon enough for Jeremy, though the need for vengeance was no longer spurring him on. Instead, he'd begun to fear that the deal that had cost Jake and Laura their lives might result in irreparable damage if he didn't succeed in getting it stopped.

*   *   *

Though Janis too had undergone a change of attitude, moving on to yet another country was not in itself a positive step, and made to seem the less so by her zany companion.

Also by my own apathy, Janis reflected when she found herself – how better to describe it? – in the Canadian capital. Unable to decide between Ottawa and Toronto, nor to say why she had selected those two cities, Claudia had tossed a coin and Ottawa had won.

While Claudia was arranging her nursing training, Janis, still undecided in that respect, spent her time exploring the city, charmed by the plethora of gardens and parks.

"You should see this in springtime," said an old gentleman pausing beside her on the lawn surrounding the Peace Tower, on Parliament Hill.

"It looks fine in summertime, to me!" Acres of brilliant green sward were visible on all sides, the neo-Gothic Parliament buildings seeming majestic against a blue sky.

"But in May, we always get tulips and daffs from the Dutch government. They haven't forgotten Canada's hospitality to their Royal Family during the war, I guess. Oh, and I forgot the crocuses! You should just see Confederation Square when they're out.

"You a tourist?" he asked, taking off his ancient Panama, to mop his brow with a blue polka-dot handkerchief.

"Sort of," she answered wryly.

"Did you notice the gargoyles on the Peace Tower?"

"Since they were several feet high, they'd be difficult to miss!"

He bade her a courteous farewell and went on his way – halting again, beside a plump, middle-aged couple, she noted, and engaging them in conversation while they gazed up at the Tower.

Was this how the old gentleman filled in his days? There

was something about him that despite his cheerfulness bespoke an inner loneliness. A kindred spirit! thought Janis. But her compassion for him mustn't be allowed to spill over into self-pity. The bulk of his life was now behind him. Janis still had long years ahead of her, and what she would make of them was up to her.

Meanwhile, she was still allowing events to buffet her from place to place, devoid of the reassuring anchor everyone needed, be it a person or a career.

Claudia, however, seemed to have found hers, returning triumphantly that afternoon to the furnished flat Janis had rented on Rideau Street.

"Well, I've done it, Janis. I've enrolled!"

"But will you stick with it?"

Claudia tossed her crimson beret on the sofa and eyed Janis witheringly. "What a bucket of cold water you are!"

"I'm trying to keep your feet on the ground."

"The bedpans will do that – and all I've done is change my ambition," Claudia declared. "I've never been one to give up easily, Janis, but I finally had to accept I wasn't going to make it in the theater."

"What makes you think you'll make it as a ministering angel?"

"How can I know I won't, till I try?"

"A negative approach, if ever I heard one," said Janis.

"But more productive than having *no* approach to life," Claudia countered, "which I'm hoping is only temporary with you, Janis."

"I'm still licking my wounds, aren't I?" Janis answered defensively.

"But it'll take something a lot more positive than that to heal them," said Claudia, "and I'm utterly guilt-ridden because I'll be living-in while I'm training. Instead of staying here with you."

"This won't be the first time I've lived alone in a foreign country."

"But what will you *do*, Janis? Wealthy you may be, but you're not the lady of leisure sort." Claudia glanced at her wrist, the gold Omega she had worn in Paris conspicuous by its absence. "Would you mind lending me the cash to buy a serviceable wristwatch, by the way?"

"You ought to've let me buy your plane ticket, instead of hocking your parents' twenty-first birthday present to pay for it," Janis rebuked her.

Claudia replied with a shrug, "It wasn't the right watch for my new career. And I simply can't take advantage of your generosity, Janis – which I am doing, of course, by living here for free."

"Will you stop this?" Janis interrupted. "We're friends. If our financial situations were reversed, wouldn't you do the same for me?"

"Sure, but my only chance of ever being wealthy, since Daddy cut me out of his will, is to marry for money. Like my sister did," Claudia added with disgust, "though she's still *in* the will. If and when I marry, it will be utterly and completely for love."

Janis, gazing through the window at the Rideau Canal winding its way through the heart of the city, turned in astonishment. "I can't believe what I'm hearing, Claudia!"

"I'm not expecting to be off men permanently, Janis. For a passionate female like me, it wouldn't be practical. How about you?"

"My feelings on the subject remain as they were in Paris."

"And are you *sure* that Jesse's being a doctor isn't stopping you from becoming a nurse?"

"Right now, the only thing I'm sure of is I hate his guts!"

Claudia tossed Janis an apple from the bag she had brought in with her. "Gnash your teeth on this and pretend it's him!"

They burst out laughing, as they had at the lunch table on the Rue de Rivoli.

"Who's going to rouse me from the blues when you're no longer living here?" Janis asked wryly.

"You're not thinking of moving on, then?"

"Where would I move on to?"

Janis glanced again through the window. Traffic was now streaming homeward at the end of another working day. Would she ever again know a place that felt like home to her? Or experience the fulfillment that went with a worthwhile career?

"I truly hope that nursing will prove meaningful for you," she said to Claudia, "and forgive me for being the wet blanket I've been."

"What's brought this on, Janis?"

"Though once it wouldn't have occurred to me, it strikes me now that every woman should have something that's hers alone, as men do. That will still be there to occupy and sustain her if things go wrong in her personal life."

"Then take your own advice."

"I would, if I knew how."

Claudia sat down on the sofa, her peacock blue dress a violent splash of color in a room whose decor was nothing if not subdued. "What did you study at college, Janis?"

"Psychology. I even got my degree!"

"There you are, then," said Claudia, "you could get positively oodles of jobs with that qualification. Including personnel work with a big company and you could end up married to the boss –"

"Men again!" Janis exclaimed. "And what you just said equates with you dreaming of marrying the hospital administrator –"

"Not if he's the chap I saw coming out of an office with 'Administrator' on the door," said Claudia, "but some of the young doctors I passed on the corridors certainly gave me the once-over."

"Would you mind not mentioning doctors to me!"

"Does that mean you wouldn't come to my wedding, if I married one?"

"Dependent upon how long it takes you to catch one, I may be over my hang-up in time to be your bridesmaid – and what a bloody ridiculous conversation this is!" said Janis. "Why is it that no matter what we begin talking about, we end up discussing men?"

"We're women, aren't we?"

"And that's no help to me."

A telephone call from Bessie then distracted Janis and Claudia went to take a shower.

"Remember the birthmark I have on my arm, Janis?"

"You're ringing up from Israel to ask me that?"

"I hated having it, didn't I? But now I'm glad it's there," Bessie went on excitedly. "It's evidence that I'm my father's daughter and I may have found him –"

"Hold your horses, love," said Janis. "I'm trying to make sense of what you're saying."

"There's nothing to make sense of," Bessie declared. "They do run in families, and Hildegard mentioned a new customer who eats every night at the restaurant who has a birthmark exactly like mine, in exactly the same place.

"Grandpa was cross with her for telling me," Bessie added. "Like Grandma Shirley, he'd rather I didn't find my father!"

"Because the outcome, if you do, might not be the one you

hope for," Janis said in their defense, "and that worries me, too."

"But I can't go on not knowing, Janis — not unless I have to, and that man could be him."

"Thanks for telling me, Bessie."

"And I'll keep you informed."

Janis had had to stop herself from saying she would come to Israel, from offering Bessie comfort and support. But her resolve in Paris that she and her brother and sister must each live their own lives must be maintained.

How I envy Jeremy and Bessie the sense of purpose that I continue to lack, she was thinking when another telephone call interrupted her reflections.

"Miss Bornstein?"

Her father's lawyer, his fruity voice instantly recognizable.

"I appreciate your leaving your new address with my secretary," he said when they had exchanged pleasantries, "and may I say that in that respect you are more considerate than your brother."

"You certainly may, Mr. Adams!"

"Having agreed on that, I hope we shall reach agreement on the subject of this call, namely, the Foundation for which your late father had set money aside. A great deal of money, I might add, and he had requested that I be the Foundation's administrator. Would that arrangement be suitable to you and to your brother?"

"I don't see why not."

Mr. Adams cleared his throat before continuing, "Since your father specified only that it was to be a medical foundation, his heirs must decide exactly how the money will be spent. Perhaps you'd discuss the matter with your brother, Miss Bornstein."

If I can find him! "There's no shortage of medical projects in need of money," she said, "and a clinic for AIDS patients would be high on my list."

Mr. Adams replied, "Would your father have wished his name to be associated with such a clinic?"

"Both he and my stepmother would have approved. But if you'd prefer not to administer the Bornstein Foundation, in view of my intention, other arrangements can be made."

A pause followed during which Janis imagined the portly lawyer seated at his desk, trying to decide between his conservative reputation and the money his firm would forego if he picked up the gauntlet she had just tossed over the transatlantic line.

"Other arrangements would be preferable," he said eventually.

A man of principle – for want of a worse way of putting it!

"I'll let you know when I've engaged your replacement," Janis told him frigidly, "and it will probably be a law firm here in Ottawa. I'll be taking a personal interest in the Foundation and I'd like to get on with it."

Janis replaced the receiver and stood with her words echoing in her ears. When was there last anything in my life that I wanted to get on with? But the Foundation was a way of making amends for whatever her father might have done to cause his and Laura's terrible end. Janis had found her sense of purpose.

Chapter 2

A. P. was inspecting the camp site prepared for his young guests when his father appeared at his side.

"Sorry to startle you, A.P.!"

"When did you get back from the States, Dad?"

"We flew in this morning and came straight here. To tell you we tied the knot a couple of days ago," said Martin Dean.

The girlfriend A.P. hadn't met was now his stepmother!

His father put an arm around his shoulders. "You'll like her, I promise –"

"But why wasn't I invited to the wedding?"

"Can I talk to you man to man?"

"The last time you said that to me," A.P. recalled, "was when I was ten and you told me about the birds and the bees. I didn't let on that I already knew."

They shared a laugh and went to sit on the upturned boat beside the lake, where an ancient oak provided shade from the midday sun.

"This weather is as good as we left behind in California," Martin remarked.

"Well, the summer of 1989 isn't the usual British kind –" said A.P.

"Nor was it in *sixty*-nine."

"I was about to add that global warming is now affecting weather patterns worldwide and –"

"No need for an ecology lecture!" Martin cut in with a grin. "My bride and I have stopped using aerosols –"

"How can you remember what the weather was like in '69? A.P. harked back. And why are we *discussing* the weather? Like the strangers we're not. As if we're carefully treading our way back to familiar ground that can never be quite the same again."

"One tends to remember the details attached to major moments in one's life," Martin answered, "and the summer of '69 was when I asked my mother if she'd mind her grandchildren being Catholic.

"We were sitting on a bench in her garden," he recalled with a faraway look in his eyes, "and the air was heavy with the scent of roses. Your gran was dressed-up for a dinner party she and my father were giving for some of his clients and hadn't expected me to walk in and begin eating the cocktail snacks she'd prepared for the guests –

"She slapped my hand to stop me! As for *why* I'd walked in on her, A.P., it was your Grandfather Kyverdale's birthday and your mum, not yet my wife, had gone to a family celebration. To which I wasn't invited. So there I was, all alone on a Saturday night . . ."

"Did Mum get invited to *your* family celebrations before you were married?"

"Need you ask? She was always made welcome in my parents' home. My first visit to Kyverdale Hall, though – and that's what it felt like – was on my wedding day," Martin said brusquely. "The reception was in the banqueting room, though it was to have been in the garden. I remember the weather on that day, too," he went on, "and me standing alone beside a window, while your mum mingled with the upper crust guests!"

"What was Gran's reply to your question about giving her Catholic grandchildren? If I've been a source of sorrow for her, she hasn't shown it," said A.P.

"You've been anything but, so get that out of your head," said his father, "and her answer to me was that all she wanted was for me to be happy. I was thinking of it while I stood watching the storm, wondering if it was an omen – and so it turned out to be."

A.P. said after a silence, "Do you still blame Mum for all the unhappiness you shared?"

Martin shook his head. "We were doomed from the start, A.P. I was never really accepted by her parents."

"Do you think I didn't know that?"

"And *she* felt swallowed up by the clan I'm part of, is the only way I can put it. Guilty, too, for marrying out of her faith – which I didn't feel since my mother had given me her blessing."

Martin switched his pensive gaze from the shimmering lake to his son. "This time, though, we've both toed the religious line."

A.P.'s mother was now Mrs. Hugh Bellingham.

"What's her new husband like?" Martin inquired.

"*You* would call him a self-opinionated, upper crust ass, Dad, and I'd agree."

"Sounds the sort her father would've thought right for her! But she can now be at peace with herself. That's what your mother needs, A.P. And Trish is what *I* need. She pets and pampers me like you wouldn't believe."

And you look like the cat that's got the cream, thought A.P., noting his father's beatific smile. "Is the man-to-man talk over?" he said.

"Not quite. You asked why you weren't invited to the wedding and the reason is, it wasn't yet on the agenda. But Trish found she was pregnant, and in some ways I'm still an old-fashioned guy."

His father's living with a woman had come as a shock to A.P., and he recalled Jeremy's saying when they discussed it, "Why should we expect our elders to behave differently from us?"

The joke, though, was that A.P. was probably the only male virgin of his generation in the land! Thanks to Mary Lou.

"Where *is* your bride?" he asked his father.

"I left her sitting in the car, while we had our chat."

"Did she mind?"

"She isn't the minding sort," said Martin as they climbed the lakeside bank and headed for the house.

"After Mum, that must be nice for you. And you're looking great, Dad. Including your outfit."

Martin glanced down at his designer jeans and shirt. "Rodeo Drive is where my clothes now come from, and Trish does the shopping."

"She's certainly made you over!"

"In more ways than one," said Martin.

And A.P. was grateful to her for the revitalizing aspect of that. As he had to be to Hugh Bellingham for transforming his mum from the unhappy woman she was.

Oh, the healing power of love, A.P. reflected. But the unrequited kind could have the opposite effect.

"I was amused to hear that Bill Dryden's daughter had joined your commune," said his father, telepathically.

"Why amused?"

"Well, you and Mary Lou didn't hit it off too well when you were kids, did you? Which Bill and I attributed to your both being only children accustomed to getting your own way."

Martin added dryly, "Left it a bit late to remedy that for you, haven't I?"

"When is the baby due?"

"Not till next spring. And it will be born and raised in its mother's country, A.P. I've decided to buy the house I've been renting in Beverly Hills and you'll always be welcome there."

"As you will be here, Dad."

Would this remain for Martin, as it would for A.P., one of those major moments he had mentioned? Father and son side by side, striding along a tree-lined path, the sun beating down upon them and the smile they had just exchanged sealing their closeness, despite their ever more separate lives.

"Can you stay till the kids get here for the camp, Dad?" he asked. "Ben will be one of them –"

"And I'd love to see how he's turned out, but I have to be back in L.A. for a recording tomorrow."

"I appreciate your making this flying visit to tell me your news. And I'm looking forward to meeting Trish – most women would bash a chap over the head for leaving them sitting in a car this long!"

"But *she* won't," said Martin, "and she looks on this trip as the honeymoon we wouldn't otherwise have had – though we'll have spent a chunk of it aboard Concorde."

"Concorde, eh? You must be doing extremely well."

"And spending most of what I earn," Martin replied, "but

as Trish would say, it's only money. If and when it's gone, we'll still have each other."

From what A.P. had heard about marriages in his father's new habitat, he wasn't too sure of that. But he wasn't yet acquainted with the woman concerned – who was gone from the limousine waiting on the forecourt.

"Mrs. Dean said she needed the bathroom again," the chauffeur relayed.

"And she isn't taking a bath!" Martin said to A.P. as they entered the house. "We had to stop several times on the way here, and it was the same with your mum when she was expecting you. I remember her frequently getting up in the night and me getting no sleep –"

"And now you'll have to go through all that again."

"All that and what comes afterwards. And before you know it, the infant that kept you awake when it was teething is a teenager giving you a different sort of sleepless night."

"When did I give you sleepless nights, Dad?"

Martin was saved from replying by Henry Moritz's emerging from the corridor they were about to enter.

"If you're going to ask me what I'm doing here, Martin, that's a question I'm still asking myself! Your charming wife is in the kitchen, drinking coffee. Allow me to congratulate you – and if you'll excuse me, I must dash to a meeting."

"A meeting with whom?" Martin inquired, watching Henry's receding back.

"He's co-ordinating the camp leisure activities with the work program committee –"

"And dashing," said Martin with a grin as they went on their way, "was always Henry's style in more ways than one!"

But "charming" was not the adjective A.P. would choose to describe his first impression of Trish, who was for him yet another shock.

Perched on a corner of the kitchen table, her long legs revealed by a white mini-skirt, she was "holding court" – as the late Lady Kyverdale might have put it – and her male audience roaring with laughter about something she had evidently just said.

Gary Potter, who was spending his college vacation at the commune, remarked to the others, "I don't recall the coffee breaks here usually being this entertaining."

"The girls, though, seem to've made their escape," said Trish dryly, "and back home that wouldn't happen, would it, Mart?" she added, patting her pink coiffeur.

"When Trish is around, the women cling on to their men like limpets."

"And when I breezed in here and said I'm your stepmom, they didn't seem to believe me," she told A.P. "Going to give me a kiss?"

"I wouldn't mind deputizing for him," said Gary.

"It won't be that kind of kiss."

More laughter from the lads while A.P. pecked her cheek, she tousled his hair, and his father watched approvingly.

"Promise you'll come visit us," she said when eventually he went with them to the car.

"And let's talk more often on the phone," said Martin.

A.P. watched the vehicle bear them away, he not yet recovered from the encounter. He'd visualized Trish as a woman nearing the end of her child-bearing years suddenly finding herself pregnant. Not the sexy young girl she'd turned out to be.

He emerged from his thoughts and saw Mary Lou leaning against a tree. "Got nothing better to do?" he joked.

"I thought you might need someone to talk to, when they'd gone," she said, coming to join him.

"Very perceptive of you, Mary Lou!"

"Well, it makes you think, doesn't it?"

"Makes you think what?"

"Come off it, A.P.! I know how you feel. The last couple of times I went home, Mom and Dad didn't seem to be hitting it off like they used to – could be the menopause, male and female both. Whatever, when I saw your mother's replacement, I thought, oh God, supposing what's happened to you happens to *me*?"

"A stepmother of my own generation, you mean?"

"She's hardly what you'd have chosen for your dad."

"Nor is Hugh Bellingham to my taste, but we're no more entitled to harbor expectations for our parents than they are for us, wouldn't you say?"

"You and your bloody fair-mindedness don't take into account human nature," Mary Lou responded. "Have you heard from Jeremy lately?"

"How did he get into this conversation?"

"Aren't you pleased I've actually mentioned him?"

"If it means you'll be civil to him when he comes to stay here."

"You've asked him to?"

"Any reason why I shouldn't?"

"No, your lordship!"

A.P. then observed the first busload of children turning the bend in the drive, heads protruding from the vehicle's windows.

"Better get Henry," he said to Mary Lou, "I think it's the French lot –"

By the evening, A.P. was exhausted as were his friends, but exhilarated, too, as he and Henry made the rounds of the tents, each bearing the national flag of its young occupants.

"I thought of putting up a bed for Ben in my room," he

said, when finally they were returning to the house, "but singling him out wouldn't be right."

"Nor," said Henry, "is he necessarily the child prodigy you think him."

"You haven't yet heard him play the piano —"

"And I wouldn't consider myself a judge of musical, or any other artistic genius. What I said, A.P., was just a spot of general advice."

"About what?"

"I said *general*, didn't I?" Henry halted to glance back at the camp site, the bell tents pitched in a circle in the center of a meadow and lit by the August moon. "You're entitled to feel elated by what you've achieved, A.P., but I wish I'd said to you sooner what I'm now going to.

"If your intention is to bring together kids from different countries, why isolate them from each other when you get them here? And emphasize it with the flags?"

"They're less likely to get homesick sharing a tent with others who speak their language," A.P. replied. "As for the flags, we thought they'd be decorative —"

"Like those adorning the United Nations building in New York! But flags are the emblems of nationalism, aren't they? — Which, like religion, is responsible for many of the ills of the world," Henry said with feeling. "If you'd like me to reel off a list, I will —"

"Okay, I get your point," said A.P. "Tomorrow we'll take down the flags."

"No," said Henry, "the kids would wonder why. But next year, A.P., no flags, and mixed tents, please."

"Boys and girls?"

Henry smiled. "That you'll get happening anyway, with the older kids, so be prepared. About the language problem, on my travels I've seen people who don't speak the same tongue manage to communicate. You'll see that happening here during work projects and at play – so why not in the tents?"

Henry paused only for breath before launching into his next topic. "As to the arts school you're planning, A.P., why restrict it to only talented children? If you'd like my advice –"

"I'm going to get it anyway!"

"Since the project is still in the embryo stage, now is the time for me to offer it to you. If I were you, A.P., I'd concentrate on the therapeutic value of the arts, rather than set up something for budding geniuses who'd eventually make it without your help."

"You haven't forgotten how to deliver a lecture, have you?" A.P. said with a laugh.

"Well, I did once briefly earn my bread that way. And you'd never have thought of the arts project if you hadn't heard Ben play, would you?" Henry said as they resumed walking.

"The idea for the camp began with Ben, too. Got a stone in your sandal?" A.P. asked when Henry halted abruptly.

"More to the point, have you perhaps got a bat in your belfry?"

"Only with respect to Mary Lou!"

"Are you sure you're not reorganizing your life because you have a soft spot for Ben? He's Howard's child, not yours, A.P."

"And the way things are looking, Henry, I'm unlikely to have children of my own."

"Mary Lou isn't the only girl in the world."

"But given your still unmarried state, because you didn't get the girl you wanted –"

"I asked you not to emulate me!"

Henry strode on, his expression as intense as was his tone. "That's one piece of advice you'd be wise to heed, A.P."

"Why are you always putting yourself down, Henry?"

"I've made a mess of my life and I don't want that to happen to you."

They trudged on in pensive silence, moonlight filtering through the fretwork of treetops overhead and the dark bulk of Kyverdale Hall looming at the far end of the avenue, its mullioned windows reflecting the lamplights within.

Would the stately home he had inherited ever *feel* like home to A.P.? Not without Mary Lou.

"Without her, my work will have to be enough," he voiced his thoughts to Henry.

"Work, however rewarding, can never be enough, A.P. Nor does any situation stand still."

The situation ever in the forefront of A.P.'s mind erupted the following morning, when Mary Lou told him she would leave the commune unless he withdrew his invitation to Jeremy.

"How could I possibly do that?" he replied.

They were helping serve breakfast in the banqueting hall, now an improvised canteen, huge containers of food and plastic dishes lined-up on the ancient refectory table where A.P.'s ancestors had once eaten haunch of venison and roast suckling pig on gold plates.

"Always the perfect gentleman, damn you!" Mary Lou flashed.

"And it strikes me that you're no lady."

"But you wanted to make me Lady Kyverdale."

"I still do."

"Damn you for that, too."

They were interrupted by another batch of children queuing for homemade muesli and wholewheat toast. Then Mary Lou resumed speaking without switching her gaze from the table.

"I didn't mean to hurt you, A.P. I respect you and if I could love you, I would. Unfortunately for me, it's *him* I love. And I hate myself and him too, because of it."

A.P. had to be dreaming this. Mary Lou in love with Jeremy?

"I can't go on keeping it from you," she went on, "and my dearest wish is to find out it's just infatuation. But that still hasn't happened – And having him staying here –"

She burst into tears and fled.

A.P. emerged from his stunned state and saw Gary Potter watching him from the other end of the table.

"Go after her, you dope!"

Mary Lou was leaning against one of the trees bordering the forecourt, and said when A.P. handed her his handkerchief to dry her eyes, "I suppose I've made you now hate Jeremy –"

Did he? No, it would take more than a girl, even Mary Lou, to drive a wedge between them.

"But I feel better for telling you."

The same could not be said of A.P.

In the days that followed, his plan to bring together children of different nationalities unfurled like a colorful tapestry before his eyes; youthful friendships made working side by side in the orchards and the fields, campfire singsongs in the evenings, and above all the tolerance he had feared might be the missing ingredient, as too often it was with adults.

But these kids would have this experience to look back on and how could it not influence their adult attitudes? he thought as the first week drew to an end. Henry was right though, work satisfaction wasn't enough, and how was A.P. to come to terms with Jeremy's unwitting role?

Chapter 3

What are you doing here? As if I didn't know!" said Bessie's grandfather when she dropped in to the restaurant, a falsely nonchalant expression on her face and wearing her best frock.

"But Professor Harim hasn't yet arrived," said Hildegard, glancing at an unoccupied table by the window.

"My father's a professor?"

Peter Kohn glared at his wife. "Why did you tell her the poor, innocent fellow's name! The conclusion you're jumping to," he told Bessie, "could land you in court on a slander charge, and the mud will stick to me, too."

"All I want to do is look at him, Grandpa."

"And then what?"

"I don't know."

"But *I* do. For the first time in my life I agree with your grandmother. The dad your mum gave you couldn't have been a better one, Bessie. He treated you like a blood daughter, didn't he? Even in his will."

"But my opinion," said Hildegard, "is that Bessie's nonetheless entitled to know who fathered her."

"The scandal wouldn't bother you?"

"Did you let that bother *you*, when you left Shirley to marry *me*?"

They exchanged a smile reminiscent of young lovers, though love for each other had come late in their lives.

"My grandmother probably gave Grandpa a dog's life," Bessie correctly surmised, "and I'm glad he's now happy."

"But you're not and we can't have that," said Hildegard, while placing portions of Sachertorte on a tray, beside glasses of lemon tea. "For table four, Peter –"

"And I and they have been waiting for it long enough! There's no time to stand gossiping this evening, Bessie. We're short of help, Shoshannah's got one of her migraines."

"Then why don't I give you a hand? I'd be willing to any time."

"That wasn't why we gave you a home," said Peter before departing with the tray.

Hildegard's response was, "Get yourself an apron, Bessie."

"Where do you keep the clean ones?"

"In *my* kitchen you won't find any soiled ones."

Hildegard was stationed at the serving hatch dividing the restaurant from the cooking area, the appetizing aroma of her homely cuisine drifting from the stoves ranged behind her.

Bessie tied a starched, blue apron around her waist and went to stand beside her, her gaze drawn as if by a magnet to the still unoccupied table by the window.

"Grandpa will take the Professor's order and you can take him his meal," said Hildegard. "Meanwhile we have other hungry customers to serve, so let's get on with it."

Bessie was kept busy carrying trays to and fro until ten o'clock, when Hildegard told her to take a break.

"You and Grandpa aren't having a break –"

"We never do," said Hildegard, garnishing the veal schnitzels she had just transferred from the frying pan to large oval plates, "and I have to laugh when I remember how I was waited on, in my Viennese youth. Peter, too. We had cooks and maids.

"Our families lived next door to each other, did you know that, Bessie?"

"Grandpa never speaks of those days, but he did tell my mum that you and he went to school together."

Hildegard added creamed potato and spinach to the plates. "He doesn't speak of them even to me. And I sometimes think that what we afterwards went through erased Peter's happy memories. We were lucky to escape with our lives and that can give a person a special sense of values."

"You're telling me this for a reason, aren't you?" Bessie sensed.

"And he's just come into the restaurant."

Bessie saw an elderly man walk with the aid of a stick to the table by the window and lower his tall, thin frame onto a chair.

"Shalom, Professor," she heard her grandfather say, but a sudden buzzing in her ears shut out the professor's reply.

Hildegard eyed Bessie's agonized expression. "It took time for you to pluck up courage to do what you're doing, my dear, and this is a big moment for you. But as one swallow doesn't make a summer, a birthmark doesn't ensure that he is your father."

"It seems fated for him and me to meet, though. Me coming to live with you and Grandpa, and him having his meals in *your* restaurant."

"Forget fate, Bessie. Why he eats here is he enjoys my cooking, like the other men who come each evening while their wives are away, or after they're widowed.

"But what I said about a sense of values – though you are a very rich girl now, I know in my heart that no matter what the money can buy for you, you won't enjoy it till you know who you are.

"And by the way, the professor is a linguist, Bessie, you can converse with him in English."

"You seem to know a lot about him."

"I made it my business to, but don't tell your grandpa!" said Hildegard as her husband came to the hatch to give her the professor's order.

"While he's waiting, he'd like his usual bottle of water," said Peter. "Bessie can take it to him."

Despite his reservations, Grandpa, like Hildegard, knows I *have* to find my father, thought Bessie, surveying with gratitude the aging couple who had seemed too busy to remember she lived under their roof.

She watched Hildegard, a dumpy little woman who must once have been a pretty girl, begin preparing the professor's salad, while Peter fetched the mineral water from the refrigerator, his appearance still boyish if you didn't count his lined face.

"Thanks for everything," Bessie said to them.

"But I need my brains testing," said Peter, "and my wife her bottom smacking for even mentioning the professor to you!"

He put ice and lemon into a glass, opened the bottle and noted Bessie's trembling hands as she picked up the tray. "Mind you don't spill it on his lap!"

Such was the tension within her, the warning was necessary, the more so when she reached the table and the professor said, "You must be the English granddaughter Mr. Kohn told me was standing in for Shoshannah."

Her grandpa had paved the way, and the man who might be her father – though the only resemblance between them was the star-shaped birthmark Bessie was now eyeing – was giving her a friendly smile.

"My mother was the photojournalist, Laura Kohn," she replied while pouring the water.

"Really?"

"She died last year."

"I'm sorry to hear that."

Though he was unlikely to confess a long-ago love affair, Bessie waited with bated breath.

"She once did a magazine feature on the other professor in my family, and I remember how nervous he was about posing for pictures."

"My mum knew how to put people at ease."

"So Zvi said, when he got back from London."

This nice old gentleman wasn't Bessie's father. But she now had a name to attach to the hope in her heart.

"Zvi was never the self-confident sort," he told her.

And I'm just like him.

"Your mother was the first and last person to persuade him to sit for photographs."

Bessie couldn't imagine any man resisting Laura when she'd turned on the charm – and it was probable that photographs weren't the only results of Zvi's trip to London.

"He is a brilliant archeologist, by the way," said Professor Harim, "and at the time had just completed a remarkable dig, I recall – which accounted for the flurry of media interest in him."

"Does he live in Tel Aviv?" Bessie asked, trying to keep her tone casual.

"If you can call it living," said the professor with a sigh. "My poor brother is afflicted by a terrible sickness of the soul."

"I'm not sure what that means –"

"And I don't find it easy to talk about Zvi – I try not to think about him and why I am discussing him with you . . . ?" He took off his pince-nez and regarded them pensively. "What it proves, I suppose, is it doesn't take much to bring everything back.

"I haven't seen him for years, my dear. None of the family has. He doesn't want visitors, you see, and there seems nothing to be done for him."

Bessie could not stop herself from saying, "But *I* must see him. He could be my father."

The professor then noticed the birthmark on her forearm and said, "Good God!"

She left him to recover while she fetched his meal and said, after placing it before him, "Grandpa won't mind my sitting with you while you eat, if *you* don't."

"By all means do, though it's a whiskey I now need, not food!"

"But please eat your dinner, or Hildegard will be upset," Bessie said, sitting down opposite him.

"I'll do my best. And you can't be the only young person nowadays wanting to know who fathered them," he answered with another of the sighs that punctuated his conversation.

"My brother, however," he declared, collecting himself, "was a devoted family man – or he might not be in his present plight. After losing his wife and his sons, he did what is commonly called 'taking to the bottle,' though he was never more than a social drinker till then."

"How did he lose them?"

This time, the professor's sigh was accompanied by a weary shrug. "The way many Israelis have lost dear ones over the years. A bus they were traveling in was hijacked by Arab terrorists. The gory details I'll spare you."

He stopped picking at his schnitzel and put down his fork. "About the birthmark, Zvi doesn't have it, though our mother did –"

"But it's no longer just the birthmark, is it?" Bessie cut in. "Not now I know that your brother knew my mum. If I've upset you, Professor, I'm truly sorry."

"Upsetting me doesn't matter. And would I be sitting here giving you my family pedigree, if I hadn't put two and two together?"

Professor Harim drank some water and contemplated the slice of lemon in the glass. "Even the most unlikely of men have been known to have their moments, but that's hard to relate to my brother."

"Do you happen to remember when it was that he went to England?"

"Ordinarily I wouldn't, but he returned to Israel on the eve of the '73 war."

"I was born in 1974."

"Did I ask you to provide more evidence?" he said with a tetchiness that Bessie sensed was a mask for his emotions.

"Does that mean you'll let me have your brother's address?"

"If I didn't, a determined girl like you would find out, anyway."

"Nobody ever called me that, before."

"Then they evidently didn't know you and I wouldn't mind being your Uncle Moshe. If you'd like me to, I'll take you to meet Zvi. Who knows that finding he still has a living child won't do for him what the liquor can't?"

Chapter
4

Janis had wasted no time in finding an Ottawa law firm to administer the Bornstein Foundation.

"Any special reason you requested a woman lawyer?" asked Isobel McLeod at their first meeting.

"You certainly know how to ask a direct question!"

"And if you can't handle that, I'm not the lawyer for you."

"Okay. I'm off men at the moment."

"That's fine by me," said Isobel. "If you weren't, I wouldn't have been assigned to administer a wealthy foundation, and that's one up for the women in this firm."

They exchanged a smile and Janis glanced around the cubicle into which Isobel had invited her. "Why not use it to get yourself a better office?"

"That had already crossed my mind. Shall we now get down to business? And I'd better warn you that my Scottish thriftiness won't allow you to just throw money around.

"Once the Foundation becomes public knowledge," Isobel went on, "we shall have to deal carefully with representatives of heart-rending causes pleading their case to be included."

Janis mentioned her plan to build a clinic for AIDS patients.

Isobel's reaction was, "You're sure one on your own."

"Someone in my family died of the disease."

"Babies are now dying of it," Isobel said with feeling, "but the righteous are still turning their backs."

"With one notable exception, mine isn't a righteous family," said Janis, blotting out a picture of Shirley at her worst. "We all stood by the person I mentioned. I'd like to help those whose families deny them that support."

"And we'd get the project off the ground faster by buying a building, instead of erecting one," said Isobel, making notes. "Have you decided where the clinic will be situated?"

"I hadn't given it a thought. But why not in Ottawa, since I'm currently living here?"

Isobel took off her spectacles to polish them, which transformed the sober appearance enhanced by her gray, tailored suit.

"I only wear contact lenses when I let my hair down," she said with a smile, patting her dark chignon, "at parties where I don't run into my male colleagues!"

"A man, though," said Janis with disgust, "can be himself in his working world."

"Not necessarily," Isobel replied. "In mine, the right image is required of men, too. Shall we discuss it further over lunch? Right now, you're paying for my time.

"And before setting the ball rolling on the clinic project, can I double-check with you on your split-second decision to site it in Ottawa?"

"What is there to check?"

"When our senior partner briefed me, he mentioned that

you'd be taking a close interest in the work of the Foundation. Since Canada isn't your permanent base, and your reason for requesting a woman lawyer has to be called an emotional one, I need to be sure you're thinking with your head."

Janis smiled wryly. "I no longer have a permanent base. And all I'm interested in is the good work the Foundation can do. Geography doesn't enter into it, though I see no reason why the money shouldn't be put to use in numerous countries. Disease knows no national boundaries.

"The AIDS clinic is just *one* of the projects I have in mind and, though my father specified it was to be a medical foundation, I'd like to help sponsor the work being done by ecologists here in Canada. I've heard that the rivers close to Niagara Falls are now so polluted, local people are scared to eat the fish."

"And this is beginning to sound to me," said Isobel, "as if you'd like the Bornstein Foundation to help cure diseases and also to rescue the world."

She put down her pen and added warmly, "I share your feelings, but even with the huge sum of money at your disposal it can't be done. You're going to have to decide whether to give just a few causes a great deal of benefit, or sprinkle it around. I know which I'd do."

Janis put away the long list she had taken from her handbag. "Thanks for straightening me out."

That evening, Janis heard from her brother for the first time since his disappearance.

"The family grapevine can always be relied on to know where you are," Jeremy joked when she answered the telephone.

"But not where *you* are."

"I needed time to think – without any sisterly interference."

"Was the anxiety you've caused your sisters included in the thinking?"

"When you next see me, I'll be wearing my new hand."

How could he sound so nonchalant? But it was just a mask.

"Unless you'd care to pay me a flying visit now? I'm sitting in the lap of luxury at the Wellington."

Janis hardened her heart and matched his style. "The pub or the hospital? Whichever, I'm far too busy to come."

When she began telling him she had engaged a Canadian lawyer to administer the Bornstein Foundation, Jeremy cut her short.

"I'll leave all the decisions to you, Janis. Just let me know if you need me to sign anything."

"If I can find you! Bessie and I could be forgiven for assuming all you care about is your damned vendetta – and you were right about Jesse. I found out he's in cahoots with Lola, so watch your back!"

A pause followed, the crackling on the line heightening the sudden tension.

"When I left Caracas, I was positively paranoid," Janis said, "looking over my shoulder in case I was being followed – and I still feel as if something sinister is hovering over me."

"Which won't go away until we know who planted the car bomb and why."

Chapter
5

*A.*P.'s belief that even Mary Lou could not drive a wedge between him and Jeremy was shaken when he visited Jeremy at the hospital, though the poison had entered his soul before then.

What is it about you that's set Mary Lou alight, he thought resentfully while Jeremy outlined a plan to seduce information from Lola – and A.P. didn't doubt he would succeed.

"I find what you propose to do disgusting," A.P. declared, and with a rancor never before present in their relationship.

Jeremy offered him some fruit from the bowl on the table, helping himself to a peach when A.P. declined. "All's fair in love and war, as the Bard said. Was it the Bard?"

"What the hell do *you* know about love!"

"This happens to be war, though I think I'm in love with Lola."

"But nevertheless prepared to use her," said A.P. watching him sink his teeth into the ripe fruit – and how symbolic that was!

"Too much is at stake for me to be what you'd call honorable," Jeremy replied, "which Lola doesn't know the meaning of."

"You, neither," said A.P., "well, not where women are concerned."

"Where has your honorable attitude got you with Mary Lou?"

They were sitting on the balcony outside Jeremy's room. A stone's throw away was Lords cricket ground, but the time when A.P. and Jeremy in their boyhood had gone with their fathers to watch a test match now seemed like another life.

"It's got you nowhere, is the answer," Jeremy continued. "And what this conversation reminds me of is when we were together in West Berlin, before we went up to Oxford."

They had done the rounds of the night clubs and discos with a couple of attractive girls, but the evening had not climaxed as Jeremy had assumed it would.

"I couldn't believe it when you suddenly chickened out," he reminisced. "The blonde was the one I fancied, but I'd let you have her and made do with her friend."

"What a sacrifice that must have been for you!"

"But I didn't even get to lay the one I was with, did I? You went all honorable at the last minute and put paid to it for both of us."

"Honor didn't enter into it," said A.P., turning to look at Jeremy, sprawled in his chair and clad in a red silk dressing gown, now popping succulent black grapes into his mouth, one after another. "And what *you* remind me of is a Bacchanalian orgy!"

"Minus the women, unfortunately."

"I'm coming to think that 'decadent' is the word for you," A.P. went on, "and I have to be sorry for you."

Jeremy stiffened. "Oh yes?"

"You'd made up your mind on that trip to Germany that I would return home no longer a virgin, hadn't you?"

"But I failed miserably."

"Because I don't tick the way you do."

"Or you'd have had Mary Lou at your mercy long before now."

"If I can't win her with love, I wouldn't want her *your* way." A.P. glanced at his watch. "And it's time I left."

"How has the camp worked out?"

"The kids are saying they don't want to go home tomorrow."

"Good for you."

"I didn't organize and run it single-handed, Jeremy, and Henry's been especially helpful to me."

"He's your new mentor, I gather."

The unspoken implication was that Jeremy no longer occupied that position, and A.P. said quietly, "You and I seem to have gone our separate ways."

"In spirit as well as physically," said Jeremy averting his gaze to a trough of geraniums brightening the balcony, "and I wish we could go back to how we were. Before you became Lord Kyverdale, and a car bomb changed everything for me."

He turned to look at A.P. "What I'm saying is we're not the same people. But we've been friends for too long for that to end now."

Were it not for the erosive matter you know nothing about, thought A.P., Mary Lou's wanting *you*.

"Can I still ask you a favor, A.P.?"

"Don't be daft!"

"I shall need somewhere private and with a suitable ambience to invite Lola to —"

"And the Kyverdale villa amid the lemon groves in Menton would be ideal?"

They shared a laugh that lightened the atmosphere, then A.P. rose to leave.

"Much as I deplore your tactics, Jeremy, I'll let you have the key."

A.P.'s return to the estate was nothing if not traumatic. The sound of children's voices, to which he had become accustomed, was uncannily absent. Mary Lou and Nina were pacing outside the house and turned on him like twin tigresses.

"Where are you when you're needed?" Mary Lou snarled.

"Leaving others to shoulder *his* responsibility!" said Nina. "The commune agreed to cooperate, but the camp project is your baby, A.P.!"

"Would one of you mind telling me what this is about?"

"Ben's gone missing is what it's about," said Nina. "Some of the kids are in a terrible state about it, his sister especially."

A.P., trying to collect himself, turned and saw Magda sitting on the terrace steps, tears cascading down her face. "Why doesn't one of you try to comfort her?"

"I don't wish to be comforted," the little girl called.

"There's your answer," said Nina to A.P., "and for your further information, Gary is leading one of the search parties and Henry the other. We decided to organize it, rather than let all the kids go trampling about on their own."

Mary Lou now turned on Nina. "Trampling on the crops, you mean, and how could that be your first concern!"

"I meant nothing of the kind."

"Cool it," A.P. said to them.

"If you'd had the nerve-wracking time we've had –!" Mary Lou exclaimed.

"And it isn't over yet," said Nina, "nobody's seen Ben

since lunch, and Gary is considering getting the police in to drag the lake."

"Ben is a good swimmer," said Magda through her tears.

"And your boyfriend isn't a member of the commune," said Mary Lou to Nina. "Gary is considering indeed!"

"But if Ben had fallen into the lake too soon after his lunch, he might perhaps have got the cramp," Magda's imagination soared, "and I wish, now, that we had not come to the camp. My parents will not think that helping to save the earth was worth losing Ben, and nor do I.

"Ben wanted to accompany you to London, didn't he?" she said to A.P. "But you would not allow it!"

A.P. then felt himself the butt of three pairs of angry female eyes.

"Your absence has had some sort of catalytic effect upon Ben," Nina declared.

"Don't be ridiculous," he replied – though she could be right.

"Ben follows you around like the little lamb in the nursery rhyme," said Mary Lou, "and when you and Jeremy were at school together, you were probably *his* little lamb, since you still run the minute he beckons!"

Mary Lou had answered the telephone that morning when Jeremy called from the hospital. But how could she know that my unreasonable resentment of him impelled me to make a visit I'd rather not have made, A.P. was thinking when Gary Potter returned with a posse of children all talking volubly in their own languages.

"I feel like the bloody Pied Piper," said Gary, his stocky figure sagging with weariness, "and this lot have tramped their feet off for long enough."

"Also I wanted to be with Magda," said her little brother,

Rudy, pushing his way through the cluster of girls now surrounding her.

"I didn't say welcome back to you, A.P.!" Gary added sarcastically. "And what now?"

Was there nobody who didn't think that A.P. had neglected his responsibility? "I'd rather not call in the police unless I have to, Gary."

"So speaks the lord of the manor, a unilateralist born and bred."

"I shall take that from where it came, and if you'll all excuse me, I'll see if *I* can find Ben."

"Indoors has been thoroughly searched," Gary called as A.P. went into the house.

But not the west wing, which was kept locked. Only a determined child, though, would have climbed the drainpipe to enter through a window.

Ben was in the drawing room, seated at the Bechstein.

"I'd have hidden somewhere else, but I wanted it to be you who found me."

"What was the point of hiding if you intended being found?"

"I don't know."

"But what you must surely know is that you've given everyone here a terrible afternoon."

"That doesn't include you and it's you I care about."

"Then let me make it clear that the way you've behaved doesn't make me happy, nor is it the behavior I'd have expected of you."

"I wanted to go with you to London!"

"You saw all the sights with the other children, when we took all of you there. That ought to've been enough for you, as it was for them."

"It wasn't the outing that I wanted! It was to be with you.

And I'm not going home tomorrow. I'm not!" said Ben crashing the piano keys to emphasize his feelings.

"Why do I have to?" he went on excitedly. "I could stay here until you start your music school and be a pupil, couldn't I?"

A.P. steeled himself to be hard with a child in whom he had, from the first, seen himself at that age. Torn between the vastly differing backgrounds of his parents and dogged by confusions and uncertainties. Discovering his own identity hadn't been easy for A.P. Nor would it be for Ben.

"You promised me," Ben prodded him.

"That we'd try to arrange for you to be a pupil if I went ahead with my idea for a music school. I have to tell you I've now decided it will be a different kind of school –"

"I thought you were my friend!"

"And I always shall be, Ben, but the sort of school I now have in mind would help children a lot worse off than you."

"Nobody could be worse off than me," Ben said passionately. "I was born in England, but now I'm here, it doesn't feel like *my* country. Nor does Germany," he went on. "How could it, after what was done to my father's people by the Germans?

"And the day our class was taken to see Dachau, some of the boys were playing their transistors while we were being shown the ovens where people were put to death.

"They're the boys who say Hitler was right, who pass remarks about my nose and sneer when I say I'm not a Jew."

How many budding neo-Nazis were there, nurtured by the propaganda of those who knew how and where to inject it? thought A.P. recalling Howard's anxiety about raising his family in Germany.

But dwelling upon the horrendous past was in A.P.'s view unproductive. There had to be a new beginning that looked

to the future and the international summer camp would be
A.P.'s contribution to that. A means of children learning to
see each other only as fellow human beings.

"I haven't noticed any German kids behaving badly to the
Jewish ones at the camp," he said, going to sit beside Ben on
the piano stool, "nor white ones treating black ones badly."

"I didn't say they were all like that."

"How could you, when they're not."

"And one of the Norwegian boys told me he'd never
spoken to a black person," Ben confided, "but he and the
boy from Brixton whose father is a bus driver said, this
morning, that they're going to be pen friends."

Heartening for A.P. to learn, since Olaf's father was a
surgeon, that social chasms, too, were being bridged.

"Jeanne gave me her address in France," Ben added, "but
who wants a girl for a pen friend! I would much rather write
to her brother."

"Because Pierre's a musician, like you?"

"Because I like him and I'd hit anyone who called him a
Frog, as he would anyone who insulted my nose."

"No need for violence," said A.P. with a smile, "and next
time you and Pierre come to a summer camp, you can be in
the same tent."

"You'd have me here again?"

"If you promise not to give your mother a hard time, when
you get home. Her situation with respect to you isn't easy,
Ben."

"That's her fault, for leaving my dad and taking me to
where I don't belong."

Ben began playing the Chopin nocturne he had played in
Munich.

"Is that your favorite piece?" A.P. asked, but he received

no reply. The boy was already lost in the music, caressing the keys lovingly.

A.P. went to stand beside the empty hearth that Lady Kyverdale had kept filled with laurel leaves last summer, as enthralled now as he was on that memorable evening.

To call Pierre a musician was an exaggeration, though the French boy knew how to strum a guitar. But A.P.'s assessment of Ben's talent remained unshaken.

Not just the talent, but the presence, seated at the piano, with his flowing dark hair, like a miniature Ashkenazy.

Whether or not he also had the will and the stamina remained to be seen, but Ben must have his chance. Would his mother, who wanted him in her family printing business, stand in his way? And Howard, after A.P. had discussed it with him, try not to let her?

The answer was probably "yes" on both counts, with more conflict ahead for Ben.

Chapter
6

Which one is your bodyguard?" Jeremy asked Lola, glancing around at the assortment of men streaming from the terminal at Nice airport.

He eyed the loaded trolley a porter was pushing for her. "And why so much luggage? All you're going to need is a toothbrush!"

"I hadn't realized it was that sort of invitation."

"What other sort is there, when a guy asks a beautiful girl to share his vacation?"

"The word you used when you invited me was 'recuperation.'"

"I'm feeling stronger than I was then. Now's the time to change your mind if you're going to," said Jeremy as they halted by the limousine he had hired, "before all that stuff gets put in the car boot."

Lola laughed. "Run home to my mother? Oh no, Jeremy. If you're having second thoughts about your invitation, you'll have to do better than that. I'm not easy to frighten off."

"Even when I tell you Lord Kyverdale isn't in residence at his villa?"

"I didn't suppose that he would be," said Lola, "and I'd be surprised if there's even a maid there."

"Just a daily one." Round one to Lola! thought Jeremy. For taking the wind out of my sails.

"I've given my bodyguard some time off," she told him, "and by the way, I like your new hand."

"But it's the other one I'll be using to hold yours," he said more flippantly than he felt.

Lola waited until they were seated in the car before saying quietly, "You have a lot of courage."

"So I've discovered!"

"Inner resources you didn't know you had?"

"You could say that." Including a ruthlessness I must have inherited from my father, though I'm putting it to a different use than he did.

"Nobody knows quite what they're capable of until circumstances call for them to prove it," Lola went on.

Too true, thought Jeremy.

"I couldn't have imagined myself taking over my father's company, and certainly not for the purpose that's impelling me to do so."

Jeremy, who had been gazing through the window at an idyllically blue sky, turned to look at her, his senses captivated by her beauty, the blue-black hair framing a madonna's face, and the lush body clad in dusky-pink silk.

His mind, though, was sounding an alarm bell: she set you up for those failed brakes. This time *you* did the setting up, to get to *her*. Don't let her get to *you*.

"And what, exactly, is your purpose?" he replied. Not that she'd tell him the truth.

"Reparation," she declared. "At first, like you, I was concerned only with retribution, with punishing whoever had taken from me the father I adored. *Un*like you, however, I knew in my heart he might have done something to deserve that terrible end.

"I tried to discuss it with my mother, but all she said was, 'Let God be the judge.' She must have her suspicions," Lola added after a pause, "but if that's how she's come to terms with them, I must leave her in peace."

"I'm all for reparation along with the retribution," Jeremy revealed, wondering if thought reading was another of Lola's useful accomplishments!

"And the project my father and yours were involved in is still being kept secret."

"You don't say!"

"By a man I don't trust," said Lola. "But once Senor Vargas is voted out and I'm the boss . . ." She smiled grimly. "Just one of his tactics to secure his position is his son is trying to court me."

"Would you fancy him if he weren't who he is?"

"Juan Vargas has what it takes to get any girl he wants." Jeremy experienced a stab of jealousy.

"Unfortunately for him, he knows it," Lola added, "as you do about yourself, Jeremy."

"Is that also unfortunate for *me*?"

"I'd say it depends upon the girl and what *she* wants," said Lola enigmatically. "But Juan, like his father, would go to any lengths to entrench himself permanently in the Mendez company.

"He even ended his relationship with a girl I'm sure he loves, so confident is he of winning me."

Lola paused and gazed through the window at the terrain through which they were passing on the Grande Corniche, the gleaming cliffs towering beside the snake-like road, the sea below seeming an azure millpond on this perfect, summer day.

"I guess it was Juan's craftiness that finally roused me from my grief and my torpor," she said.

But Lola herself was an expert in that department, and had to be conning Jeremy right now. "Go on, I'm finding this interesting," he answered.

She turned to look at him. "If all you're finding it is interesting, I'm wasting my time telling you! I accepted your invitation not just because I care for you, it's time for us to work together, Jeremy."

Oh yes? – On both counts.

"When your sister came to see me," Lola recalled, "I told her there are *two* other sides, and one of them is the man now running my father's company –"

Information Janis hadn't bothered relaying to Jeremy, but he had by then deduced it for himself.

"I don't think she believed me."

Nor was Jeremy yet prepared to believe that Lola was on *his* side.

"If Janis hadn't stalked off the way she did, I'd have told her what I'm now telling you," Lola continued. "How is she enjoying being in Canada?"

"More to the point, how did you know she's there?"

"An acquaintance of mine mentioned it when I last spoke with him."

"The mysterious Dr. Cohen?"

Lola smiled. "There's nothing mysterious about Jesse."

"Tell that to Janis."

"It's for him to tell her, not me."

"He'll be lucky!" said Jeremy. "And everything points to his being on your payroll."

"The last thing Jesse would do is take money from me,"

Lola answered. "Shall we leave it at that, and get on with our own concerns?"

One of Jeremy's was to make love to her. But business came first and a business meeting – with Lola in the chair – was how this felt.

"Let's deal first with our mutual wish for retribution," she said as if a written agenda was on her lap. "It's no longer just the assassin that I want to punish.

"Your father and mine have paid with their lives. But Senor Vargas is still living –"

"Do you also have a hit man on your payroll?"

"I'm not in the mood for melodramatic jokes, Jeremy."

"What makes you think I'm joking, or being melo-dramatic? If I've learned nothing else from my experiences since the car bomb, it's that anything is possible in the world I didn't know my father moved in – and I ended up losing my hand in an accident that wasn't one."

"You think I set you up, don't you?"

"Since you mention it, yes."

"And in a way, you're right."

"In a way? Either you did, or you didn't."

"Vargas used me to feed you disinformation."

"Which makes you the two-faced bitch I let myself hope you weren't!"

"Protecting my father's company was initially of great importance to me," Lola went on, despite the insult. "That was how Vargas got to me. I'd hoped to ensure, too, that our family would not be smeared. I have sisters, remember –"

"Me, too," Jeremy interrupted, "but that consideration didn't stop me from seeking the truth."

"When you began, you had no conception of what the truth might be."

"And I doubt that you are being truthful now," said

Jeremy, appraising her. "Were you working for Vargas when you accompanied me to the public hospital, to help me find the man who was my father's bodyguard?"

Lola shook her head. "That was an impulse I afterwards regretted. But Vargas learned I'd gone with you and pleaded with me to help the company, not you.

"I continued doing so even when I realized he wasn't to be trusted and had made up my mind to oust him."

"Why?"

She turned to look at him. "Do you still not realize what we're dealing with, Jeremy? Cunning must be met with cunning."

"And you're a mistress of the art."

"When I said I'd set you up for the car crash *in a way*, I meant that I was the instrument – getting you to Caracas or wherever to meet someone who'd lead you to yet another red herring was what I'd been doing for some time."

If ever a man had been led by the nose to nowhere! But not all of the clues Jeremy had followed had come from Lola, or he might now be renewing his early hope that his dad hadn't led a double life.

"Your phony informants weren't the only ones prepared to talk for a price!" he replied.

"And greed on a grander scale is the reason for the secrecy about that multimillion dollar deal."

Possibly including yours, thought Jeremy, which made Lola no different from the picture she'd painted of Vargas.

"My trying to match cunning with cunning, though," she went on, "didn't include envisaging Vargas engineering your demise. When he asked if I'd be sending the limo to meet your plane, I told him you were arranging for a self-drive car. And when I learned what had happened to you . . ."

Lola's expression was now anguished and tears had sprung to her eyes. Could she be that good an actress?

"I'm never going to forgive myself. And I almost went to pieces because of it."

"Me, too!"

"But you didn't, and that served to strengthen my resolve also," said Lola. "What do you intend doing about your father's business, Jeremy?"

"I haven't given his *legitimate* business a thought, though there's still a secretary sitting in his London office."

"It's my intention to eventually sell the Mendez company," Lola declared. "Once the reparation I mentioned is made, I shall want no part of it."

"Reparation to whom?" Jeremy asked as they entered Menton, the tang of lemon trees now drifting in through the car windows.

"That," said Lola, "is the multimillion dollar question."

Chapter 7

While Jeremy was considering whether or not to let his heart rule his head, his younger sister could no longer deny her love for the boy next door.

But when would Sim begin seeing Bessie as more than a friend? she thought, eyeing him longingly en route to the West Bank kibbutz where her cousin Chavah would be married that day.

"It was nice of your dad to lend you his van," Bessie said.

"And still nicer of Chavah to invite me when she hasn't met me."

"It was probably her gran's idea," said Bessie shrewdly, "she wouldn't think it right for a young girl to make this journey alone, and I'd have had to go by bus."

Sim glanced at a group of Arabs watching them pass by. "Well, let's just say I'm glad it isn't my mother's car I'm driving. The van would be more protection."

"Do you think we'll get stoned?"

Sim laughed grimly. "A word that in Israel doesn't mean what it does everywhere else, and the answer to your question, Bessie, is anything could happen on the Hebron road, not to mention once we're in the territory we're headed for."

Bessie wanted to tell Sim that she felt safe with him, but said instead, "I'm never going to get used to the Israeli buses."

"To what people eat on them, you mean! When I first lived here, I remember getting off a bus because I was overpowered by the smell of garlic. That's a pretty dress you have on, by the way."

But he had only just noticed it and the compliment was an afterthought. "Well, I had to dress up for the wedding, didn't I? It will be the first Israeli one I've been to."

"They're not all alike," said Sim, "and if Chavah's is what they call a love match, I'd be surprised."

Bessie averted her gaze to the glossy white shoes that pinched her feet, but enhanced her slim ankles.

"What've I said?" asked Sim.

"Nothing."

"Come on, I can read you like a book, Bessie!"

Not quite, or you'd know that just the mention of love, from you . . .

"Look, I wasn't casting aspersions at your cousin," said Sim, "only making a comment about the ultra-orthodox way of life, and I was thinking about a cousin of my own who now lives in Mea Shearim."

"Hildegard calls that community an Israeli Golders Green," said Bessie, "where I sometimes went shopping on a Saturday with my mum, and we'd see families of 'shulgoers' pass by dressed in their Sabbath best.

" 'I admire their piety, but I couldn't live their way,' Mummy once said, and I wasn't quite sure what she meant,"

Bessie went on, "till I met Chavah and Anit, and Anit said things to her sister that opened my eyes."

"The cousin I just mentioned," said Sim, "was married off when he was sixteen, to a girl his age whom he didn't even like."

"Is she beautiful, at least?"

"I thought so when I saw her at their wedding," Sim replied, "but since then she's had six kids, one a year. At that rate, her physical beauty's unlikely to last, I'd say, and I'm as sorry for her as I am for him.

"You wouldn't catch me getting married just for God's sake! It would have to be the right girl."

Would he waken one morning and realize she lived right next door to him?

"Did you hear yet from the professor," Sim asked, "about taking you to see his brother?"

Bessie shook her head. "And he hasn't been back to the restaurant since the night he promised to."

"Perhaps he's had second thoughts, Bessie. Maybe you should, too. When I encouraged you to do what you felt you had to, well —"

"Well, what?"

"The worst outcome I anticipated was you'd find your father and he'd want nothing to do with you, but at least you'd know who he was."

Bessie glanced through the window at some Arab children playing by the dusty roadside and voiced her own fear. "That could still happen."

"But given what you learned from the professor, his brother might instead latch onto you, Bessie."

"What on earth do you mean?"

"You're a very wealthy girl, aren't you?"

"How dare you insult my father, Sim!"

"*If* he turns out to be, and it isn't certain yet, the fact remains that you don't know what kind of person he is."

"He's ill and he needs me is all I have to know."

"Exactly what I'm afraid of for you," said Sim. "Haven't you been through enough, without complicating your life with the burden an alcoholic father would be for you?"

"You wouldn't see it that way if your dad was an alcoholic!"

"I owe my dad a lot, don't I? Ask yourself what your still anonymous father has done for you and the answer is you owe him nothing."

"If it weren't for him, I wouldn't exist, would I? And I sometimes wish I didn't," said Bessie, bursting into tears.

Sim pulled up by the dusty grass verge and gathered her close, ignoring the shouting and horn-honking of drivers who then had to steer their vehicles around his.

"What am I going to do with you, Bessie?"

"My problems aren't yours, you don't have to do anything –"

"But you yourself have become my problem, didn't you know that?"

"I'm not sure what that means."

"Nor am I, quite."

Bessie then received her first kiss and thought she might die of joy in a dirt-streaked van on the road to Hebron.

"Someone has to watch out for you and I seem to have elected myself," Sim said with a grin when they were again on their way.

He hadn't said he loved her, but for Bessie, the kiss and what he *had* said were enough to be going on with.

Chapter
8

Janis made herself a cheese sandwich and switched on the TV news, nowadays a daily saga of the painful, piece by piece unshackling of Eastern Europe.

A year had slipped by since a car bomb in Caracas had its devastating effects upon Janis's life. In the meantime, Poland had acquired a non-communist Prime Minister, the first in the Soviet bloc and Hungary, now allowing East Germans to cross the border into Austria, could be next.

As for the picture now filling the TV screen, who would have believed it possible? A massive demonstration taking place in Leipzig – and the commentator prophesying that Erich Honeker would be forced to resign.

There were times, like now, when Janis's personal problems seemed to her unimportant. In June, when the Tiananmen Square massacre of young people like herself had shocked the world, she had thought, what's losing respect for your father, compared to being mown down by tanks because you've dared to fight for the right to be free?

Such objectivity could not be expected to last; human nature dictated otherwise. And Janis had soon learned the lesson that A.P. had: work, however rewarding, was not enough. Immersed though she now was in initiating the Bornstein Foundation, loneliness remained her constant companion.

She was beside the window, pensively watching the leaves scurry along the canal bank in the autumn wind, when the doorbell rang.

"I've come to drag you on a double-date," said Claudia discarding the plaid wrap enveloping her. "Like my little black dress, Janis?"

"What there is of it! And no thanks, Claudia."

"If you won't come, I shall have to go out with the two of them —"

"Why are you complaining?" Janis said with a laugh. Claudia's disenchantment with men had quickly evaporated. "You'll be able to play one off against the other."

"That," said Claudia, "would be too utterly selfish of me, when you're sitting here all alone. I've no idea what *my* date's friend is like, Janis, but he could be the answer to your prayers, couldn't he?"

"A man is the last thing I'm praying for!"

"And it's turning you sour," Claudia informed her.

"Thank you for your too honest criticism."

Claudia sat down on the sofa, fingering the turquoise pendant enhancing her cleavage. "I'm your friend, Janis, and I don't like what's happening to you. It isn't what we came to Canada for —"

"I seem to recollect that you came because you wanted to see Niagara Falls!"

Claudia responded, "Be funny with me if you must, but what I'm saying to you is serious. Have you taken a good

look at yourself lately? If I'd been able to continue living here
– well I wouldn't have let it happen."

"Let *what* happen?"

"Okay, I'll be more specific," said Claudia, rising and
propelling Janis to the mirror above the sideboard. "When
did you last use a conditioner on your hair? It used to gleam
like silk and now it's as dull as straw.

"Also, there's a button missing from your blouse –"

"So what?"

"And I bet if I inspected your shoes, I'd find that they
need repairing," Claudia went on.

"So what, again!"

"You don't give a damn, do you, Janis, and that's what
worries me. When I ran into you downtown, with that
frumpy female you introduced me to, you weren't wearing
make-up –"

"Nor was I when you ran into me in Paris," Janis cut in.

"In Paris we were both utterly, utterly at rock bottom, but
if I've managed to pry myself out of it, why can't you?"
Claudia demanded. "I detect absolutely no raising of your
spirits, Janis. In fact the signs are to the contrary, and you
absolutely and imperatively have to get over the lying sod
who's responsible –"

"Would you like to tell me how?"

"My infallible recipe for forgetting a man is to blot him out
with another, however transient, so how about coming on
that double-date tonight?"

Janis managed to smile. "Thanks for caring, Claudia, but
you're not me and I'm not you. As for calling my lawyer
frumpy –"

"Okay, so I was exaggerating."

"As you often do."

"But not about how you're letting yourself go, Janis, as if

nothing matters to you except the medical foundation you're setting up."

The following day, a telephone call from her lawyer jolted Janis from her personal apathy.

"I think I've found the right person to head the AIDS clinic," said Isobel, "a Dr. Jesse Cohen —"

"Are you out of your mind!"

"I beg your pardon?"

"I wouldn't have that man within an inch of the clinic," Janis said vehemently.

"He's highly recommended and you're going to have to explain that to me."

"On the contrary, *you* are going to have to accept your client's instructions without questioning them."

"The day I do that," said Isobel, "I'll be ready for retirement. My clients must accept the lawyer they've engaged, or find themselves a replacement.

"You left it to me to interview the candidates," she went on, "and in my opinion, Dr. Cohen is the best of them."

"But the second best will get the job," said Janis.

"If your first priority isn't the clinic, fine —"

"And you can tell Dr. Cohen that I congratulate him on his chutzpah."

"Why not tell him yourself? He managed to wheedle your address from my secretary and is now on his way to see you."

"Your secretary should be fired!"

"For helping a guy in distress? It's time you came clean with me, Janis. Like Dr. Cohen did when I interviewed him."

"What, exactly, did he tell you, Isobel?"

"Sufficient for me to put two and two together. You'd said you wanted a woman lawyer because you were off men at the moment —"

"And he, no doubt, turned on the charm! He had me fooled, too, and he isn't getting a second chance."

The doorbell pealed as Janis replaced the receiver and she felt like making a hasty exit via the fire escape stairs outside the kitchen window.

Instead, she sat down and tried to calm herself. If she didn't open the door, Jesse would eventually go away.

She had not reckoned on his tenacity. Fifteen minutes later the bell was still ringing – and driving Janis crazy!

When she could bear it no longer and flung open the door, the irate words on her tongue petered out. Tears were streaming down Jesse's face.

"So much for the handsome hero you once called me!" he said, fumbling in his pocket for a handkerchief.

"And I must have had too much wine when I did," Janis replied. "You'd better come in, till you've pulled yourself together."

He thrust the bunch of red roses he was clutching into her hands. "These are for you."

"But 'say it with flowers' isn't going to work," she replied as he followed her to the kitchen, where she was glad to have something with which to busy herself, nipping the ends of the stems and stripping off the lower leaves, before putting the flowers in a vase, aware of Jesse drying his eyes.

"Mind you don't prick your finger on a thorn," he said, "like you did the last time I gave you roses. I never saw anyone go to the trouble with flowers that you do."

"My stepmother used to do this," Janis recalled, and briefly it was as if Laura's warm presence was beside her, with it the memory of the simple home life the Bornsteins had lived, despite Jake's wealth.

How did I get from that to this? Janis asked herself, again

assailed by the unreality that had dogged her since the assassinations.

Though she had left home and roamed the world after breaking her engagement to Kurt, she'd lived the way other young people did after fleeing the nest. On the cheap, but enjoying their independence – only it hadn't been independence that Janis was seeking.

Nor was it now. A loving husband and family was all she'd wanted and when Jesse came along . . . She'd thought him her salvation, but how wrong she was!

"Dammit! I *have* pricked my finger on a thorn –"

"Do you have any antiseptic?"

"An Elastoplast will do."

Jesse went with her to the bathroom and watched her open the wall cabinet.

"Is there nowhere you won't follow me!" she exclaimed while opening a packet and finding it empty. "A friend of mine who stayed here had a blister on her heel and must have used up all the dressings – Why am I bothering to tell *you*!"

"And meanwhile you're dripping blood –"

"A Dracula like you must find that exciting!"

Jesse grabbed Janis's hand, turned on the wash basin tap, and rinsed her finger. "Is that towel on the rail a clean one?"

"You made a fuss like this the last time!"

Jesse decided against the towel and carefully dried the wound with paper tissues. "I'm a doctor, remember –"

"How could I possibly forget, since an emergency call in Haiti introduced you to my father – or so you said – and you're now trying to reinsert yourself into my life via the Bornstein Medical Foundation.

"Did Lola put you up to it?" Janis inquired while he held her finger upright and applied a tourniquet, using the immaculate handkerchief he had taken from his breast pocket.

"You certainly got yourself up for your interview," she observed, surveying his well-cut dark suit and sober tie, "and it helped fool my lawyer. I never saw you dressed that way except when we met on the plane to Sydney."

"You never saw me in my working world."

"And I'm not letting you into mine."

"Okay, it's stopped bleeding," Jesse said, removing the tourniquet.

"The heck with my finger! Compared with my invisible wounds, I didn't even feel the prick."

"Some of your invisible wounds," said Jesse, "are self-inflicted, all in your mind."

"How dare you!"

Janis strode back to the kitchen, Jesse hot on her heels.

"For one thing, you've got Lola wrong, her intentions too," he persisted.

"Oh yes?"

"Right now she's working closely with your brother –"

"And I say they're welcome to each other. As you'll have gathered I intend doing something more productive than Jeremy currently is.

"I've put the past, including you, behind me," Janis lied.

"Condemned without a fair trial," said Jesse, "and that isn't like you."

Janis averted her eyes from his magnetic gaze, sat down on a stool and said crisply, "Okay, defend yourself."

"And your smart lady lawyer would counsel you that I'm innocent until proven guilty."

"Ever heard the saying, 'The law is an ass'? But *I'm* not!"

"Circumstantial evidence, though, has been known to hang an innocent person."

"Just get on with it, will you, Jesse?"

"Because I didn't tell you I was acquainted with Lola, you

assumed, when you found out, that I'd lied to you about everything from the minute we met. That my being on that plane, in the seat beside yours, wasn't coincidence –"

"To set the record straight," Janis cut in, "I was suspicious the moment you mentioned my father –"

"If I may interrupt the prosecuting counsel," said Jesse, "your brother's vengeance trip and its traumatic consequences for him have distorted your view of everything and everyone."

"I'm over that now."

"Not with respect to me. You think I was working for Lola, but nothing could be further from the truth. There are times, though, when *withholding* some truths is preferable to damaging a relationship."

"What a person doesn't know can't hurt them, you mean? But truth has a way of unexpectedly emerging," said Janis, "as the aftermath of the car bomb proves," she added bitterly.

"Your father's double life?"

"What else! Not to mention the glance you and Lola exchanged that told me you weren't strangers."

"Is the accused going to be offered a cup of coffee?"

"If he cares to make himself one."

Jesse put the kettle to boil, spooned some instant coffee from a jar on the counter into a mug, and resumed his defense.

"That panic call you got from Lola about Jeremy's car crash was the first time you'd mentioned her to me, Janis. If I'd told you then that I knew her, what would you have thought?"

"The same as I did when later my intuition told me. That you're what my friend Claudia calls a lying sod – and part of the network Lola inherited from her father. This is getting you nowhere, Jesse."

"Nor will it, till you accept that I don't know from networks, Janis. I'm just an ordinary guy who happened to meet Lola Mendez when she was a student at Harvard, and I doing a post-grad course at the medical school.

"She was at one of the parties I got invited to and joked that Luis Mendez's daughter had a bodyguard to see her home – everyone knew her father was a multi-millionaire."

But when I was at college, nobody gave my being an heiress a thought, least of all me, Janis reflected. Nothing that had preceded her father's death had prepared her for any of this.

"At the time, I thought it *was* a joke," Jesse went on, "but I recalled it when I found myself being paid by Senor Mendez for treating your dad, in that shady set-up I told you about."

"My dad didn't carry money, only credit cards."

"So he said, and Mendez said, 'Leave it to me, Jake, it's my pleasure.' "

"And *his* bloody fault, no doubt, that my parents lost their lives!"

"Let's not get into that," said Jesse quietly. "All I'm concerned with right now is do you believe I'm not on anyone's payroll and never have been? – if you don't count my professional employers."

Janis watched him make his coffee. "You were really at Harvard when Lola was?"

"Check it out and I'll come up smelling of roses."

"I still haven't put yours in water."

"That can wait, I need your undivided attention, and was about to tell you my ex was there, too. It was when we were a pair of happy newlyweds. Before she began getting hot pants for other guys and I still don't know how far back in our marriage that goes.

"She's about to get spliced to the one I found out about, by the way. A mutual friend told me, and that they intend it to be what's nowadays called an 'open marriage' – adultery by consent! Heaven help their kids if they have any," Jesse added.

"I agree," said Janis, "but I'm an old-fashioned girl."

"And the one for me in every respect."

"Including the job you're after?"

"I was working with AIDS patients in Sydney, wasn't I?"

"But you weren't head of a clinic. How do I know you're not using me in that respect?"

Jesse's expression was as though Janis had slapped his face. "I hadn't realized you were paranoid in another way, too, thinking every man you meet could be after your fortune and what it could do for them –"

"I didn't say that."

"But you damn well implied it. For the second time in my life I misjudged a female," Jesse said coldly, "and I'm thankful I've found out in time to avert a second disaster. If we'd married, your money would have come between us."

"You don't understand how I tick and you never did!" Janis retorted.

But Jesse was already on his way out of the flat.

Chapter
9

When eventually Bessie heard from Professor Harim, he explained that he had been rethinking his promise to take her to meet his brother.

"A promise is a promise," she said, sitting down beside the telephone, aware that her legs were trembling, "and you could've let me know sooner that you'd changed your mind, instead of keeping me on tenterhooks."

"All right, Bessie, I deserve what I'm getting," he replied, "but it's you, as well as poor Zvi, I'm thinking of. If he refused to acknowledge you, you might begin hating the man you now hope is your father."

"I'm not the hating kind."

"But you'd be even more upset than if you'd never found him and that's just one of the aspects I've been considering."

"If another is what would I do with an alcoholic father, my boyfriend is worried about that. But I'm not," Bessie declared.

"Dare your possible uncle say he agrees with your boy-friend?"

"I've inherited a lot of money and –"

"You could end up paying my brother's liquor bills," the professor cut her short.

"What I'd spend it on is getting him dried-out."

"First he would have to agree," said the professor. "When I made that suggestion, if he hadn't been too drunk to punch straight, I'd have got a black eye."

"If you're trying to put me off, you haven't succeeded," said Bessie.

"And I was right when I called you a determined girl."

Bessie heard one of his lengthy sighs drift over the line. "Will you, or won't you take me to meet him?"

"How can I refuse something that means so much to you? But you're also a soft-hearted girl," said Professor Harim, "and there's something I must warn you about before you've met him: Beware of pity, Bessie, it's been known to change people's lives and not always for the better."

Bessie's first awareness, after entering Zvi Harim's bungalow in a suburb of Tel Aviv, was of an odor so repugnant she wanted to turn and flee.

"Doesn't he ever open the windows?" she whispered to the professor, beside her in the kitchen where an overflowing garbage pail had greeted their eyes, the empty bottles on the tiled floor a testament to how Zvi assuaged his grief, a moldy half-loaf on the oilcloth-covered table adding to the air of desolation, and mingling with the sweetish smell of rotting vegetables the pungency of spilled liquor.

"Open the windows?" the professor replied. "We're lucky he forgot to lock the back door last night, or maybe for you it's *un*lucky."

"You're still trying to warn me off."

The professor glanced around the room. "If this doesn't, Bessie, nothing will."

It was Saturday afternoon and the two were dressed in their best, Professor Harim having attended the Sabbath service that morning, and Bessie wanting to make a good impression on Zvi when he opened the door to them.

Instead, she had stood tensely in the grimy front porch while the professor repeatedly pressed the doorbell, eventually following him through a neglected garden, where the weeds had failed to strangle the ornamental bushes, to a rear verandah on which the kitchen door was situated.

"I feel like a burglar," she said now.

"No need for whispering, Bessie. Zvi wouldn't know if there was an earthquake when he's sleeping it off. But one day he *will* be burgled, when I came here years ago I got in like we did today – What are you doing!" he exclaimed when Bessie took off her crisp cotton jacket and picked up the garbage pail.

"Getting rid of this lot."

The professor, leaning heavily on his stick, agitatedly followed her outside, where at the far end of the verandah she found some garbage disposal bags lying beside a lidless bin.

That task completed, Bessie returned to the kitchen to fetch the empty bottles, watched by the increasingly anxious professor.

"If you're going to be Zvi's cleaner, that's something you'll get used to doing!"

"That wasn't a very nice thing to say," Bessie answered.

"And you forgot to dump that moldy bread with the rest!"

"I expect there'll be things in the fridge I'll have to dump," she said calmly, "so I'll do it then." She opened the refrigerator and shut it again quickly.

"Who are you trying to hide the contents from? Me?" said the professor with one of his sighs.

"Not the contents, just the rancid smell. And I'll have to get some proper containers," said Bessie while transferring the unwashed dishes from the sink to the draining board.

"Do you think there'll be any hot water, Professor?"

"How would I know?"

"If not, I'll have to boil some, so I can scour the sink before filling it."

Professor Harim sat down on a dusty chair, his hands resting on his stick, watching her set to work. "You'll make that boyfriend you mentioned a good wife, Bessie."

"Right now," she told him, "all I want is to be a good daughter."

"You'll be that, too, and Zvi will be a fool if he rejects you, but don't be too surprised if he does."

"That wouldn't stop me from coming back to try again."

"And if he didn't let you in and made sure you were locked out?"

"I'd bring my sleeping bag and camp on the verandah –"

"And I'm coming to think it's me you take after, not him! If he had any backbone, he wouldn't still be feeling sorry for himself," the professor opined.

Bessie, an expert in self-pity, kept her thoughts to herself. Lack of backbone hadn't accounted for her ending up anorexic, she'd wanted to feel loved and that could be what Zvi needed.

Professor Harim looked on in silence while she methodically cleaned the kitchen, trailing behind her when she entered the adjoining living room and began the unenviable task of restoring it to order.

"If you think my brother will notice the difference, Bessie –"

"What you're saying," she interrupted, "is he doesn't care. I don't need telling that. But I'll help him get back his self-respect. I can't have my father living in a sty."

The professor sat down on the shabby sofa amid some dusty newspapers, discovered an empty bottle beneath his rump and handed it to Bessie. "You still *want* Zvi to be your father? It isn't too late to back out."

"But I'm not going to. There was a time when I turned against my mother," Bessie revealed, "but I think I understand her better now. I'd have preferred my father not to be an alcoholic, but grief did that to him, didn't it?"

Zvi then appeared in the doorway and Bessie froze with a duster in her hand, affected by his belligerent demeanor.

"Am I having a bad dream?" he said, glaring at the professor.

"When you learn why I'm here, and who this young lady is, you might think you're having a good one, Zvi. She can go and make you some coffee, while I help you to think back."

Chapter
10

*S*uch was Janis's continuing apathy toward all but the medical foundation, she had not once attended a synagogue social in Ottawa, which might have led her to new friendships.

When in November Claudia became engaged to a radiologist at her training hospital, Janis was pleased that at last she had found her anchor.

I, however, am still floating, she thought on New Year's Eve, which she had chosen to spend alone, declining Isobel McLeod's invitation to a party, and Claudia's to a hospital dance.

"Don't sit by yourself being homesick," Isobel had said, and Janis had thought wryly, homesick for where?

How often, though, had she found herself picturing her little flat in Sydney, and hoping that whoever lived there now was taking care of her verandah garden? Remembering, too, the breathtaking panorama the harbor was, and the brash architecture of the Opera House.

Also the times she'd gone to concerts there with Jesse, which she would rather *not* remember. By the end of that mock trial the two of them had played out on the day he had brought her roses, Janis had no longer doubted that he loved her and was telling the truth. Why she had then said such hurtful things to him was beyond her own comprehension.

On the stroke of midnight, while she was by the window watching some warmly clad revelers play "Here we go round the mulberry bush" on the canal bank, Jeremy called to wish her a happy New Year.

"Where the hell are you?"

"The impression I got from our last chat was you don't care."

"And the answer to my question is probably Caracas. How is your vengeance trip going?"

"If you'd had your way, I'd have sat back and done nothing!" Jeremy retorted.

"And you'd still have two hands."

"I'm doing fine with just one, thank you very much, and less concerned with vengeance than with setting some wrongs right. If I succeed – Lola's helping me – I'll let you know."

Janis was left prickling with an all too familiar apprehension that she had not allowed to impinge on her new life in Ottawa. Who was she kidding? A life it wasn't, and her brother was still risking his.

As for her sister, now undertaking adult responsibilities that Janis would have thought beyond her – but were they any longer?

Bessie had called last week to let Janis know she intended moving in with her alcoholic father. Was this the same girl who had thrown a tantrum in Shirley's flat, exactly a year ago? Unable to decide where she would make her home from then on?

Come to that, am I the person I was? Janis reflected. And Jeremy certainly wasn't.

Janis took her troubles to bed, glad to put 1989 behind her.

A.P., too, had received a New Year greetings call from Jeremy, and had himself called Janis and Bessie, which his gran would approve, he had thought with a smile. Marianne wouldn't want the family to disintegrate with A.P.'s generation.

Bessie had sounded happier than A.P. had expected, given the problematic outcome of her search for her father. He had sensed in Janis, though, an emptiness that matched his own.

With the end of the summer camp, the commune had reverted to its former routine and A.P. to his former boredom.

But it wasn't just that, he thought when Mary Lou remarked that a televised speech he had made in the House, before the Christmas recess, was distinctly lackluster.

"I'm well aware of it and you're responsible," he told her.

"Because I encouraged you to embark on a life you're not enjoying? But once you get the school you're planning off the ground –"

"You're responsible because all I seem able to think of is you."

"Despite what I told you?"

"It might have been kinder if you hadn't."

A silence followed and A.P. was assailed by déjà vu, watching Mary Lou continue setting mugs on a tray, while he shoveled tea into the pot.

Again they were sharing kitchen duty and how many traumatic conversations had they, by now, had in this domestic setting?

"Kinder to let you go on hoping, though it's Jeremy I want?" said Mary Lou.

"He isn't good enough for you."

"And *I'm* not good enough for *you*."

"Let me be the judge of that."

"You still want to marry me?"

"I still want to marry you."

"But *I* wouldn't marry Jeremy if he went down on his knees and begged me to."

"Then you're mistaking something else for love. And the picture you just painted of Jeremy as a romantic suitor makes me want to laugh! Though he's now entangled with Lola Mendez, he'll disentangle himself when it suits him to and I'm sorry for the girl he eventually marries. What a dance he'll lead her!

"Marry *me* and I'll show you what love is, Mary Lou."

"I never heard you sound so passionate, A.P., and if you're like that in bed —"

"There's more to marriage than bed," he cut in, "and not least is the friendship that some marriages lack."

"You sound like a marriage counselor!"

"I'm qualified to be one," A.P. replied, "since I grew up listening to my parents air their differences and came to realize they had nothing in common but me."

A.P. made the tea and stirred it, absently watching the leaves swirl. "Since I got the idea for the camp and the school, and you made me see it was because I wanted to work with children, I've done a lot of thinking about my own childhood, Mary Lou.

"How I was always needing someone and somewhere to run to. Though the Bornsteins lived close by, they were such a happy family going there used to emphasize my own plight.

"Instead, I went to my Grandma Marianne's flat and it became my second home. If she was working on a novel – which she usually was – I'd do my homework at her kitchen table and later we'd have something to eat and a chat.

"I don't know how I'd have got by without her," A.P. went on pensively, "and I'm probably a lot less scarred, because I had her to go to, than the kids from broken homes who'll be among those having a happy interlude at the Kyverdale school.

"As for my own kids –"

"That you haven't yet got."

"There's no way I'd put them through what I suffered and I refuse to give up hope that you'll be their mother."

"But I'm in no hurry to be a mother," said Mary Lou. "While the camp was going on, and especially when Ben did his disappearing act while you weren't here, I began to think I didn't like kids.

"Thank heavens for Henry, I thought, watching him sort out squabbles in foreign languages and all the rest that he did without batting an eyelid or losing his cool. Henry's a great bloke to have around," Mary Lou declared.

When a few days later Henry packed his shabby holdall and bade the communards farewell, A.P. drove him to Bridgewater to catch the London train.

"It's been an interesting experience for me, but moving on has become my way of life," he apologized for his defection, "and you know me! I like to be where the action is. Reconstructing Eastern Europe is going to be an uphill struggle," he went on, "and the execution of the Ceausescus hasn't left Romania squeaky clean. That's where I'm heading for now."

"And you'll be missed by your friends at the commune,"

said A.P., pulling up to let a stout farmer shepherd his dairy herd across the narrow lane, "including Mary Lou."

"May I offer you some parting advice, A.P.?"

"I'm not to emulate *you*!"

"A little more specific than that. If in the end you don't get her, settle for another girl as I ought to've done in my youth. A different loaf has to be better than no bread."

Chapter 11

*L*ola had carried through her intention to become chairman of the Mendez company and was now working with Jeremy to uncover the project they believed responsible for the car bomb.

"Without your Harvard business course, we'd be sunk," he said during a lengthy session in the executive offices.

"Didn't you use computers at Oxford?" she asked, her gaze remaining riveted to the screen.

"Sure, but I wasn't the wizard at it that you are. For my purposes I didn't need to be."

"The joke is I never expected to make use of that course," Lola replied, "and it'd help if I had even the slightest idea of what we're looking for."

"Maybe we should find a way of making Vargas tell us."

"Resort to his tactics? Oh no, *querido*."

When she called him "darling" in Spanish and one of her caressing glances accompanied it, all Jeremy wanted was to make love to her, recapture the ecstasy they'd shared in

Menton and the carefree abandon they had allowed themselves for that brief while.

Now, Jeremy was again a guest in her home, occupying the suite he had on his previous visits, lying sleepless in those sumptuous surroundings and sometimes wondering if the interlude amid the lemon trees was just a receding fantasy.

"In my mother's house propriety reigns," Lola had instructed him.

"If I came to your room she wouldn't know."

"But I would know I'm committing a sin under her roof and that I'll never do."

Jeremy switched his mind to the present, aware of Lola coolly concentrating on her task and of his own edginess. There were times when he wondered which of them had seduced the other into this grim partnership. The two of them isolated together in what felt to Jeremy like a brightly lit fish bowl set against the velvety darkness outside.

"If there was anything incriminating to find, Vargas would have erased it," he said, "and he has to know you stay late at the office and I keep you company —"

"Of course he knows," Lola cut in, "but I've taken care of that. As for the first part of your supposition, he wouldn't expect me to look as far back as I am — and I've allowed him to assume I'm taking my chairmanship duties too seriously, which since I'm a woman he probably finds amusing."

Lola removed her hands from the keyboard and thoughtfully clasped them beneath her chin. "What did you say you and Janis and your parents were known as, when you were a kid in South Africa, Jeremy?"

"The four Jays, since my mother's name was Julia."

Lola pointed to the computer screen. "Would it be overimaginative to connect your father with Fourjay Enterprises, Zurich?"

"Not in the least!" Jeremy said bitterly.

"Setting up a Swiss company isn't illegal," said Lola.

Jake Bornstein's reasons for doing so, though, must have been, and his employing the family nickname for his nefarious purposes was another sickening blow for his son.

"What I've turned up," Lola told him, "is a deal between the Mendez company and Fourjay made in 1982."

The year Dad married Laura and took Janis and me to live in England, thought Jeremy. But he was up to no good long before then though my mother was a lawyer, regardless of whether she'd get struck-off if he was found out.

"There's no indication of what the deal was," said Lola, "and it isn't necessarily the one we're looking for, but now we know about Fourjay we might make better headway tomorrow."

"Why not stick at it tonight?"

"Vargas has invited us to a party."

"I'm not bloody going!"

"You really must learn to play things my way, Jeremy," Lola replied.

"Match cunning with cunning, you mean —"

"And I faltered only briefly in that respect. Speaking my mind to Vargas was a mistake and I afterwards changed my tactics."

"You and your tactics!" Jeremy exclaimed.

"Where did your bull-in-a-china-shop delving get you? Though it doesn't always suit us to let men know it, the female mind is a good deal more manipulative than the male," Lola declared.

And was she, perhaps, manipulating Jeremy?

"To lull Vargas's suspicions about your continued presence in Caracas," she went on, "and your spending time with me at the office, I told him we're getting married and you're getting the feel of the company, since you'll be joining it after our wedding."

Jeremy was stunned by the *depth* of her cunning.

"Vargas said that though his son would be broken-hearted he wishes us well – and would the Mendez and Bornstein companies also be getting married to each other?" Lola relayed with a laugh.

"When I said that was highly likely, I could hear the cash register tinkling in his mind as he envisaged the value of his shares in such a powerful organization."

Jeremy pulled himself together and asked tersely, "What happens when the news of our fictitious forthcoming marriage reaches your mother's ears?"

"Does it have to be fictitious?"

"Was that a proposal?"

Lola came to wind her arms around his neck. "One of us had to make it and I'm growing impatient, *querido*."

The Vargas party was Jeremy's introduction to the Caracas social scene and he had wanted to run a mile from it.

"Some of my friends will be there with their parents," Lola, looking stunning in white chiffon, had told him en route to the mansion the Vargases called home, a five minute walk from her own home, but they were nevertheless chauffeured there.

As though, Jeremy thought on the way back, arriving in style is written in the scenario, and how far removed from the real world that champagne and caviar scenario was.

In retrospect, the gathering he had reluctantly attended seemed to him a glittering montage of silk-suited men and the women who were their expensive appendages, of crystal chandeliers competing with diamond necklaces and cigarettes stubbed out on platters of rich food.

Lola, though, was chatting about the party as casually as Jeremy might about one of the take-away pizza get-togethers he and A.P. were sometimes invited to in North London.

"Serena Silvera, by the way, was my arch enemy at school and I like her no better now," Lola said.

"Which one was she?"

"The skinny blonde in the red dress who kept giving you the eye, and I wanted to say to her, 'Lay off, he's mine,' which she'll find out when we announce our engagement."

"*If* and when."

"Because we're of different faiths?"

"Among other things."

"I've always believed there's nothing that love can't overcome."

With her fingers entwined with his, Jeremy too was prepared to believe it.

"And my mother would put my happiness first, provided we married in church."

"That," said Jeremy emphatically, "you'll never manipulate me into doing."

Chapter
12

*B*essie's relationship with her father was a good deal
more complicated than his unquestioning acceptance of her had foretold.

"So my past has caught up with me!" he had said with
bravado when she returned with the coffee on the day she
met him.

"And you should count yourself a lucky man," said his
brother.

"That depends on what she's expecting of me."

"I'm not expecting anything of you."

"Then you won't be disappointed."

"But I'd like to help you."

"Already she's telling me I need help!" he flashed to his
brother, and to Bessie, "Can you bring back my wife and
sons?"

The rest of that traumatic afternoon was to Bessie a painful blur of Zvi comforting himself from the bottle he had
immediately reached for.

By the time his unwelcome visitors left, he was in a drunken stupor, barely noticing their departure, and the professor had advised Bessie against returning.

Advice she had eschewed, gradually inserting herself into the unhappy existence of a man who seemed not to care if she was there, or not.

There was, however, consolation and significance in Zvi's never having told her to go, and little by little, he had grown accustomed to her presence.

"You need some new clothes," Bessie had eventually dared to tell him.

"Who cares what I look like?"

"I do and I'd like to take you shopping."

"You won't succeed in making a new man of me," he had replied.

"But there's no harm in trying."

To her amazement he had gone with her, albeit resignedly, on what was for Bessie another memorable Saturday afternoon, showing no interest in the items they purchased from stores in the Dizengoff Center, a motley collection of shoppers milling around them.

"Did you use to come here with your wife and sons?" Bessie asked him and saw his lifeless expression come alive with pain.

"And afterwards, we'd buy sandwiches and sit on the benches at Dizengoff Circle, and eat them," he said, after nodding.

"Then why don't you and I do that?"

"Whatever you'd like to do, Bessie."

Again he had spoken resignedly, but that was better than his not bothering to reply, as if a shrug was enough.

"What sort of sandwiches would you like, Zvi?"

"I used to be partial to pastrami."

"If you'd told me, I'd have got you some to have at home."

"You're a good girl, Bessie."

But even that was said with resignation.

Later, while they sat at the Circle munching the sandwiches cheek by jowl with old ladies gossiping in Yiddish, children racing around clutching ice cream cones and the traffic reminiscent of Oxford Circus, Zvi allowed Bessie another glimpse of the memories locked inside him.

"Batya and I — we married when we were very young. We met on a dig in Israel, but she was British, like you. Her parents called her Beatrice.

"I visited them in Birmingham when I was in England for the photo session."

His acceptance of Bessie had not yet included mentioning her mother's name. Would it ever? Or had he permanently blotted out the details of her conception?

"After our sons were born, Batya put them before her career," he went on. "She was that sort of woman and never showed a trace of envy about me pursuing mine. The kind they call a real homemaker, because that's what she chose to be."

Zvi's gaze roved the scene around them, parents and children predominant among the crowds thronging Dizengoff Street, the cafes and ice cream parlors doing a roaring trade. In Israel the Sabbath was a family day even for the nonreligious and in Tel Aviv they were the majority.

It's the family atmosphere that's triggered off Zvi's telling me what he has, Bessie reckoned. She then learned something of her half-brothers who had died at the hands of Arab terrorists.

"My two boys were very different from each other," Zvi said wryly. "Avi, he was the younger, was a born archeologist and had already been on one or two digs with me. Yosef, though, wanted to be a professional footballer."

"Was he good enough?"

"What does it matter now if he was, or not? Or that Avi was looking forward to seeing Ephesus in his school holidays. I'd promised to take him there, but neither of us got to see it."

"Where's Ephesus?" Bessie inquired.

"It's an ancient trading city now an archeological site," Zvi told her, "in the part of Turkey that used to be called Asia Minor."

"What's stopping you from visiting it now? If you like, I'll go with you."

"All of a sudden you're interested in archeology?"

Bessie could think of no suitable reply. And the familiar mask with which Zvi hid his feelings, when they weren't obliterated by drink, was back on his face, shutting her out.

Bessie was recalling that sole outing with Zvi when, a week later, she let herself into his bungalow with the key he had reluctantly given her and set down her suitcase in the hall.

She had not told Janis that he didn't know she intended moving in with him, nor had she mentioned that to Hildegard and Peter.

All three would have advised her against presenting Zvi with a *fait accompli*. But I'm grown up now, Bessie told herself, over sixteen and capable of making my own decisions.

She didn't want people trying to protect her. Well, except for Sim, but that was different, a boy's feeling for his girl included wanting to take care of her.

Last night, Sim had helped her put Zvi to bed and to clear the debris of another binge, before escorting her home. From now on, though, this would be Bessie's home and the truth was, she wasn't looking forward to it. But there was no chance of Zvi's changing his ways while he lived alone.

Would the time come when Bessie began thinking of him as "Dad"? No. That title would always be for her attached to Jake Bornstein, who'd been a real father to her in all but the blood sense.

She had expected that when she met her blood father, love for him would be kindled in her heart. Instead, Zvi was just a man she felt sorry for – and beware of pity, his brother had warned.

As for Sim's continually saying that Zvi was wallowing in *self*-pity, who wouldn't in his position? Everything he'd once had, his family and his career, now gone? Sim, who'd never had cause to pity himself didn't understand, but Bessie had had plenty of cause to feel sorry for herself.

Now, though, those days were behind her. Though Sim still hadn't said he loved her, she was letting herself believe he did, reliving over and again the ecstatic moment when he had kissed her.

She had Sim and she'd found her father. What more could *I want?*

A *different man* for my father, Bessie answered her own question, entering Zvi's living room and stopping short.

But you can't choose your parents and the tidy room on which Bessie had closed the door last night now looked as if a tornado had swept through it. Chairs upturned and books swept higgledy-piggledy from their shelves, pictures askew on the walls, nuts and crisps strewn on the carpet, and lying on its side in a pool on the table, the vase of flowers carefully arranged by Bessie, the petals as bruised as her feelings.

Zvi had evidently wakened in the night thirsty – and not for water! An empty whiskey bottle almost tripped Bessie when the doorbell rang and she went to see which of his neighbors had called to see if he needed anything from the supermarket. Someone had to be fetching his liquor when his legs wouldn't carry him.

Instead, she found Sim standing in the porch and beside him was her cousin Anit.

"Remember me joking to Anit at her sister's wedding that if she ever wanted to run away I'd help her?" said Sim. "It'll teach me to keep my big mouth shut!"

"You didn't say that when I rang up and asked you to come and get me," said Anit.

The smile the two then exchanged caused Bessie to prickle with alarm. "You're welcome to come in," she said, "though the place is a real mess."

"What, again?" Sim dumped Anit's suitcase beside Bessie's and went to survey the wrecked living room, his expression tight-lipped.

"When Zvi's drunk he doesn't know what he's doing," Bessie said more airily than she felt.

"Or could he be trying to tell you something?" said Sim. "Like, 'Stop trying to tidy up my life.' "

"How it looks to me," said Anit, joining Sim in the doorway, "is he just went wild. Does he do this all the time?"

"Since he's drunk most of the time, you'll get used to it if you stay here," Sim told her.

"And I shan't mind helping Bessie with the clearing up. Remember when I came with my gran and my sister to visit you," said Anit, turning to Bessie, "and we talked about you and me sharing a place in Tel Aviv?"

"Chavah and your gran will remember that, too. When they tell your parents, your dad will call Grandpa and come here to get you."

"My dad threw me out," Anit answered, "though I *would* have run away if he hadn't. There was a terrible family row early this morning, which ended with Dad praying on my behalf for God's forgiveness, and Gran and my mother begging him not to banish me.

"By then, Chavah was throwing up in the bathroom. She's already pregnant."

"Mazeltov," said Bessie, "you're going to be an auntie. I'm looking forward to when Janis, or Jeremy, makes me one. Do Chavah and her husband live with your parents?"

"And the baby will be able to have my room," Anit replied, grimacing at her reflection in the hall mirror. "What a mess I look!"

"To me you look great," said Sim, and again Bessie was assailed by disquiet.

"But I can't say I *feel* great," said Anit, "what I actually feel is hungry. Sim picked me up at the petrol station I called him from," she told Bessie, "and there was nothing there but the pumps and the phone, not even a candy bar machine."

"I didn't have time to eat breakfast, myself," said Sim. "How about feeding us, Bessie?"

"If Zvi hasn't emptied the cornflakes onto the floor and the milk as well," she said, leading the way to the kitchen.

Though the packet of cereal was intact and the milk she had bought yesterday still unopened in the refrigerator, sugar and lentils crunched underfoot when they entered, a broken jar of honey had spilled its contents on the work counter and adorning the table was a frying pan in which two fried eggs had congealed in burnt fat.

"I didn't know Zvi could cook!" said Sim.

"Would you mind not making cracks?" Bessie turned to Anit. "As you'll have gathered, my father's an alcoholic —"

"I put her in the picture on the way here," Sim cut in.

"But you had no right to! It was for me to tell Anit."

"Why are you lashing out at *me*?" Sim asked, sounding hurt.

Perhaps because our twosome is suddenly a threesome and I don't like the feeling, thought Bessie, remaining silent.

Anit declared warmly, "I'm really glad I'm here to support you, Bessie. We're not just relatives, we're friends and I won't let you down. Like I knew you'd have me to stay, when my dad told me never to darken his doorway again."

"He actually said that?"

"Not in those words, but it was what he meant. I think the final straw for him was when Gran said hopefully that he'd change his mind when he calmed down and I said I'd rather he didn't.

"A husband has been found for me, you see, and I said the hell with that – the first time I'd used a swear word in my father's presence."

While they ate breakfast, Anit went on with her tale. "When Dad got his breath back, he said, 'Why can't you be like your sister?' and I said, 'God forbid.' "

"It isn't that I don't love Chavah – I'm sorry for her – but when Dad began listing her virtues, telling me she's an example of what a Jewish woman should be, it was too much for me.

" 'Then be thankful you have one perfect daughter!' I yelled at him, and he said that from now on he only *has* one daughter.

"Odd, isn't it?" Anit added wryly to Bessie. "You moving in with a father you've only just found, on the day mine shows me the door?"

"But a girl has to do what she has to do," Bessie said as the sound of footsteps overhead told her that Zvi had dragged himself from his bed.

Chapter
13

*B*y the spring of 1990, the Bornstein Foundation was functioning from a suite of offices in downtown Ottawa, and had not gone short of publicity bringing in its wake a deluge of applications for grants.

Janis was working at her desk when her secretary buzzed her on the intercom.

"There's an Irish guy on the line who won't state his business, but says it's important he speaks with you."

"Okay, put him through."

"I'm sorry to be intrudin' on yer good work, an' may the Lord bless ye fer it," said the caller, "but there's something I wish fer ye to see, Miss Bornstein."

"If it concerns a grant, you must first write to me," Janis replied. "I have a very busy schedule."

"Too busy to inspect the damage yer father's venture has done and will continue to do?"

Janis's stomach felt as if it had somersaulted. Had Jake

Bornstein got on the wrong side of the IRA? Was she talking to the assassin? "Who are you?"

"Just a priest who's decided to act on behalf o' his parishioners, my name is O'Brien."

"Where is your parish?"

"In Venezuela."

Where else? And it was for Janis grimly ironic that she, not her brother, was now in possession of what could be the crucial clue, she thought when the priest had told her the name of his village.

"I'm hopin' fer a visit from ye soon, Miss Bornstein," he said before ringing off.

Like it or not, the aftermath of Caracas that had taken so long to recede was back in the forefront of Janis's life.

Still trying to pull herself together, she dialed Lola's office number.

"Is Jeremy with you, Lola?"

"No, he's in Zurich following up some leads."

"When will he be back?"

"Your voice is trembling, Janis —"

"So might yours be, if you'd got the call I just did! I have to discuss it with my brother."

"Since I'm his future wife, you can discuss it with me."

"Does he know yet that you're his future wife?"

"That's an unkind thing to say, Janis. Why are you still so hostile toward me?"

"Perhaps because Jeremy and I used to be close, but that's now in the past like a lot of other things —"

"And you blame *me*?"

"I blame everything that's happened since the car bomb and it's difficult not to include you," Janis said with feeling.

"That must have been some call you got, the way you're

letting off steam," Lola replied, "but I'll excuse you if you let me in on it."

Her response to learning what the priest had said was, "This could be a trap."

"And your thinking so is typical of you and Jeremy and your bloody intrigues," said Janis, "you've been plotting and scheming separately and together for eighteen months and where has it got us?"

"You don't understand the world my father and yours moved in, Janis, and you never will. How ruthless it is. Arms dealing and industrial espionage are only the half of it.

"Transactions that result in putting thousands out of work take place over lunch," Lola went on, "and Jeremy and I still haven't found out what that multimillion dollar deal involved."

When a week later Janis arrived in Caracas, she found A.P. awaiting her with Jeremy and Lola. Then Jesse appeared as if from nowhere and took her arm.

"What's this, a welcome committee?" she managed to joke.

"I offered your brother my support in what could be the last lap of his crusade," said A.P.

"Me, too," said Jesse, "when Lola let me know about it. But that isn't the sole reason I'm here, Janis."

"And may this be your happy reunion," said Lola.

But there could've been a better scenario for it, thought Janis as the five made their way to a hired minibus and Jeremy began meticulously inspecting the vehicle, the driver eyeing him, when he slid flat on his back beneath it, as if he had gone mad.

"This is the second time he's seen Jeremy check the bus," Lola told Janis.

"Why is he doing so again?"

"The guy went to get himself a sandwich, while we were meeting your plane, so there's been an opportunity for we-know-what."

She spoke to the driver in Spanish and he replied with a silent shrug.

"I said Jeremy was once let down by a car, didn't get to where he was going and is ensuring that doesn't happen again," she translated.

"An edited version of the truth that'll do no harm," Jesse said to Janis with a meaningful smile.

"But let's not get into that!" And Janis would always associate this traumatic experience with the singing now in her heart. Joy and trepidation at one and the same time.

"Why do we need a driver?" she asked Lola.

"The village is up in the mountains. A treacherous route if you're not accustomed to that sort of driving, as you'll see for yourself, Janis."

Jeremy joined them, brushing down his clothes. "Okay, let's go," he said tersely, "and let's hope the priest, if he *is* a priest, hasn't gone off somewhere for the day."

"We ought to've let him know when we'd be coming," said Janis.

"Are you out of your mind?" Lola and Jeremy replied in unison.

"They're convinced it could be a trap," A.P. put in.

"So much so that I'm toting a revolver," Jeremy told him.

"I don't like the sound of that."

"Me, neither," said Jesse.

"And Dad would turn in his grave if he knew," Janis said to her brother.

"A sick joke if ever I heard one!" Jeremy exclaimed. "But

the revolver isn't loaded," he added after a silence, "it's just for show, if necessary."

The idea of her brother carrying a gun was nevertheless anathema to Janis. In order to get to the truth, he and Lola had let themselves employ the tactics of those peopling the world that Jake Bornstein and Luis Mendez had moved in.

Was it worth it? Janis thought not and it struck her now that their shared determination to find the assassin might be all they had in common. What sort of basis was that for the future together they were seemingly planning? Janis wondered, with Jesse's arm reassuringly around her, his being here proof that he hadn't stopped loving her and was back to stay.

Though his meeting her father, in the circumstances he had, was initially all that Janis and Jesse had in common, their time together in Sydney, the outings and the intimate Sunday lunches, the conversations about this and that, had revealed they wanted the same things from life.

Things money can't buy, Janis thought now.

"How's the commune going?" she asked A.P. when they were on their way.

"Our organically grown produce is selling very well to supermarkets," he answered without enthusiasm, "also our free range eggs —"

"And how bloody boring it all sounds," Jeremy interrupted. "If it weren't for Mary Lou Dryden, you'd probably have packed it in by now."

"Who is Mary Lou Dryden?" asked Lola.

"A girl who for A.P. can do no wrong, he's besotted with her!"

"You don't think *I* can do no wrong, do you, *querido*?"

"And I shouldn't think Jesse has that attitude toward Janis."

"But that doesn't mean I'm not besotted with her," said Jesse, fondling Janis's cheek.

A.P. folded his arms and surveyed the two couples, Janis with her head resting on Jesse's shoulder, and Lola smiling up at Jeremy.

"I'm beginning to feel like a gooseberry on this trip! Would anyone mind if I took a nap?"

"You may as well, it's a long journey," said Lola, "and we're all going to need sweaters when we get there. I remember my father's chauffeur making sure I had one with me when once I went home with him for the ride."

Jeremy's expression was astounded. "He came from the village we're going to?"

"And I know what you're thinking," Lola replied calmly, "but I couldn't have been more than ten when I accompanied him to visit his parents and they've now been dead for years."

"That doesn't mean there can't be a connection and you ought to have told me," said Jeremy.

"Don't be ridiculous, *querido*. Poor Pedro lost his legs when the bomb went off, didn't he? He'd hardly have been the one who planted it."

They fell silent and Janis could feel the tension building within the bus as it ascended the narrow, twisting road, on their left a sheer drop and ahead the mountain view shrouded by mist, the driver hunched over the steering wheel and the reek of garlic drifting from his direction.

"All that you two seem worried about is we might be walking into a trap," Janis wanted to say to Jeremy and Lola. Her own fears were centered upon what the priest had wanted her to see . . .

A.P., his hair a bright blob in the gray light, seemed now

to be asleep and soon Janis too, jet-lagged as she was, closed her eyes and drifted into a brief oblivion.

When she awoke, the others had put on their sweaters and Jesse had taken hers from her holdall and wrapped it around her.

The driver had pulled up outside the village inn and Lola was speaking to him in Spanish.

"I told him to go get himself a meal," she said when he had departed with alacrity.

"Let's hope he doesn't get drunk, as well," said A.P., "or one of us will have to drive back and I wouldn't like it to be me!"

They alighted from the bus into a small square, in the center of which was a stone statue of the Madonna and child. The buildings too were of a mellowed stone, an open-fronted carpentry shop and a general store occupying one side and a hospital and a school another.

Opposite the inn the church, set back behind a low wall, was screened by tall trees, its steeple silhouetted against a sullen sky.

Despite her warm sweater, Janis was shivering, but the temperature didn't account for it, it was the atmosphere pervading this place. Apart from a nurse who had just entered the hospital, there was nobody around.

Lola, similarly affected, was glancing at a steep, cobbled street rising from beside the inn. "Pedro's parents lived in one of those little houses, but he didn't take the car up there, we walked and I remember seeing women sitting on their doorsteps gossiping, as we passed by —"

"Let's just get on with what we're here for, shall we?" said Jeremy brusquely, leading the way to the church from whose open doorway a priest was visible before the altar.

Father O'Brien rose from his knees and turned to watch

them approach down the aisle. "I've prayed every day fer ye to visit us," he said, shaking hands with Janis. "I recognized ye from yer photo in the paper where I read of yer good work. An' ye'll be Miss Mendez, I reckon," he said to Lola. "Ye've a strong likeness t'yer mother."

"You've met my mother?"

"Sure I have. Didn't she accompany Pedro when he came back fer his poor parents' funerals? An' a fine contribution to the church fund she made in their names, may the Lord bless her fer it."

"Does whatever you've invited Miss Bornstein to see concern me, too?"

"How wouldn't it, since yer father an' hers were in it together? But I reckoned she'd be gettin' in touch wi' ye —"

"Our families have been in touch since the bomb incident," Jeremy interrupted, introducing himself, Jesse, and A.P.

"Aye, there's that an' all," said the priest with a sigh, "but first things first, an' if ye'll kindly follow me —"

He led them through the vestry, as dimly lit as his church, across a mossy path to the village cemetery where he halted, head bowed, beside a row of small graves.

It took but a minute for his visitors to register that every grave in this section of the cemetery was occupied by a child and Janis would not forget those rows of neat headstones, nor the pathetic graves themselves, adorned with flowers.

Oh God, what did my father do to bring this about? Had Jesse not been holding on to her, her knees might have buckled.

A graphic shock of another kind awaited them at the village hospital.

"If ye'd left it much longer t'pay us a visit, the evidence'd all've been buried," said Father O'Brien as they entered the children's ward, the empty beds lining the narrow room lending a terrible credence to his words.

At the far end, a nurse was watching over the two remaining patients.

"Stay here, you don't have to see this," Jesse said to Janis.

"It's what I came for, isn't it?" But Janis's imaginings could not have encompassed what she had seen in the cemetery and was about to see.

Moments later, Janis and Lola were weeping and Jeremy and A.P., white-faced, shepherded them away from the dying children, whose emaciated appearance was made the more pitiful by their huge, staring eyes.

Only Jesse was capable of objectivity, talking quietly with the priest.

How can their parents bear it? thought Janis, noting the resigned expressions of the couples seated at the bedsides. One of the women — clad in black, had she already lost a child? — was suckling a baby. The other was fingering a rosary, and her burly husband now gazing at the wooden crucifix on the wall above the bed. What but prayer was there for these simple folk to resort to?

But someone had resorted to violence and Janis didn't blame them. On the way to the hospital, Father O'Brien had said that the tragedy in this village was caused by toxic paint.

Later, in a living room incongruously reminiscent of a Victorian parlor, Father O'Brien gave them tea and spoke with nostalgia of his home in Tipperary.

"How long have you been here?" A.P. inquired.

"Long enough fer my hair t'go gray. T'were carroty as yours when I left my native shores. An' lest ye be wonderin' how I acquired a Venezuelan flock, the glut o' Irish priests accounts fer it."

The afternoon had slipped into twilight and he rose to light an oil lamp atop the bookcase, his slight figure sagging with weariness beneath his cassock.

"I'm sorry t've caused ye such distress," he said, returning to his chair and surveying his young guests, "but it had t'be done."

"Our distress is unimportant," said Janis.

"But there remains a great deal for Father O'Brien to explain," said her brother, "starting with how the toxic paint was linked to Dad and Senor Mendez."

"At first," said the priest, "the cause o' the children's sickness was a puzzle. As I told ye at the hospital, Dr. Cohen," he added, turning to Jesse, "the practitioner who visits the village once a month, or in an emergency, couldn't fathom out why none o' the adults were goin' down wi' gastroenteritis."

"Since it usually infects the whole family," said Jesse, "I'd've been foxed, too, though I'd have looked for some significance in only children of school age being affected."

"But it turned out not t'be an infection, didn't it?" said Father O'Brien grimly. "Though t'were not till an adult did go down wi' it – the teacher – an' then the lad who'd painted the classroom, that the doctor connected it wi' the school an' Senora Mendez sent a specialist from Caracas t'get t'the bottom o' it."

Lola was astonished. "My mother knows?"

"She learned o' the epidemic from Pedro, an' a saintly lady she truly is. If ye can save her from knowin' yer father's part in this, I'd be obliged."

The priest absently smoothed the red chenille tablecloth before continuing, "Pedro too played a part in it, but his was an innocent one.

"He'd overheard Senor Mendez and Mr. Bornstein discussin' a new, wonder paint they expected t' make them a lot o' money —"

"When was that?" Jeremy interrupted.

"I wouldn't know exactly, but t'were when he was drivin' them somewhere. What I do know fer sure is t'were Pedro who provided the paint that did such terrible damage.

"He knew the schoolroom was always given a fresh coat in the spring, an' I remember him arrivin' in the village wi' some cans he'd bought, an' the teacher tellin' me he'd said t'was an Easter gift to the school."

"Can you recall what year that was?" Lola asked.

"Sure an' all I can, t'was in 1985. In '86 an' '87 the schoolroom didn't require new paint, the wonder-stuff had lived up t'what was printed on the can: 'Guaranteed to last a lifetime.' How that was achieved, though, was by shortenin' lives!"

Father O'Brien picked up his cup with a trembling hand and swallowed down some tea to help calm himself. "An' I may as well tell ye death didn't come quickly. The families had t'watch their dear ones slipping away an' naught t'be done fer them. The teacher was the first to go, an' then the painter — a fine lad o' seventeen — an' I reckon it sent his father out o' his mind. T'were him who planted the bomb."

"He confessed to you?" asked Jeremy.

"If he had, I'd've been prohibited from telling you," the priest replied.

Lola said to Jeremy, "The confessional is sacrosanct, *querido*, as you must surely know."

"Even when murder is involved?"

"What you're still calling 'murder,' " said Janis, "I now see as retribution."

"What did Laura do to deserve it?" Jeremy demanded. "Or Pedro, who lost his legs? But the perpetrator didn't care who else was in the car! He must be brought to justice."

"Since he hanged himself – two weeks ago – only God can now be his judge," said the priest.

"But my brother lost a hand, seeking vengenace," said Janis bitterly, "and all that remains now is for us to make reparation as best we can."

"Not quite," said Lola. "Jeremy and I must ensure the removal of the toxic paint from the market."

"Thanks be t'God fer a Bornstein-Mendez partnership that isn't an unholy alliance," said the priest, giving them a wan smile.

He went on, after supplying the trade name of the paint, "Guaranteed never to fade, along wi' the rest o' what'd tempt folk t'buy it, an' such a beautiful color the schoolroom was."

"Like people buy the beautiful apples that are piled in supermarkets," said A.P., "without realizing that the pesticides they've been treated with have penetrated the skin."

"Lord Kyverdale is an organic farmer," Lola informed the priest.

"Is that a fact?"

"Well, that's one way of putting my current occupation," said A.P. "But what I and my friends are doing is just one aspect of trying to cure the ills Man has inflicted upon the world –"

"We don't have time for one of your House of Lords speeches," Jeremy cut in edgily.

"What I've seen here will strengthen my elbow," A.P. replied, "and it would be interesting to find out why no reports of poisoning elsewhere have been related to that paint."

"The likely answer," said Jeremy from the depths of his experience, "is that silence, like information, can be bought."

"An additional answer," Jesse put in, "could be that the paint is being marketed only in third world countries where, among other dangerous commercial corruptions, pharmaceutical products known to be harmful to children are sold over the counter to unsuspecting parents."

"If my father was into that, too, I'd rather not know," said Janis, "and given what we now *do* know," she added to the priest, "why did you wait so long before contacting me?"

"I wasn't in possession o' the facts, Miss Bornstein, till I read the letter José left for me. Pedro was his cousin an' had told him about the conversation he'd eavesdropped on —"

"But Pedro would never have pointed the finger at my father officially," Lola interrupted, "or have helped engineer his death. He wouldn't have done anything to hurt my mother."

"An' imagine his distress, poor soul, that t'was himself who'd bought the paint an' brought it to the village.

"As fer José," the priest went on, "t'were after his son who'd painted the classroom died that he did his evil deed, an' before he ended his own life, he buried the last o' his six children.

"Sure an' all there's no denyin' that grief can send a person off the rails . . ."

When Bessie knew about this, and she'd have to be told, thought Janis, she'd be thankful that Zvi Harim had done nothing worse than take to drink after losing his family.

"In the envelope wi' José's letter," Father O'Brien relayed, "was a newspaper picture o' Mr. Bornstein bein' met at Caracas Airport by Senor Mendez, an' José had underlined the date of a convention they'd be attendin' together before Mr. Bornstein left for a vacation wi' his wife."

"His opportunity to get them both with one fell swoop," Jesse remarked grimly, "and though he might not have expected Mrs. Bornstein to be in the car, he surely knew that Pedro would be driving it."

"But how did he plant the bomb, Father?" asked A.P.

"Not only did José show no concern for Pedro, he used him," the priest said sadly, "an' in the unholiest o' ways. Pedro'd always admired the wooden shrine José had carved fer outside his house.

"Ye'll see many o' them in this village, but none so beautiful as José's, wi' tears runnin' down the Virgin's face an' angels at her feet," he briefly digressed.

"On that terrible day, José took it t'the the Mendez company's garage in Caracas an' gave it t'Pedro, who accordin' to José's letter put it in the car boot –"

Lola's expression was horrified. "He hid the bomb inside the shrine?"

"In the hollow base, an' well padded t'muffle the tick o' the alarm clock he'd taped t'the gelignite, he wrote as if he'd wanted me to know how clever he'd been. An' when I picture him taking the shrine apart for his evil purpose . . ."

"My interpretation of that," said Jesse, "is he no longer believed in God."

"And if Father O'Brien will excuse me for saying so in his presence, who could blame him?" said Janis. "My little sister found it hard to forgive God for letting our parents die as they did," she told the priest.

"An' I'd be tellin' ye a falsehood were I t'say I'd never questioned Him," he answered surprisingly, "but my experience is that the Lord's ways truly are weird an' wonderful and He somehow arranges fer good t'come out o' evil."

Father O'Brien surveyed his young companions' strained expressions and sipped the tea that had gone cold in his cup. "If between ye, ye can make sure the toxic paint does no more harm than it already has, the painful events that brought ye t'my parish won't've happened in vain."

"You may rest assured on that score, Father," Lola replied, "but it won't rid me of the guilt I inherited."

"Nor me of mine," said Jeremy.

"And the *money* I inherited will now go into the Medical Foundation. I want no part of Dad's ill-gotten gains," Janis informed him.

"Sure an' all, isn't that good comin' out o' evil?" said the priest.

Chapter
14

Jeremy had remained in Caracas until he and Lola had released to the press the grim story of the toxic paint. Compared with which his personal souvenir of his father's dubious deals paled into insignificance, he thought glancing at his artificial hand – which the man seated beside him on the flight to London was endeavoring not to do.

Being maimed, though, and the way some people reacted to you, was just another of the things Jeremy must come to terms with. Like no longer having a place that felt like home. And the possibility of there being no future for him and Lola together.

She had accompanied him to the airport in her family's limousine, her close proximity as heady as her perfume and her conversation no less manipulative than Jeremy had come to expect.

"How can I reconcile blackening my father's name with the commandment that says I must honor him?" she had said.

"That sounds like one for your padre to sort out," Jeremy had replied.

"You've broken the commandment, too, so let's go see him together."

"If I required spiritual guidance, I'd see my rabbi."

"I'm still hoping you'll convert to my religion, *querido*."

"That's the only thing I wouldn't do for you."

"Then you wouldn't mind us living in my mother's house?"

"I sure would!"

Jeremy was returned to the present by a doe-eyed stewardess with a plastic smile. "More brandy, Mr. Bornstein?"

"Why not?"

"My own attitude egshackly," his neighbor said unnecessarily. "What elshe ish there to do on theshe goddamn flightsh but tie one on?"

"And try to sleep."

"Okay, I guesh I can take a hint!"

Sleep, however, eluded Jeremy, nor did the in-flight movie serve to divert his thoughts. His lengthy ordeal since the first time he flew to Caracas seemed now as if he had been to hell and back.

What Jeremy now wanted was to be just an ordinary guy again, living the ordinary life he once had. But he also wanted Lola Mendez and the two didn't jell.

What a pair of mutts A.P. and I are! he reflected. Each of us falling for the wrong girl. But Jeremy was now on his way to spend the Spring Bank Holiday at Kyverdale Hall and maybe they'd succeed in talking sense into each other.

Mary Lou was lolling on one of the stone benches that flanked the entrance to the house, fanning herself with a ragged straw hat.

"You've returned in the middle of a heat wave, Jeremy."

"You don't say!"

"And A.P. isn't here to welcome you."

"If he asked you to deputize for him, you're not making a very good job of it."

"I didn't want him to invite you."

"But you're not Lady Kyverdale yet and for A.P.'s sake, I hope you never will be."

"Unfortunately for you, though, that's up to me."

A hostile pause followed, during which Jeremy registered that Mary Lou's white tee-shirt was clinging to her unfettered breasts. And the tip of her tongue wetting her lower lip – if he didn't know she hated him, he'd think she was giving him the come-on!

"Okay," he said brusquely, "so A.P. isn't here right now, when will he be back?"

"As soon as he's sorted things out for young Ben. He got a panic call from the kid this morning and rushed off to Munich. You know A.P.!"

"I both know him and value him," Jeremy declared, "but do *you*?"

Mary Lou bit back a sharp retort as Gary Potter emerged from the house.

"Well, if it isn't my old pal, Bornstein, back from the wars!"

Jeremy mustered a smile. "In a manner of speaking."

"I should've called it your own private war," said Gary, putting a fraternal arm around Jeremy's shoulders, "and the lads're looking forward to celebrating with you, when you get back to college."

"Any excuse for a celebration, I seem to remember!"

"Come off it," said Gary, "and it won't be you standing us the drinks. To tell you the truth, you've surprised us, since you never gave the impression there was a whole lot to you."

"That remains my impression," said Mary Lou.

"But who gives a damn what *you* think!" Jeremy flashed.

"Evidently *you* do, or what I just said would've washed over you. And talking of washing, you look as if you could use a shower," she added, eyeing his sweat-stained shirt.

"In a minute she'll be offering to scrub your back," said Gary with a grin.

"He should get that lucky!"

"Me, too. But just to conclude my speech," he said to Jeremy, "congratulations about what you told the press despite your father's involvement in it. That took the sort of guts not too many folks have. You'll never be thought of as just a good-time-Charlie again."

But learning he had been viewed that way was a shock to Jeremy. Do we ever see ourselves as others see us? he pondered while showering.

Though Mary Lou hadn't bothered mentioning it, A.P. had left him a note. And – touchingly – the key to the west wing, with instructions to consider it his private quarters for as long as he cared to stay.

Could a guy have a more thoughtful friend? There was food in the refrigerator and wine from the Kyverdale cellar. No need for Jeremy to socialize with the communards over dinner tonight, all dressed up in his artificial hand.

"Something else you haven't yet come to terms with," he told his reflection in the bathroom mirror, before donning the toweling robe provided by A.P.

He was eating quiche and coleslaw when the house phone rang.

"Enjoying your meal?" said Mary Lou.

"Is that your way of telling me not to talk with my mouth full?"

"What a nasty piece of work you are!"

"And you, of course, are all sweetness and light."

"Believe it or not, I'm doing my best to be nice to you."

"Why?"

"A.P. wants you to have a quiet recuperation."

"In that case, stay out of my way!"

Several glasses of wine later, Jeremy still hadn't recovered from her impinging upon his peace. But the animosity between them had begun when they first met. At the Seder night Janis had carefully planned and cooked for, so the Passover would not go uncelebrated in their home, though their parents were gone.

Just one of the multitude of memories Jeremy must lock away and get on with his life. Himself and his sisters together for the last time, before going their separate ways. Smiles on our faces masking our emotion. And the unwelcome stranger A.P. brought to the table.

Any stranger would have been unwelcome on that poignant occasion, but it wasn't just that, Jeremy thought now, nor my reaction to Mary Lou's influencing A.P.

But would Kyverdale Hall now be a commune, were it not for Mary Lou? The answer was no, and A.P.'s sole personal satisfactions were the summer camp he hoped would be an annual event, and the arts project to be housed here in the west wing – if it ever got off the ground!

Briefly, Jeremy fantasized about A.P. and himself taking off for wherever and living a simple life, uncomplicated by love and responsibilities, a couple of carefree beachcombers blithely strolling the sands of time.

Could Jeremy live without Lola? Maybe he'd give it a try. But A.P. was never going to give up on Mary Lou.

When Jeremy awoke in the night and found her in bed with him, it seemed another kind of fantasy. But wasn't this part of the chemistry between them? Lust along with the loathing, which he had ignored because A.P. wanted her for his wife.

All Jeremy wanted from her was what they were now doing was his last coherent thought.

"I'll leave the money on the dresser," she quipped when it was over.

"Kindly don't add insult to injury!"

"If you'd like the truth, I'm disgusted with myself."

"Since I'm not in the habit of double-crossing my best friend, me too."

"I've decided to marry A.P.," she said while pulling on her jeans, "and for his sake, you and I must make a pact."

"Including that what he doesn't know can't affect him?"

"It's already over and done with."

A remark that tempted Fate, Mary Lou reflected when she found herself pregnant. By then she was Lady Kyverdale.

Epilogue

The consecration of Laura's and Jake's tombstones took place on the second anniversary of their deaths and for their children, it was as though the roller coaster of events following the car bomb had finally halted.

While the rabbi conducted the service, his gown billowing in the autumn wind, A.P. saw Janis and Jeremy exchange a glance. How could they not be recalling that other cemetery, as he was? Where the terrible evidence of their father's guilt had confronted them.

Janis, now married to Jesse, might eventually put it behind her. Together they'll build a family, like Mary Lou and me, he thought, smiling down at his wife. But Jeremy had never looked more lonely.

"It's hard to tell which of those girls is expecting first," Shirley whispered to Marianne, glancing from Janis to Mary Lou. "As for Bessie's having the nerve to bring *that man*!" She averted her gaze from Zvi Harim. "And Jeremy looks as if he hasn't shaved for a week."

"Maybe he's growing a beard."

"But he could have tried to look presentable today."

For Shirley, appearances mattered most. But the three young people who'd had to begin again when tragedy struck had each in their own way proved their worth. As A.P. had got to grips with his inheritance *his* way.

Marianne was proud of them all.

A former journalist, Maisie Mosco began writing fiction in the sixties and is the author of fourteen radio plays. *NEW BEGIN-NINGS* is her twelfth novel. Originally from Manchester, she now lives in London.

HarperPaperbacks *By Mail*

READ THE NOVELS
THE CRITICS ARE RAVING ABOUT!

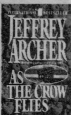

AS THE CROW FLIES
Jeffrey Archer

When Charlie Trumper inherits his grandfather's vegetable barrow, he also inherits his enterprising spirit. But before Charlie can realize his greatest success, he must embark on an epic journey that carries him across three continents and through the triumphs and disasters of the twentieth century.

"Archer is a master entertainer."
— *Time* magazine

FAMILY PICTURES
Sue Miller

Over the course of forty years, the Eberhardt family struggles to survive a flood tide of upheaval and heartbreak, love and betrayal, passion and pain...hoping they can someday heal their hearts and return to the perfect family in the pictures from the past.

"Absolutely flawless." — *Chicago Tribune*

PALINDROME
Stuart Woods

Seeking an escape from her brutal ex-husband, photographer Liz Barwick retreats to an island paradise off Georgia's coast. But when a killer launches a series of gruesome murders, Liz discovers that there is no place to hide—not even in her lover's arms.

"Moves along with hurricane velocity."
— *Los Angeles Times Book Review*

THE CROWN OF COLUMBUS
Louise Erdrich • Michael Dorris

Vivian Twostar—single, very pregnant, Native American anthropologist—has found Columbus' legendary lost diary in the basement of the Dartmouth Library. Together with her teenage son Nash and Roger Williams—consummate academic and father of her baby—Vivian follows the riddle of the diary on a quest for "the greatest treasure of Europe."

"Compelling entertainment."
— *The New York Times*

BILLY BATHGATE
E.L. Doctorow

In the poverty-stricken Bronx of the Depression era, gangster Dutch Schultz takes young Billy Bathgate under his crooked wing. With grace and vivid realism, Billy Bathgate recounts his extraordinary education in crime, love, life, and death in the dazzling and decadent world of a big-time rackets empire about to crumble.

"Spellbinding." — *The Boston Herald*